The girl in the doorway

Brian Smith

This novel owes much to the characters of my childhood and I am grateful to my family for giving me such a colourful collection of memories to draw upon. However, it is important to note that my story is ultimately a work of fiction.

Editing by Phil Lyndon.- phil@columncomm.co.uk

Front cover photograph by Shirley Baker
©Nan Levy for The Shirley Baker Estate

ISBN: 979-8-56-034073-5

DEDICATION

To Collette, my big hearted little sister.

ACKNOWLEDGMENTS

To Bryn for his insight and honesty, to Luke for his creative input, to Jess and Deb for listening to me go on and on about my book, to my brother Paul for his support, to Kate and James for their artistic voice and to Sally for encouraging me to publish.

.

PAINTING A PICTURE

There's no such thing as a bad colour...everything depends on the colour combination but I don't paint with any theory in mind. I've never been inclined to research someone like Goethe and his theory of colour and light nor do I pay too much attention to any general rules about ratio or colour harmony. It's partly because I am lazy but also I never like to be too formulaic and I've always encouraged my students to break the rules.

I love getting lost in it. I like the way that all sorts of things go through your mind; sometimes I don't even know what I've been thinking about. I couldn't tell you but on this occasion, with this portrait, I know that my mind will go back to the past. It is inevitable.

And now it is time, everything is ready, all is arranged as it should be...the tea, the biscuits, the brushes. I really want to get this one right for all sorts of reasons. It's not just about likeness, it needs to capture something more, maybe the soul of a person if such a thing exists. I prop the board on the easel next to the desk, take a sip of my tea and stare at the roughly-painted cobalt blue background and time moves backwards. It is the year 2001...

It's not that Olive had a trust issue with me and my sister Belle, she just wouldn't let herself be reassured. I told her "everything's gonna be okay." I don't know why she was so agitated as there was little to pack away and there was nothing of any great value anyway. She needn't have worried but she scrutinised every move we made. She sighed. It was an impatient, irritated sigh. We were clearly annoying her so she marched out of the kitchen through the narrow hallway and planted herself on the front doorstep.

With her back to me, her diminutive figure stood solid like stone except for the rhythmic rise and fall of her upper body caused by the long slow drags of a roll up. I could sense what she was doing. She was surveying the red-bricked council estate through those suspicious eyes. There was nothing new about that, Olive was always suspicious. If mother Teresa suddenly appeared with a sack full of provisions for the poor it would be in her words "too bloody sweet to be 'olesome."

Legs stiff and unbending with one hand on her hip, her stance remained uncompromising. The old lady was definitely in a mood. Hard grey puffs of smoke seeped out from the top of her head rising slowly upwards and then ground to a halt unable to escape the dank Manchester air. Undeterred, these wispy tendrils of malice seemed to reach out sideways searching for freedom only to be hauled back in by an invisible hand. I watched, fascinated. My mother was an evil jinn bringing the wind, air and smoke of a dull Wythenshawe day under her command. Suddenly the sound of a smashed pot reverberated through the bare rooms of the old 1930s terrace.

"Shit!"

The eerie spell cast by the wraith-like vapours was suddenly broken. Olive charged back inside to see me and my sister quickly picking up the fractured pieces.

"Mum it was an accident. Just a cup," said Belle, relieved that it was nothing valuable. Olive tutted and then went over to inspect.

"See, just a cup," repeated her daughter but the old lady wasn't satisfied as she realised that it was one of her favourites – the 'kiss me quick' one from Blackpool.

"It can easily be replaced," I said quietly as I placed the other cups carefully into a packing box. I was hoping that the quiet assurance of my voice would ease her anger. She sometimes listened to me.

"Okay," said Olive begrudgingly. She paused for a second and then issued a command. "Just don't bloody throw anything away. I know what you're like!"

"It's fine mum. Trust us," said Belle but she could see that her mother was not fully convinced.

My sister turned to me and looked for guidance so I walked over to my mother, pressed my hands around her shoulders and looked fondly into her small brown eyes.

"Don't worry mum it will be fine. This move…it's the right thing to do. We're just helping you to sort a few things out." I smiled to reassure her and in return she looked back at me and nodded hesitantly. Her frown dissolved a little. She was appeased but still needed to have the last word.

"Just don't bloody throw anything away," she demanded.

This time it was not said with quite the same bite. But her tone was still firm and left me and my sister in no doubt that she was still in charge. Olive then sat down on her favourite nicotine-stained armchair and took a last deep drag of her fast-fading roll up, becoming less agitated as she did so. She watched as Belle could not resist pressing down on the head of a dwarf-like figurine to release a golden stream of orange juice through a small shrivelled penis.

"Leave my little friend alone," joked Olive, her mood lightening. Belle laughed. Neither of them seemed too concerned as the contents splashed all over the bare floorboards.

"Do you want these mum?"

I held aloft a couple of badly-painted clay ornaments that had flanked le pis manikin on the old coffee-stained window sill. She stared angrily at me.

"I'll take that as a yes then."

Belle chuckled just enough for me to hear as she picked up some old sticks of Blackpool rock that had coagulated into a sickly mess on the mantelpiece.

"What about those mum?" I asked pointing at Belle's handful of sugary slop.

Olive paused and probably sensed that there was a hint of the ridiculous in my question.

"You can stick 'em up your arse for all I care."

Me and my sister laughed. We both loved her outbursts but Olive was not amused. My sister then made a slightly suspicious looking move towards me. It was spotted by Olive who looked irritated that she was not close enough to be a part of any conversation that might take place. Olive then frowned as she saw her daughter put her hand over her mouth and pretend to scratch her lip. Sure enough Belle wanted to say something that Olive couldn't hear.

"I think she's losing it more than we thought."

"What do you mean?" I whispered.

"The 'oles gone missing from her arse."

"I beg your pardon," I said, mystified but laughing at the same time.

"Arse'ole," said Belle, "it's usually stick 'em up your arse'ole."

I laughed to myself. It wasn't just that it was comical. It was unlike Belle to be that sharp and sarcastic, she was far too nice. My older brother Johnny on the other hand was much more acerbic. He could really dish it out but he was funny. We once made a list when we were kids about Olive's usage of the word arse'ole. It's there somewhere in my box of memorabilia.

But Olive was familiar with all forms of the expression and would be considered an expert in its usage. It was by far her most commonly used term. According to Olive, "the world is full of all kinds of arse'oles."

This was an essential part of my early education – a tenet passed down from mother to son. But unlike my mother I could never quite master the usage of arse'ole. Whenever I said it, it

6

never sounded right. No timing, no real feeling. I tried it once in front of my mates for effect but it was embarrassing. Back then I was never any good at swearing. I never really wanted to be. Johnny on the other hand was very skilled. He did have a couple of years' experience on me but it came easily to him. Guttural and passionate but subtle and sardonic when needed…all part of a good Mancunian's armoury but unfortunately my cupboard was pretty bare.

Funnily enough, Olive never used the 'F' word as she thought it was too crude. She went ballistic if she ever caught us using it. It was bad enough if she heard us swearing at all. Johnny was careful never to swear in front of Olive but he never thought twice about swearing elsewhere. He even used the 'F' word and it seemed fine when he did it.

Once I told on him for using it though I don't know why I did it. He got a slap from Olive. "I'll wash your mouth out with soap and water you dirty little bastard." Even aged ten I understood the irony of the statement but I had been stupid. Johnny was mad with me and gave me a right crack. I remember crying. He dared me to tell Olive. "Fucking tell 'er…go on fuckin' tell 'er." I never did.

I remember…I remember it well. I don't think I'll forget the sting of his fist in my ribs. Memory is like that. It seems to allow you to remember pain more than joy.

I squeeze some yellow ochre from the tube and unhurriedly mix the colour around. I am slow and deliberate to begin with. There is no need to rush. I am quite careful. The paint feels smooth and luxurious under my brush. I am determined to have some grip over what I think so that I can make sense of what happened all those years ago. I don't want to come away from my painting with fragmented episodes and a jumble of memories. If possible I want some clarity. Maybe if I start at the beginning but I'm not sure when that is.

For all my deliberations, as soon as brush hits canvas I am lost. I cannot help myself; a slow wave of subconscious carries me to a time and a place of my growing up in north Manchester some forty years ago. I am there in the back room of the shop – "Olive's Offy." It is nearly at the beginning but not quite.

1971. FRESH FROM WARBURTON'S

"She can be a right twat," said Johnny. She didn't need to 'ave a go at dad like that." He looked at his seven-year-old sister who seemed upset. "Sorry Belle," said Johnny, "cover your ears. You shouldn't need to hear that." But it wasn't so much what he said, it was the way that he said it. There was venom in his tone.

"Well she is," said Stacey. We looked puzzled so she explained. "What Johnny said, you know...the T word." My sister rarely swore but felt okay about agreeing with it. We all nodded. Olive had just berated her husband Ted for tripping over the worn edge of a piece of frayed lino. He did it in front of her customers as he entered the shop which really pissed Olive off.

The worst thing was that it wasn't just a small stumble. He went arse over tit. It didn't help that Ted was in his slippers and the lino floor had just been mopped. The trip turned into a slide...it was like watching Bambi on ice. As he reached out to rescue himself, one arm swiped two cans of baked beans from the shelf and sent them shooting across the floor just missing old Mrs Harris. The sleeve of his other arm got caught on a hook and half tore his old blue cardi. In the end he was left quite literally dangling by a thread.

"For Christ sake Ted! You gormless git! Fix the bloody lino. It's been like that for bloody ages!" yelled Olive, oblivious to his predicament. As we came running in to see what had happened, Olive made some quip to the customers about only bringing her husband out for special occasions. "Usually as Coco the Clown to entertain the kids." Everybody in the shop laughed. Ted did too but it was clear he was embarrassed not so much for his accident but because he appeared to have little sympathy from Olive.

"She's in a mood," said Derrick quietly. He nearly always spoke quietly. He was often drowned out by Johnny who was far louder and more demonstrative. Johnny could easily dominate a crowd and even though Derrick was the eldest he didn't seem to be able to stop that from happening.

"I wish I'd seen it," said Johnny suddenly seeing the funny side and giggling slightly. "Coco the bloody Clown," he muttered out loud," she's not far wrong with that one."

"Poor Ted," said Stacey trying to hold back the laughs.

Even Belle started smiling. We used to be like that. All of us laughing and joking together but of late that didn't happen much any more. Something had changed. It was hard to pinpoint exactly when it happened but it was somewhere near the time of Michael's death. *That would make sense.* Everybody knew it was there…this atmosphere, particularly with my brothers and Olive but nobody talked about it. That day was an exception. Just for a time tensions eased and it was almost as though it was forgotten.

"Get some Black Jacks, our kid," said Derrick looking over at me.

"I'll 'ave an Arrow bar," said Stacey.

"And what about you Belle. Marshmallow?"

Olive didn't mind us going into the shop and helping ourselves to sweets but if she was in a mood then I would generally be the safest bet to fetch them. Derrick, Stacey and Johnny were all in agreement with this. In their eyes I was the favourite and there would be a good chance that I would be able to deliver. As I walked in I saw her standing imperiously behind the counter, all five foot and a tea leaf of her. Bacon slicer to the left and a crate of Holt's pale ale on the right, I remember being struck by her self-assured presence. There was no doubt that she was mistress of all she surveyed. She was a larger than life character with peroxide blonde hair and a confident swagger. She was pretty and could be quite glamorous but she had also inherited the curse of the Jones 'flat nose' courtesy of her father.

Olive was eying up a customer, a fairly non-descript woman with a yellow scarf. This woman had the temerity to be testing the bread. She was feeling and prodding with bony fingers putting her mits all over the batch. Olive always hated customers feeling her bread. It was always fresh from Warburton's. Everybody knew that. There was no doubt that this woman was pissing her off but Olive appeared to be more aggravated than usual.

From the back room Johnny heard a few mutterings and knew by Olive's tone that something was going to happen. He came up and peered through the thin strands of a red, white and yellow PVC curtain. I was close by so I could see him but nobody else in the shop could. As I watched the wrath of Olive descend with a mixture of macabre fascination and embarrassment, I could see my brother's shadowy figure out of the corner of my eye. I didn't need to see too clearly to realise that he was doing his vampire impression from one of those old Hammer horror films in which Dracula is about to feast on his prey. The plastic strands of the curtain obscured his face. It didn't matter, I knew that his dark brown hair would be brushed back, his lips would be curled up, and he would have that weird satanic smile. His eyes too would be wide and bright, full of fake menace. I could feel myself going.

I tried to ignore him but I couldn't resist looking, just one look. I can still see it now; that gawky spindly frame rising up and down on creeping toes. I tried to turn away but couldn't. Grimly fascinated I peered through those wispy strips to see claw-like hands either side of his pointy chin. Somehow he managed to look like Olive and Christopher Lee at the same time.

Oh please Lord don't. Don't make me laugh. Not while mum's having a go. Too late – gone! I loved and hated Johnny at the same time. The fits started. I made a dash and got back behind the curtain just in time. I'd had to clamp my hands over my mouth in a desperate attempt to try to contain my giggles. Just as I heard the swish of PVC behind me, the snot that had been oozing out through my fingers, shot out with the force of a valve being released from a pressure cooker. Johnny was disgusted and gave me a dig in the ribs but he loved that he could reduce me to such a blubbering mess.

After taking a minute or two to recover I saw the denouement of Olive's little contretemps. A low growl that ended with a final ultimatum. "Now then, are you gonna cough up with the money and buy that bloody loaf or are you just gonna piss off?" We both saw the frightened face of the woman who, clearly intimidated, paid up and then ran from the shop with her loaf clutched to her stomach.

"Mouse," said Johnny aiming his comment at the wounded customer. "No backbone. I would have pissed off but not before feeling every twatting loaf in the batch." It was clear that he wanted to see more resistance from the woman and he was so disappointed when it didn't happen. In his mind he was the only one that really stood up to Olive.

Later on that day Johnny played the scene out to all of us in his own special way. We loved his little enactments and he in turn would love to entertain us. He entitled his short cameo, "Arse'ole or not an arse'ole? That is the question." Johnny explained that he would act out the parts of both Olive and the interviewer. We all made ourselves comfortable on the settee in the upstairs living room. Belle shuffled along and sat on Stacey's knee and all went quiet. Johnny coughed. "Oh by the way, the interviewer could be a policeman with a southern accent". He coughed again and then began. First he was the interviewer.

Interviewer: So you were in the shop and a woman entered the premises.

Johnny then jumped half a yard to his left and pretended to be Olive.

Olive: Yes.

We all nodded. It was a pretty good imitation of our mother's tone of voice. He then hopped back again to be the interviewer.

Interviewer:- What was the first thing she did that annoyed you? (another hop back)

Olive: Well the first thing this arse'ole did. (quick hop back)

Interviewer: Excuse me but we have not yet decided whether or not she was an arse'ole. (everybody laughed)

Johnny then paused and mimicked Olive's gorgon stare at Belle who chuckled and then buried her face in Stacey's chest. Johnny then gave Olive's reply.

Olive: This ARSE'OLE shook the rain off her umbrella onto my shop floor. (hop to the side)

Interviewer: What, your beautiful lino? (hop back)

We laughed. It was the same tatty lino that Ted tripped over. Johnny had timing. He let the laughs die out before continuing.

Interviewer: *The woman may not have realised...(quick hop to the side)*

Olive: She was still a dozy bastard and therefore an arse'ole. (titters from the audience)

Interviewer: Did she apologise?

Olive: No.

Interviewer: Not even a bit?

Olive-: No. There was no doubt in my mind...she was definitely an arse'ole.

Interviewer: You did give her the stare...the one known as the gorgon. The one that can turn people to stone. Was that fair? (More titters from the audience)

13

Olive-: She was squeezing my loaves!

And with that Johnny made a suggestive squeeze of his hand near Derrick's genitals. Everybody quickly scattered but then laughed nervously. Johnny continued.

Olive: I looked at 'er and thought to myself, no you bloody don't. 'Are you buyin' that bread or touchin' it up' I said. I couldn't 'ave been any clearer. (Forgot to hop)

Interviewer: What did she say?

Olive: Uh uh uh. (plenty of laughs)

Olive: I told 'er: 'you've got fingers like Doctor Crippen. I don't want you anywhere near my bloody loaves.' I said 'are you buyin' 'em or touchin' 'em up?' 'What do you mean?' she said so I said to 'er 'only you're givin' 'em a bloody good feel.'

Interviewer: She looked a bit frightened. Did you feel sorry for her?

Olive: Who do you think I am? Bloody Mother Theresa? She should have known. My bread is FRESH IN FROM...and then Johnny paused and we all joined in...WARBURTON'S!

There was a great cheer and then Johnny continued.

Olive: 'Now then', I said, 'what are you doin' coughin' up or pissin' off?'

Johnny then hopped to his right instead of his left and put on a posh woman's voice.

Posh woman: Well hi ham pissing awff. But not before doing this!

And with that, Johnny ran round feeling anything he could get his hands on, bits of arm, bits of leg shouting out "is it fresh from Warburton's? Is it fresh from Warburton's? Is it fresh from Warburton's?" Stacey screamed. I ran. Derrick smiled and Belle cried. We were all in stitches apart from my little sister but she soon perked up. Oh and Derrick. I know he found it funny but it was almost as though he didn't want to laugh.

"Derrick smiled," I *mutter out loud as I rinse the yellow ochre from my brush. The first few marks are fine. A basic outline is there. I stand back to look and squint my eyes.*

Derrick never laughed like the others. He hardly ever laughed out loud but that was Derrick. Back then I could never picture him laughing wholeheartedly. I'm sure he did but I always had the impression that he never really let himself go. Not at that time anyway. He was quite a serious sixteen year old and that's probably because he took himself so seriously. I don't think he was always like that.

I used to think it was something to do with being the oldest…all that responsibility shit. That may have had something to do with it but there was something else, and it was in that smile. It was so half hearted and so begrudgingly given. Maybe it was because it was Johnny who was at the centre and Derrick just didn't want to find him funny. But for all his lack of openness he was kind to me. Not like Johnny.

Occasionally Derrick could be surprisingly sensitive. He was the one who suggested that Olive was in a mood because her fortieth was approaching. He was right in some respects and I could see why he said it. Life was passing her by. The swinging sixties had been and gone and five children had at times got in the way. And now the seventies were rolling in and the colours that life was beginning to paint had too many shades of grey. The shop that she had insisted on purchasing had not been a roaring success and the future wasn't looking great. But that wasn't the sole reason she was in a mood.

The whole business surrounding Michael was still there in the background. Even though the tragedy happened a good two years earlier, it had never really gone away And Frank – Frank had just disappeared.

There were no suspicious circumstances surrounding Michael's death said the report in the paper. He'd wondered down to the old railway line behind Smedley Fields and got himself electrocuted. The reason it wasn't treated as suspicious was that we all used to do it. We told the police that. We were never supposed to go down there. We were warned and there were signs but it was one of those things...you tell kids not to do it...it's dangerous so they do it.

It was odd that he'd wondered down on his own but he was a bit of a loner and he would do things like that. He was even spotted by some of the lads at the youth club clambering over the fence to go down to the track. He looked as though he was on his own. There may have been someone with him but the police ruled it out.

"On Sunday June 2nd the body of 15-year-old Michael Jones was found dead lying near the railway track behind Smedley Fields. A young couple walking their dog spotted the body late on Sunday afternoon. Death was by electrocution. Police are not viewing this as suspicious circumstances."

Manchester Evening News

I don't remember much about Michael. I only saw him a few times. All I remember was this awkward gangly figure with longish hair and odd jumpy movements. I think Johnny was friends with him. Not really good friends but they seemed okay with each other. Occasionally, when Terry, the youth club leader, would call round to pick up Johnny and Derrick, he would have Michael in tow. They all seemed to get on.

What was puzzling is that Olive never really knew the boy Michael well. She saw him from time to time with Johnny, Derrick and Terry but it wasn't as though she was attached to him. Yes, it was a tragedy but she had no emotional connection unless there was something we didn't know about. But his death really got to her. She tried to cover up her feelings but she was angry after it happened, very angry. Johnny was too. They seemed to take it out on each other and fought like cat and dog. They were always arguing but it got worse as time went on. It wasn't right.

In all of this Ted was the calm in the eye of the storm, almost oblivious to what was going on but he was so important without really knowing it. He was the light comic relief in an otherwise unrelenting drama and was happy to play a minor role. He never wanted the limelight. In a pantomime he would be more than content at being the back end of the horse.

SAINT TED

Playing second fiddle to Olive came quite naturally to Ted, not that he had much choice in the matter as his wife packed such a powerful punch. You would take her on at your peril. But Ted, poor Ted so meek and mild he never did argue back. I can still hear him saying "she who must be obeyed. You know what she's like."

Quite simply Ted did what Olive said. He was a kind man and would help anybody out but in truth he wanted nothing more than an easy life. He had lost the zest of youth in his looks although his smile was still warm and friendly. Years of stomach ulcers (probably brought on by having five children) had left their mark. His face, even then, was gaunt whilst his figure was quite thin. He was a good deal older than Olive anyway.

But he didn't help himself. His hair was slicked back with dollops of *Brylcreem* and sadly this revealed a front hairline that was triangular and peaked. He also had hideous thick black-rimmed spectacles and looked like a comic version of a short-sighted Count Dracula and he wore the most dreadful clothing.

The worst were the cords that were far too big for him. You always knew Ted was coming your way without even seeing him. The billowing cords used to rub together…shump, shump, shump. His slightly knocked knees added to the friction. The sound was like the repeated shunting of a train being sick. Me and my brothers were always embarrassed to be seen in public with him but Belle and Stacey were very fond of him and his appearance didn't bother them as much.

We all questioned why on earth our parents were together. We used to call them the odd couple. Over the years I understood a little more about their relationship and one particular discovery changed everything but I don't want to get ahead of myself. I stop and take a step back.

I'm not bothered about flesh tones yet. Instinct tells me that some broad sky blue blocks of colour would set down a good marker. I use the same brush as it's my favourite. The brush picks up the paint and the flow on canvas is creamy. I laugh and cry. When I think of Ted, comedy and tragedy are never far apart.

Ted was once late coming back from an errand. It wasn't long after the incident with the woman and the loaf of Warburton's. I remember he'd taken the car and Olive was always secretly worried. She never liked Ted driving on his own. Stacey seemed to catch her mother's mood. She was quite sensitive in that regard and had no idea about many things but she was definitely a people person. She had bags of tea and sympathy, overflowing at times and had a good heart.

"Dad's late," she said.

"The rubbin' of those bleedin'cords has caused 'is legs to spark up and self-ignite," quipped Johnny. "He's probably being used as some human torch. Along with that haircut they've whipped him off to be some extra in 'It Came from Outer Space.'" Despite their animosity towards each other, even Olive chuckled as she knew that Johnny had inherited her cruel wit. He could be particularly hard on Ted but you couldn't help laughing. However, as time passed we all became concerned. It wasn't like him to be this late. Eventually about two hours later than expected Ted staggered in looking as white as a sheet.

"What the bloody hell!" came the collective cry.

"It's okay. I'll be okay," said Ted and then groaned in agony as he eased himself onto the red leather chair in the back room of the shop in true martyr-like fashion.

"Where's the bloody car?" bellowed Olive apparently impervious to his pain.

"Mum, mum. Can't you see he's in shock," said Stacey clearly alarmed at Olive's lack of feeling. She then looked around and frantically asked if someone could get him a brandy. Olive's nostrils flared for a second as her daughter appeared to undermine her. On this one occasion she dismissed it as there was something more pressing. Olive slowly repeated the question with a little more deliberation.

"Where's the bloody car, Ted?"

Ted looked at Olive imploringly and then told about how a lorry had driven into the back of his car just as he was getting out of it. He was hesitant and faltering in his delivery. If this was designed to elicit maximum sympathy from his family then it worked. We all nestled around Ted patting his brow, rubbing his hands and passing him his brandy to sip. All except Olive who looked on stony faced and emotionless.

"The car, Ted. The car," said Olive, even more slowly and deliberately.

Ted then let out further groans as he clutched his back. It wasn't just the physical pain, Ted was clearly trying to avoid Olive's interrogation. Derrick the most responsible of all of us could sense his father's distress and desperately tried to think of some way of saving him. He knew that once Olive got the bit between her teeth, there was no stopping her. And then he had a brainwave.

"You could get compensation!"

It worked as suddenly the focus shifted.

"Yeah dad, you could," added Belle without really knowing what compensation was. And then everybody started to join in seeing something positive in the midst of Ted's terrible ordeal. All except Olive who stood there arms folded tapping her foot menacingly on the floor. Despite the hordes agreeing with Derrick she said nothing, hoping that it would die down but the chorus continued.

"It's true dad. Joe down the road got a couple of hundred quid and there was barely a scratch on 'im."

"You could sue the lorry driver."

"I bet there were witnesses."

"We could get a brand new car!" (the old Rover was a rust bucket) shouted Belle who had quite a loud voice for a seven-year-old. She then walked deliberately over to Ted and gave him a great big cuddle as though he were a large shaggy pet.

"No. No, I'll be alright," replied Ted in his now customary self-sacrificing fashion. It was a phrase he had repeated throughout. "I'll be alright." Even I found it irritating. Olive couldn't stand this tea and sympathy any longer.

"For Christ's sake Ted. What about the BLOODY CAR!"

Ted then whimpered something about it being a crumpled heap outside Norman's hardware store and with that, Olive stormed off.

"What a heartless bitch," Stacey whispered out loud as our father looked broken. "Never mind dad, you've still got us," she added.

Ted simply nodded his head and spent the remainder of the afternoon milking the sympathy of his two doting daughters. Stacey sat on the arm of the chair stroking his arm. Belle sat between his ankles playing with her beads. Every so often she would glance up to see if Ted was okay. And there it was right before my eyes: a full scale re-enactment of Mary and Martha at the feet of Christ! I once saw a painting by Vermeer entitled 'Jesus at the house of Mary,' and I swear that my sisters had exactly the same stance, the same pose and that same tender gaze and Ted, well Ted had that same benevolent acceptance of their love. The scene might as well have been entitled 'Belle and Stacey at the feet of Saint Ted.' Belle the infant had such cherubic features anyway. She would have quite easily fitted into one of those old Italian Renaissance works of art.

I remember saying all this to my parents when I was looking over some old photos of my sister. I was at art college at the time and was just getting into artists and the history of art. Belle was so beautiful as a child that it was easy to make the connection. But actually saying this out loud in front of my parents…it just kind of came out…like some unguarded thought.

"Belle. She looks as though she could be a part of Giotto or a Botticelli. There's actually a Vermeer that…" And then I stopped and instantly regretted what I had said. Olive looked at me with a mixture of scorn and disdain and set to work on ridiculing my utterances…

Botty 'oo. Botty oo?

Botticelli mum.

And what was the other? Ted, what was the other one?

Jotty something, I think.

Close mum. It was Giotto actually.

Whatever. Botty and Jotty. Ha ha.

Very funny.

What was the other one. Vermin? Christ what's all that about?

Vermeer. It was Vermeer mum.

Oo would 'ave a bloody name with Botty in though?

'E's not an arse bandit is 'e? Ted?

No Olive. I don't think so.

Jesus! What are they bloody teachin' you?

About artists mum.

If those are real artists then my arse is a Chelsea bun. Botti and Jotti. Christ!

I don't think I mentioned the names to impress them. It's just as well because they clearly weren't. I just wasn't thinking. I took no offence at their scornful remarks. In fact I am sure that we all ended up laughing. As much as they would mock me, I would bait them. I once brought home a poster of a Rothko knowing full well what Olive's reaction would be. One word beginning with "A."

I never could convince my parents of the validity of modern art but I had some fun trying. Fun was never a word used with my brothers and Olive in respect of their relationships. Some of the anger between them subsided over the years but there was a strange indifference that replaced it. If only they'd just talked or been more honest, but that was never going to happen, not then. Olive did however make one confession.

Years later after Ted died, she eventually told us why he didn't want to tell us about the car or make any kind of claim. According to Olive "The daft bastard never took his driving test. Scared stiff he would fail because of his poor bleedin' eyesight. Mr Ted bleedin' Magoo couldn't even find his own arse'ole."

The result, according to Olive was that Ted had "no license, no insurance and no idea." And with regard to the incident she simply said, "POOF! Any money comin' our way blown up in bloody smoke!"

It all made sense. He was so panicky about being pulled up by the Old Bill that he used to creep along, driving at no more than 25 miles an hour at any given time. Occasionally he would put his foot down and go up to 35 in the slow lane of the motorway but that was rare. Slowmo Ted, as we used to call him, made the car crawl into an art form. Olive could have explained this to us at the time and that would have made her response understandable she but chose not to. She was happy to be cast as the villain and it saved Ted from huge embarrassment. She hid things well but I am not sure that she always had the best of intentions for not revealing the truth. *How much did Ted know?*

The car or lack of it only exacerbated Olive's foul mood. The old Rover was a complete write off and without insurance we couldn't claim for a new one. During this time we were left to fend for ourselves with regards meals. That wasn't a problem as we just dipped into the tins of processed pleasures stacked up on the shelves of the shop as and when we pleased. A tin of macaroni cheese on toast or a Fray Bentos pie would often suffice. If, however we were feeling particularly ambitious we would mix these two together to form the most disgusting gooey mess that was wrong on so many levels. Johnny even invented a name for it where he joined parts of the words together. I can still hear him shouting, "LET'S HAVE THE MAC-FRAY!" And I can still hear the collective "yeah" from me and Belle even though we didn't quite know what it was.

"Yellow and brown shite!" were Olive's words for Johnny's glorious concoction, but we ate it thinking it was something exotic. I tried it again once when I was much older and surprisingly it wasn't that bad!

THE FART

Olive's mood eventually lifted when she found out that Irish Edna from up the road had been caught moonlighting whilst claiming benefits. Olive never liked that woman and did not hide the fact that she was pleased at her misfortune. You could see clearly that this was the case as Olive walked jauntily into the back room of the shop, hoisted up her skirt and pushed her backside towards the heat of the fire. She was reasonably careful that the front part of her skirt covered up what was necessary. Then she let out a cackling rasping fart.

"Christ all bloody mighty!" blurted Johnny.

We both looked astonished. It wasn't the uncouth manifestation of Olive's course manner that caused our response. We were used to it. What made the event so remarkable was that we both saw bright red and yellow sparks spit out and flicker angrily in response to the fart. Oblivious to our reactions, Olive proclaimed, "I am happy today. My arse is full of little chuckles." She then thought for a moment and reflected on the enormity of her fart. "No, I am so ecstatic that my arse is full of rip-roaring laughter."

My brother looked at the satisfied expression on our mother's face and shook his head in disgust. I looked baffled.

"It's Irish Edna. She's been nabbed," whispered Johnny, trying to explain.

"Is that why she's so happy?" I said.

"What the fuck do you think?" said Johnny, annoyed at the naivety of my question.

It seemed an over-the-top response but that was quite common from Johnny. Sometimes I didn't need to do much to wind him up. I didn't think the question was that stupid but it obviously pissed him off. I am not sure what my brother expected of me then. I couldn't be anything else other than what I was. Unfortunately for some of the time that was pretty vacant. He used to thump me on my shoulder when he caught me day dreaming.

"You've got no idea," he would say. "You don't know what it's like in the real world."

"I don't want to," I would answer. "I'd rather be in my own world." I always expected Johnny to hit me again when I said that but strangely enough, he accepted it. Sometimes I wished that I was more like Johnny. He had so much more awareness of what was going on around him. He was practical where I was not. Sometimes I used to think that if I were more like him, he wouldn't be so angry with me.

I once forgot to bring a ball for our cricket game. It was my job as he'd brought everything else. I remember the uneasy feeling I had when I had to confess my mistake. I tried to explain that I could run back home. It would only take a few minutes but that didn't stop him laying into me. "You gormless bastard. Only one pissin' thing to worry about." It didn't stop there. "You fuckin' waste of space. I'm not playing with you again."

Johnny went on for a good few minutes and needless to say I was in tears afterwards. My punishment was harsh and strange because he could also be incredibly protective of me and in many respects he looked out for me but I guess he just took stuff out on me. There were times when I felt that everything that he bottled up was poured over me.

My base layers are on. They will probably be painted over. You can't always see the underneath in a painting but the layers are important. I often go as close as I can to some of the great paintings as you can learn so much more by seeing what's underneath. Sometimes chinks of that underneath show through but it isn't obvious at first. Sometimes it's intentional and sometimes it isn't but if you don't look, you'll never know. I would go so far as to say that with some paintings you can never fully understand them until you see what's underneath. It can be quite revealing.

I tell my students not to be fooled by what's on the surface. Sometimes what's underneath can be just as important.

There were layers with Johnny – an underneath but I didn't look closely. I was blinded by his comic talent and I was too young to see. If I could have frozen moments of time like a painting and I was a few years older, I might have been able to go up close and see what lay beneath the surface and then I would have understood. I asked Johnny about Michael a few days after he was 'found'. He just shrugged his shoulders and said that "he was alright. Not a bad lad. He was funny but 'es dead now so there's no point." It was clear that he didn't want to talk about him or events around that time and I never got to the bottom of it until years later.

THE POLICE

I am not sure how much of the sky blue I want to remain. I am not sure whether or not my way of working is normal. I start with colours that I don't necessarily want to be seen and then work over or take away. This time I take away with a scraping tool. I then use my thumb to smooth out some of the area, being careful to leave any happy accidents. What is normal anyway?

In one sense it wasn't odd. In fact it seemed perfectly normal to see lots of police round at the shop. It never felt weird to walk in the back room and find one, two or even three sat there supping a cup of tea as they were always calling in. For whatever reason, Olive was like a magnet and they loved chatting to her.

My mother had a strange relationship with the police. I know she enjoyed the "crack" but she never hid the fact that she believed most of them were as "bent as a nine bob note." Nevertheless she still encouraged them to seek sanctuary in the back room of "Olive's Offy." All the while she would tempt them with hot drinks, custard creams and her own brash charm. She in turn found out what was going on and picked up tit bits of local gossip. But some women love a man in uniform.

What was her name?"Betty," I say out loud.

From nowhere she appeared. She was a vivacious bubbly blonde about my mum's age with an ample bosom and short skirt. I can't remember how but she seemed to become our friend in a very short space of time and soon became a very intimate friend of the police. To be fair she often helped out and was always a good laugh. I still cringe when I remember Johnny asking me to ask her about how she found being the police bike.

I'd no idea what the expression 'police bike' meant so I was hesitant at first. "Go on," he said, "she likes people asking her about her little hobby." I was so gullible that I went along with his request.

I was so earnest. "How do you find being the police bike?" I asked. I can hear my voice now; all innocent but as soon as I said it I knew something was wrong. Betty went bright red and looked over to Johnny who was smirking. "Fine," she said sharply "fine" and then tried to give Johnny a slap but he was too quick for her and darted out of the way.

I smile to myself. Johnny used to try to get me in so much trouble. I rinse my paint brush and tell myself that it's not just about Johnny. The police, they're an important part of it all. There were clues.

Some broad tones to model the nose and cheek bones. Quickly done as I don't want to lose the energy.

I feel myself going back to the time just after Ted's accident with the old Rover. The bell of the shop door rings and a voice calls out across an empty shop.

We didn't need to see him to realise who it was. The voice was cheery and familiar.

"Evenin' Ol." We all recognised it straight away. It was Bill, our friendly policeman.

"For Christ's sake," uttered Johnny beneath his breath. "Who the bloody 'ell does he think he is, Dixon of Dock Green?"

It was funny but also quite sarcastic. Johnny could be like that.

"That's 'evenin' all," said Ted who emphasised the "all." He clearly had not got the joke. Johnny just shook his head in disbelief and on his way out turned to Ted.

"You can hear when you want to then."

29

Ted didn't respond.

Bill's heavy footsteps gradually drowned out my brother's lighter quicker ones as they passed each other in the shop front. Johnny was nipping out to see his mate Andy.

It was the swish of the coloured PVC curtain that heralded the appearance of Bill or rather Bill's head in the back room of the shop. He never came all the way in, not straight away. He sort of poked his head in to see if all was OK first. Bill would consider it bad manners, even if he had known the family for many years, to simply walk in without some respect so a head first was more polite than the whole body. Sometimes it appeared odd as though Bill were just this disembodied head wearing a ridiculous policeman's helmet floating up the side of the wall with coloured curtain strands wrapped around his ears like some sort of celebratory garland. And then it would talk.

"Ok if I came in?"

"'Ello Bill," said Olive who was pleased to see him. And as Bill pulled the strands of plastic further apart there appeared another policeman alongside him.

"Who the bloody 'ell's this?" said Olive to Bill. "Christ, he doesn't look old enough." Olive then turned to the fresh-faced copper. "Are you sure you're mum's let you out this late luv? Isn't it past your bed time?"

The young man looked sheepish and mumbled something like "Well, urm." Olive loved it.

"Well park your arses then," she said briskly.

The two largish figures did as they were told and sat down on the old tea-stained, red-cushioned settee.

"It's not just a social," said Bill "It's about the car. Ted's accident."

"Stacey, put the kettle on!" commanded Olive who sat down opposite the two policemen. "Now about the car," she stated in business-like fashion, "It's..." Olive suddenly broke off and turned to her husband and told him "Ted would you mind serving in the shop a minute?"

"But there's no one...," Ted was unable to finish his sentence as his wife overrode him.

"Just do as you are told, there's a good husband." She then turned to Bill and rather patronisingly suggested that Ted was better off in the shop. Ted got the message and wondered slowly out of the back room to stand behind the shop counter even though there wasn't a customer in sight. He looked like a lost soul, all alone with no one to serve but he would never relinquish his post nor would there be any dereliction of duty until Olive gave the order to re-join the main party. Anyway, he was more than happy to let Olive do the talking. Given his circumstances it was a wise course of action.

Meanwhile, Stacey my precocious fourteen year going on seventeen-year-old sister, took an instant shine to Bill's partner, a very attractive young man in uniform. I'd noticed just recently how she was taking more of an interest in boys. Stacey was definitely changing and developing fast. Her figure had become curvier but she was still slim. I saw her a few times watching herself in the mirror practicing standing in a certain way, pouting her lips and bringing her brown hair over the sides of her face.

She was trying it now. It was pitiful really. It was so forced. But she forgot the pout and instead let her jaw drop. She might as well have been drooling. She couldn't stop staring at the young man. Olive had clocked this from the very moment that her daughter had entered the room. Two whispered words were all it took from Olive which were uttered quietly but very threateningly in her daughter's ear.

"Piss off."

She got the idea very quickly and scurried up the stairs. I was told to make myself scarce as well, so I did. Eventually when me, Stacey and Belle came back half an hour later everybody was laughing and joking and I knew everything was OK. Somehow Olive had smoothed things over. With Bill's help she had managed to get a little money from the manager of the truck company and amazingly Ted was still allowed to drive! Bill even got Ted a good deal from the scrap merchant for the old Rover.

The young policeman, who had said nothing then mumbled something about the toilet. Olive was busy in conversation with Bill and gestured towards the back door. Suddenly, Stacey elbowed me in the ribs.

"Quick, quick!" she gasped and motioned me to come upstairs and look outside the window. "It's the young copper 'e's going to use the outside toilet and it's just getting dark." And with that Stacey sniggered. We both knew the perils of that short journey from the back door to the outside toilet. We waited in anticipation. Stacey could hardly contain herself. He was such a dishy young copper but she was just dying to see his reaction from what was surely about to happen. We both waited for the pained outcry and sure enough it came.

"Shit, shit, shit, shit!"

"What's wrong?" cried Olive, feigning innocence.

"Can't you clean up this bloody dog shit," said the young man swearing as he tried to scrape off several squelchy brown turds from his freshly polished black shoes courtesy of our Jack Russell who was a regular shitting machine. Nobody ever cleaned up Kimmy's shit for two reasons. One, Kimmy was quite territorial over his little turds and chances are he would come and give you a nasty little nip if he saw you cleaning them up. Two, the dog ate too much (Belle used to feed him when Olive wasn't looking) and consequently it was always shitting and there was lots of it. Thankfully it was just in the yard.

It didn't help that nobody ever took the dog for a walk as he was always starting fights with other dogs. The only reason we kept it was Olive. There seemed to be a mutual admiration for each other's feistiness. Kimmy was her "lovely little arse'ole" (a rare but justifiable use of the word) but for us it was a malicious little git. I swear it used to save up its worst kind of turds…the walnut whips and deposit them in the places where it would be most likely to be trodden in (usually the top step).

Eventually when it got too much and the yard was literally a minefield of crap, Ted would go out with a peg on his nose and a long-handled poop scoop. He operated it at arm's length with expert precision like a topiarist skilfully crafting a hedge. Sometimes the clean-up took him a good half hour. The finale would be a grand hose down and big bottle of disinfectant poured liberally over all areas of the yard floor. We only ever used that outside toilet if we were desperate.

"It's supposed to be lucky!" shouted Olive.

"What is?" bellowed an indignant voice.

"Stepping in shit. Anyway you lot are on some nice little earners. You can put up with a little shit now and then." Olive laughed to herself happy in the knowledge that her dog had done its job. Quite literally.

"Sorry," said Bill to the young policeman as he hopped inside. "I forgot to warn you."

"Don't worry," said the young man still frowning, "I'll remember next time." He then looked around….

"Have you got a bathr…?"

"Upstairs first right," said Olive cutting him off." She watched him closely as he made his way up the stairs. "And don't tread any shit in my carpet. I know how ignorant you lot can be."

Bill and Olive laughed.

"He'll be alright," said Bill quietly to Olive. "Gary's new but he's not a bad lad."

"He just seems a little bit too straight," said Olive, smiling.

"That's the problem," said Bill, "Everybody is too straight-laced."

He said this looking directly at Belle who didn't quite know what to make of that comment. Bill suddenly laughed and Belle found herself laughing back. It was difficult not to. Bill's laugh was infectious.

I step back and view the deeper tones, I put the end of my paintbrush in my mouth and contemplate. It's an old habit that helps me to think.

He was little known to us then. He was just a bit-part player but Gary, that wet behind the ears policeman, would go on to become a big part of our lives. In this scene he only had a walk-on part but years later he was important. He helped Belle a lot, that's for sure.

Bill was great company for us youngsters. He was friendly and always seemed to see the funny side of things. It was surprising given the job he did and the sights he must have seen. Perhaps experience had taught him that a sense of humour was a good way of surviving. He had found a kindred spirit in Olive, that's for sure. Bill was fondly thought of and had been a family friend for a few years. He had graduated from sitting on hard chairs in the back room to loafing in the upstairs lounge on a very tatty but comfortable couch. (A cast off from my rich Uncle Ernie whom Olive slagged off at every opportunity). It was Bill's favourite place. I used to watch, fascinated by the way in which his large arse sank down into the cushioned seats. I knew when Bill had stayed late because there was that huge dip in the settee. There were also piles of Holt's pale ale bottles left scattered around the room the next morning. I would often tidy them up. I didn't mind. I liked Bill. In fact he gave me my first camera and later on bought me a photography book. He encouraged me to take photographs. I was even allowed to take some of the family ones. Looking back I have a lot to thank Bill for. He probably helped fuel my love of art.

Sometimes I wished Bill was my dad. He seemed so warm and real.

Bill's wife, Margaret invited us all down for Sunday lunch once. I think she was curious as to what her husband found so interesting that he should spend so much time with us. My older siblings refused to go but as the youngest, me and Belle had no option. We had to attend.

We got a bit of a shock. The house in Prestwich was posh. Gravy was served from a jug, butter was in a dish and they had something called side plates. To be fair I think Margaret found Olive quite entertaining but there would never be a chance of them becoming friends. Olive wouldn't fit in with the blue rinse brigade and I always got the feeling that we made the place look untidy.

Bill talked to Olive about Michael. Bill had a way with him as he knew how to elicit trust. Most of the community trusted him. Bill took time to talk to lots of people including Terry Evans, the youth club leader. Terry was the one who was most upset about Michael's death. I saw it in his bloodshot eyes and witnessed Ted giving him a hug. But there was something secretive going on. I heard a lot of hushed voices and saw a lot of doors close as I was about to walk in.

I heard Frank our lodger's name mentioned a few times but nothing of any significance. But I wasn't that interested. I barely knew Frank anyway. We used to call him the owl as he only came out at night and by then I was usually in bed. I remembered a few things which made sense later but at that time it all seemed vague and unfocussed and Frank was just a blur.

THE SMELL

Now that the acrylic base and outline are complete it is time to change medium. (I like to use acrylic first because it dries quicker) I reach for a couple of tubes of oil paint – burnt umber, titanium white, and alizarin crimson. With each one I unscrew the cap and squeeze. The paint comes out differently to acrylic, it's firmer and the colour seems to have more body. Sometimes I use the paint straight from the tube...impasto. I may well do that later on but right now I need to thin it with linseed oil or turps. I take the lid off the linseed oil and poke my nose over the top. It's delicate but that familiar nutty scent of seeds and flax fills my nostrils. I do the same to the turps. It's not household turps although I am fond of that smell too but this is refined turpentine that has a rich and gorgeous odour of pine resin. A memory is triggered.

"Jesus! What's that fuckin' smell?" said Derrick forcefully. He never swore much but such was the offensiveness of the odour, it was completely justifiable. Johnny was just about to say that his brother's nose was too close to his arse when he got a whiff.

"Christ!" was all he could say and then a few seconds later heaved. "What the fuck?"

They both screwed up their faces and looked round in disgust, before Derrick worked it out.

"It's your bloody socks," he said looking at me and pointing sharply to a couple of 'rags' draped over the fire guard.

"Look at 'em. They're steaming."

I looked over at the gas fire roaring away, virtually cooking my footwear. My brother was right. The vapour given off was very physical. I'd made the mistake of not washing them properly in my bath water. It was Johnny's fault as he knew it was bath night but he still ran a deep bath. By the time I'd jumped in after him it was freezing and all the hot water had gone. I had to get out quickly so my socks only got a quick dip in pretty murky water. The fact that I'd been wearing them all week made matters worse.

Stacey went up close. She always had a morbid curiosity and took a couple of short sniffs. Her face became quite pained. "Good God. I want to be sick."

"I think that's exaggerating things," I said.

"Exaggerating!" Johnny exclaimed. "Exaggerating. Just wash the fuckin' things properly you gormless bastard."

Head drooped in pathetic fashion I moped over to collect the offensive clothing.

"Look, "Johnny said, "It's like a child playing in its own nappy. It don't mind its own shit." And at that point my brother poked me in the ribs and flicked the back of my ear. I let out a yelp. It was painful.

"Steady on Johnny," said Derrick.

"What the fuck do you know, you fuckin' piece of shit!" came the rage-filled reply. It was completely out of the blue and it was bloody aggressive. It shocked us all but it wasn't surprising as Johnny never needed an excuse with his brother. Derrick stared back icily through those thin round spectacles. Johnny walked up to his older brother who was taller and squared up to him.

"Go on then," said Johnny.

Derrick said nothing but continued to stare at his brother for a second or two but then he just walked out of the room. Although we felt sorry for Derrick we were also shocked at his limp response.

"Fuckin' coward," said Johnny as Derrick shut the door.

Everything fell silent. It was awkward. And then Stacey broke the ice.

"You wanna do something about those socks," she said in a helpful way. It eased the tension. She then hastily pulled up a window and without thinking grabbed one of Olive's brass ornaments to prop it open.

The old sash windows' cords were always breaking but it wasn't just brass ornaments that were used as stoppers – a hardback edition of Treasure Island, Ted's old tool box or an Etchasketch proved just as effective. But the whole house was like that; propped up with make shift solutions in wonky rooms. I can hear Johnny saying, "It's worse than the bloody fun house at Blackpool."

"There, that's better," said Stacey and the bad smell quickly dissipated but didn't vanish completely. The odour of my brother's fall out still lingered.

Sometimes I just wished everything was back to normal like it used to be.

Opening the window did however, let a chill blast of cold air into the room. It also made everything a little louder as the rumbling noise of the traffic from the busy road outside was heard as well as seen. We all sat there freezing for five minutes but anything was more tolerable than the pungent odour of my steaming socks and in a moment the drama was forgotten.

Maybe we stopped questioning my brothers' relationship because their enmity became normal. It is a thought that hangs in the air as I pick at some loose bristles from the large hog hair brush and pull them out.

I clean my brush with an old rag and look out of the window. I am just about able to see the sea. My view is quite different from the smoke-filled sky line and slated roof tops I saw as a boy. I have been gone from Manchester for some time but I still remember that view from my bedroom window and those peculiar urban scents.

FOREIGNERS

Whenever Mrs Singh walked past the shop window with her large brood in tow, Olive couldn't help herself, she had to make a comment. Usually it was "Christ almighty, it's gettin' more like bloody old Calcutta every day."

Although crudely put, I could see what she meant, Cheetham Hill was becoming quite "foreign." An influx of Bangladeshi and Pakistani immigrants had altered the look and feel of the area. It was more noticeable on warm summer days when bright saris were unleashed from beneath grey overcoats that otherwise kept out the shitty Manchester weather. I remember thinking that they always seemed to cook a lot as I could smell garlic and odd spices everywhere. As time went on it was not so uncommon for a waft of curry to drown out the greasy but ultimately comforting odours of the fish and chip shop next door. I viewed this invading scent and the culture it was attached to with suspicion.

It was therefore ironic that at this time I became good friends with a foreigner. He was new to the area, Nawab Haider, the boy from Bangladesh. Our friendship didn't start too well. I'd lost a small football some days earlier. Some of my friends swore that "the little foreign bastard" had nicked it. I knew that he hadn't because I'd found it and he was playing with a different one. But goaded by all around I went up to him, snatched "my ball" back and punched him in the face.

As my fist thudded into the soft cartilage of his nose I yelled out, "You fuckin' bastard." I don't know where that came from but as he hit the floor, blood gushed instantly from both nostrils. I suddenly felt sick. In that instant I would have given anything to have taken back what I did and said. It wasn't just that I was instantly ashamed of this spiteful cowardly act that, to be honest, had more than a hint of racist intent but it was the fact that I was going to get the cane. I had never had it before. I was one of the so called "good kids."

I waited all day, terrified at being asked to see the headmaster but the call never came. To my surprise and utter relief Nawab never told on me. I saw him later on that day waiting at the gates to pick up his younger sister. I'd never really noticed him before and even when I punched him I think I had my eyes closed. But now I felt compelled to look at him closely. It was my penance. He was thin and sallow looking and never a match for me. I shook my head in self-disgust.

On further inspection I could see that a neat mop of jet-black hair framed a pale brown face with a nose that was quite swollen. He looked vulnerable and slightly lost. I already felt guilty enough but there pointing towards me, accusing me was the tip of his blood stained collar peeping out from his grey pullover. I tried to walk past him but couldn't. My legs wouldn't let me so I stopped and instinctively reached into my pocket.

"Here," I said offering him some half-melted, half-eaten chocolate.

Nawab viewed me with a little suspicion but after some hesitation gently took the peace offering. Whilst this was happening his younger sister walked quietly over and positioned herself behind Nawab's legs.

"Can she have some too?" I asked.

Nawab nodded so I offered her the last bit but, as I held out my hand, she moved further behind her brother.

"It's ok," said Nawab to his sister, but his sister wouldn't come out. He then turned to me and said apologetically "Sal does not trust anybody yet."

"Well, I don't blame her," I said sheepishly, "I can see why. Look, I am sorry."

"Don't worry" he said forlornly. I suddenly realised that a part of him was used to the racist attacks.

"Shit, shit, I wish I could…"

"Don't worry," insisted Nawab, "It's fine." And remarkably it was.

I spent the next half an hour walking with him to his house. In that time the barriers seemed to lift and we got on. Nawab's English was good and it was clear that he was well educated which surprised me. I learnt that his family, who were pretty well off, had to flee from some kind of political persecution whatever that meant. We quickly became friends. Over the next few weeks Nawab told me about his father who was still in Bangladesh suffering in some kind of prison and then I thought of my own father and suddenly I was very grateful for Ted, however inept he appeared.

I told him about my family and about the difficulties in our lives…the hostility between my brothers and Olive and about some of the mysteries surrounding the time of Michael's death. About Frank too. It must have been the way I told it because it seemed perfectly natural for Nawab to ask the question.

"Do you think Frank the lodger murdered Michael?"

"I don't know," I said seriously, "he did disappear quite soon after and nobody seems to know why."

"What about the police?"

"They've ruled out foul play so it can't be Frank."

"Not necessarily. Have you asked your parents about Frank?"

"I did once and my mum nearly blew my head off. I'm not going there again."

"We have only conjecture then," said Nawab "But we can still theorise."

I kind of got what Nawab was saying. He trusted me enough to be himself and not shy away from using his extensive vocabulary. He was careful to hide it amongst others at the school but not with me and I enjoyed his way with words. He theorised about a few things. I got the idea that he liked it. I must admit that some of his notions were preposterous. At one stage he even had the church and the police in league. It was, however, good fun and proved to be light relief for me.

Nevertheless all this conjecture and theory, as Nawab put it, proved to be quite disconcerting and gave me bad dreams about Frank. The trouble was I could never quite picture him. Rather like Michael, his face was a bit of a blur which only added to the unsettling nature of any thoughts I had about Frank.

I scrape the Prussian blue off my no 10 Filbert brush on to a piece of card that I was using as a palette. It doesn't quite do the job so I get the old tea towel and squeeze hard being careful not to take the bristles off. It does the trick. As I start to mix a warmer hue with the cleaner brush, I realise that I was really quite fortunate.

If I hadn't seen Nawab as I was leaving, if he hadn't befriended me when I'd done little to help him, if he hadn't shown me kindness when I showed him cruelty, if he hadn't forgiven me when I didn't deserve it, would I have turned out differently? Would I have continued to view Johnny foreigner with fear and suspicion? His kind actions towards me made think about the kind of person I wanted to be and made me question how I viewed the "other."

I still did bad things. I went along with the gang when we put worms through Mrs Herman's letterbox because she was a Jew and I joined in when we threw marbles and smashed old Mr Hussein's window but none of these things were as funny any more. In fact they became a source of shame and in the end I distanced myself from such acts. But in the early seventies it was so easy to fall in with the crappy view of other cultures because in Cheetham Hill "they" were spreading. "All of them lot comin' over 'ere, taking our jobs, takin' over our shops, bloody takin' everythin" was a commonly-held view within many households like ours. Enoch Powell's speeches and all the stuff coming from the Conservative party resonated with many who lived in our area. We in the north were poor and angry and it was easy to blame immigrants. Olive was the worst. She would always go on about the bloody Irish or the Pakis and yet the stupid thing was that if she saw any one of them in need she wouldn't hesitate to help. She did help once and it proved to be one of the most important things she ever did.

There was also fear and suspicion from Nawab's parents. They didn't want me to mix with their son and as a consequence I didn't knock around with him much outside of school. I wasn't allowed to. His parents had plans for their son and didn't want anybody or anything distracting him from the path that they had chosen for him. In fact, as far as I knew, he didn't play out much at all. They were being protective and I could understand why.

It was a right old state of affairs so thank goodness for the genius of Johnny Speight. The TV comedy show 'Till death us do part' did more to explode the popular prejudices that existed at the time than any left-wing political counter argument, not that I ever heard any. It was pure gold. I didn't get it straight away as I was too young and just found it funny. We used to call everyone a scouse git and me and Nawab would imitate Alf by continually saying in a contrived cockney accent "it stands to reason."

When I look back I still despair at Olive saying "'es got a point though 'asn't 'e Ted? Alf's got a point about all those coloureds." I can still see Ted nodding compliantly.

The show put into words part of what I was beginning to feel. I started to question many things…my white working class background, the kiss me quick rubbish from Blackpool, bags of chips and the perceived narrow-minded view that I was surrounded with and that's probably the reason why a free-thinking art education so appealed to me. The problem was that a few months at Manchester Poly and I thought I knew it all. For a short time I was such an arrogant twat. I was never ashamed of my roots, I just thought that I was above them. Johnny soon sorted me out but that's getting ahead of myself. I was just glad that Nawab never met Olive. That was a relief.

I remember thinking that it was probably for the best. I'm not sure how a possible meeting with Olive would have panned out. God knows what ideas Nawab would have brought back into the Haider household. No, there was never going to be the remotest chance that Nawab would ever come into contact with her but his brother did. He met Olive and he was the one who caused a real stir in our household.

Jammi

It was one of the rare times that me and Nawab ever mixed outside of school and the only time I ever went to his house. Olive was not bothered about me mixing with the boy from Bangladesh. She was never too concerned about where I played and who I played with but she didn't want me coming home smelling like some "curried shit." So just before it got too late Stacey was sent by Olive to collect me from Nawab's house.

Nawab's older brother Jammi (short for Jamiruddin) was standing to the side of me and Nawab. He was watching over us, curious about the game of marbles we were playing. He looked on attentively, his chubby brown face framed by thin wispy strands of black facial hair. Jammi was an interesting character. For a start he could swear like a trooper.

"Do you want some fucking Blackjacks? Go on, bloody take some. Yes, bloody take some. And some fucking Fruit Salads." His swearing was chummy and enthusiastic as he shoved a fist full of sweets towards us. Me and Nawab laughed. It was partly to do with the way he looked. His face was quite gentle with no sign of the confrontational countenance of a hardened Mancunian and consequently his vulgar language carried no threat. In fact, it was endearing.

"What is so fucking funny you bastards? Is it the bastard sweets? They are so fucking chewing, isn't it?" Jammi carried on chuntering away for a good few minutes.

We laughed even more. Just then Stacey turned up and without a thought Jammi blurted out, "Bloody lovely."

I looked up to see my sister who looked strangely different. Out of Olive's reach and vision, Stacey had made some changes. Her skirt was hoisted up showing off her shapely legs and revealing more than a little thigh. A bit of lippy and some deft flicks of eye shadow had highlighted her pretty features. Some slingback shoes (smuggled out in a small silver handbag) completed a very fashionable look. Stacey smiled. Jammi's comment met with her approval.

"What?" said Stacey indignantly in response to my quizzical look.

"Can't a girl dress up once in a while?"

I didn't respond, I was more concerned with winning my game of marbles. Stacey then walked up to me hesitantly. "Just don't tell the dragon," she whispered. And then her bravado returned as she walked past me swaying her hips provocatively. "I'm just having a bit of fun!" she added wryly.

It was clear that Jammi liked this kind of fun and Stacey knew it. As me and Nawab finished our game I could see Stacey sidle up to Jammi. My sister was definitely flirting and before long they engaged in a peculiar activity of laughing quite loudly and then talking very quietly. It was annoying because it made me lose my game of marbles! I should have guessed. They were making secret arrangements to see each other again and in the blink of an eye Stacey and Jammi had made a secret date. What on earth were they playing at?

The date

They decided to meet at the bottom of Cardinal Street by the newsagents. It was about a mile away from their respective homes. In their minds it was far enough away to make it unlikely that anyone would see them and, besides, they weren't doing anything wrong.

Stacey didn't give Jammi's nationality or culture a second thought. She wasn't aware of how much trouble mixed relationships could be. She was naïve in that way. It was just that she found him amusing and she was sure that he would be good fun to be around but Stacey was still a little guarded. If anybody said anything, this wasn't a proper date anyway. The whole thing felt clandestine as they furtively walked around the block and took a small detour along the back of Smedley Fields. They briefly stopped at a place close by the old railway track and peered through a small gap in the fence. Close by was a park bench with a small plaque screwed to the back commemorating the life of a young boy tragically cut short.

"I fucking know him," said Jammi pointing to the plaque.

"Yes, I do too. Poor Michael."

They both stood there for a few more seconds and then dismissed themselves.

"Do you want some of my sherbet dip?" said Stacey as they trundled on down the footpath.

"Don't fucking mind if I do," said Jammi cheerily. Stacey watched as Jammi scooped some up.

"I need to get back," said Stacey.

47

Jammi simply smiled. They couldn't stay any longer as Olive was already suspicious. It was however more than enough time to arrange a second "real" date. In her own mind Stacey had already organised for her friend Linda to be her alibi.

The following week they both got the 59 bus up to Heaton Park. As soon as they got off the bus, well away from their respective neighbourhoods, they felt free and for the next couple of hours they were both stupid teenagers with all inhibitions cast aside. They threw each other into the shrubbery that lay either side of the park's pathways and laughed unashamedly at their resultant bedraggled looks. Jammi bought Stacey an ice cream and daubed a bit on her nose. Stacey reciprocated by plonking the whole of the cornet on his nose. Jammi let it stay there for a minute as strawberry and vanilla streams ran down into his mouth. If the streams in any way deviated from this path then Jammi guided them back to his mouth via an expert use of his tongue. Never once did he use his hands. Stacey was suitably impressed and they laughed again and then they laughed some more. They both had such wild and innocent fun but they knew they couldn't be too long as this time Jammi's mum would be suspicious so they reluctantly made their way to the bus stop. It was a slow but blissful walk which had to come to an end.

"It's the bastard 59 bus stop," said Jammi reluctantly.

"Yes, it is," said Stacey.

"What a fucking good date it is."

"Yes," came the soft reply.

There seemed to be something expectant in the air. There was no one around so they snogged. It was initiated by Jammi but Stacey felt a little uncomfortable. She wasn't quite sure because a part of her really didn't mind. She gently pushed Jammi away. He wasn't at all worried, nor did he feel rejected. "Bloody lovely," he said smiling away to himself.

They stepped onto the bus, aware that eyes were on them. They were careful. They didn't hold hands but they did giggle which definitely annoyed some of the elderly passengers. As they were getting off the bus they made arrangements to see each other but Stacey was still a little unsure as she had an uneasy feeling. It wasn't just the kiss, it was as if someone was watching. It was the next evening that those suspicions proved to be accurate

.

We were all watching telly when we heard it kicking off. "Open up, open up. I am demanding you bloody open up!" The shouts were fierce and angry. Banging fists then thudded against the locked door of the shop. It was a right old racket. We all rushed down to see what was happening.

"Open up!" and again more fist banging.

"Oh shit. It's Nawab's mum," I blurted out. There was another woman with her. She looked vaguely familiar. "I think it's Nawab's auntie," I said to anybody who would listen. She was dangling Nawab's youngest brother, two-year-old Fassi around her hip. Even he looked pissed off.

"Bloody open up!" Mrs Haider repeated. That swearing. She sounded like a high-pitched Jammi. Speak of the devil, there he was standing head bowed in sheepish fashion just behind the two irate women. Olive waited at the back, hidden from view and then at the right moment she strode forward and we all stepped back like Moses parting the red sea. It was dramatic. She then slowly walked up to the door, slid the catch back and very deliberately turned the lock. There was a pause, the door opened and in frank and earnest fashion Olive spoke,

"What the bloody 'ell do you want?"

Everything was contained in that statement: 1) this had better be good, 2) I'm taking no shit and, 3) watch out. I pose a threat!

"Your daughter. That floozy," continued Mrs Haider in a very proper English accent, "She has tempted my Jammi. He is a young boy, my boy and your daughter with short skirts and…your daughter is a bloody floozy!"

Olive never batted an eye lid, instead she slowly reached into her pocket and pulled out her pack of fags. She took the middle one of three, tapped it on the lid of the packet and lit it. She inhaled deeply. It was both luxurious and purposeful, she then exhaled. Not once did the dragon take her eyes off Mrs Haider and her sister. They were hypnotised as the long tendrils of smoke softly drew them in. In Olive's world they were small fry. She had had far worse to deal with in her time. The dragon's demeanour exuded the confidence of a battle-hardened warrior and it affected the two women as they began to crumble. As if to force home her advantage Olive waited and then summoned her daughter.

"SSSTTTTAAACCEEYYYYY." The cry was deep and authoritive with a growl attached to the end. All the while the dragon continued to eyeball them. She smiled as she watched her little piece of theatre take effect. In the time it took Stacey to come downstairs, Mrs Haider wilted like a plant without water whilst her sister purposely let herself be distracted by the small child. The women looked down as they avoided Olive's glare.

As Stacey came to the shop door much of their anger had dissipated. In fact Jammi gave Stacey a little wave. She acknowledged this only slightly. She had to be ultra careful not to arouse her mother.

Mrs Haider's sister then told Olive of "the kiss." Olive remained unmoved.

"Thank you for telling me," said Olive sternly, "I will wash my daughter's mouth out with soap and water because I don't know where this little bastard's been." And at that precise moment Jammi felt the full force of Olive's Gorgon glower. We all turned away. It was hideous.

Before the two women could say anything, Olive continued. "Believe me they won't be seeing each other again." Mum looked at Stacey who nodded her head in agreement. "Now, if I were you," she decreed looking at her adversaries, "I would piss off and if you ever darken my door like that again I will not be so accommodating." And with that Olive slammed the door in the faces of the two startled women.

Olive looked at Stacey. "You, upstairs!" Stacey knew what was coming. Olive went ballistic. It lasted a good half an hour. I saw her two hours later and her eyes were still red from crying. I felt so sorry for my sister. Poor Stacey. All she'd tried to do was have some fun. I think she was tired of all the stuff that was going on. I was lucky as I could just play out but Olive kept Stacey in a lot more. She was getting to be quite attractive. Olive knew what boys were like from her own experience. She didn't want her daughter getting pregnant, not to a bloody foreigner. That's all she needed. She'd got enough shit on her hands. She didn't want to have any trouble with Stacey. That wasn't going to happen.

Olive went completely over the top and crushed her daughter. It took a long time for Stacey to get over it. Derrick was good with Stacey. He tried to comfort her. He could have such a generous heart. I wanted to help but I didn't know how.

The first layer is on now. I like to rough the painting out first with fairly loose marks. I don't mind the drips from the burnt umber as it stops me being too precious. I watch as one of the drips snakes down the canvas – slow and hypnotic. On the surface it spoils but then it occurs to me that something so stained to begin with can blossom like a relationship that can appear doomed, can succeed. Who would have thought that

Jammi and Olive could have even got on but I'm getting ahead of myself again. At this moment in time Olive is upset.

She knew that she had been hard on her daughter. The old lady could be very good at covering up her feelings but on this occasion the mask slipped a little. We could all sense that she wanted to talk to Stacey, maybe comfort her a little but sadly she never did. That whole event seemed to add to the disparate nature of our family life. Derrick and Johnny at each other, Stacey and Olive not talking, Ted and Olive miles apart and me...an arty farty square peg in a round hole.

It was heavy going but it was Johnny who drew us together, perhaps inadvertently with his comedy, his anarchic humour. He made us laugh through difficult times and later on when we were much older he used it again to try to bring us together. But for my brother's comedy to work he needed a fall guy. Sometimes it was me but more often than not it was Ted. Poor Ted.

THE SQUIRREL

Keep watchin,'" said Johnny. "You'll see it move."

We all gathered round. Belle in particular was transfixed. She was young and may not have known exactly what she was supposed to be looking at but she understood the need for complete concentration and absolute silence.

"It only moves every five minutes. Blink and you'll miss it," Johnny whispered enthusiastically in true David Attenborough fashion.

"Oh, oh, the hands moved. Did you see it folks? This is incredible. We may be about to see something quite extraordinary. Ted could be going for the chocolate. This only happens once every two days."

Ted sat in the corner concentrating so hard on piecing together his tiny aircraft models that he didn't see or hear any of us but Johnny was right, Ted's hand did motion towards a piece of chocolate that Olive had given him three days ago. But then he drew back leaving us all slightly disappointed.

"Will he, won't he. Will he, won't he? That is the big question." Johnny paused for dramatic effect and then resumed. "No, he won't! I'm afraid that's it. There may not be another movement from Ted for another hour."

We couldn't contain ourselves any longer. Stacey broke first and collapsed in fits of giggles and then we all joined in.

"Bugger off you lot," said Ted clearly irritated at the bursting of his contemplatory bubble. When the dust had settled, Ted looked at his piece of chocky longingly. And suddenly we were in a scene from Lord of the Rings and I swear Golem was there whispering in Ted's ear.

"Do not eat the precious right now. No, not now, my precious. Wait, we eats it with our coffee."

Ted's ability to store unwrapped chocolate indefinitely was legendary. It would be there festering amongst the bits of modelling card, the strands of raffia and deposits of glue for days. We used to call him the squirrel. He could even do that thing that squirrels do, where they store nuts in a pouch in their mouth. Dad could do the same. He could make a piece of chocolate last an hour encased in a mucous membrane in the jowls of his cheek.

But the corner of the room that Ted claimed as his own was a real mess. "Full of all sorts of crap," as Olive would say. This was true. It wasn't just his model-making stuff. Ted was a 40-a-day smoker and a continuous coffee drinker. All round that corner, coffee stains and deposits of fag ash would pebbledash the area. It kept people away and was certainly a deterrent against stealing the old man's "precious" chocolate.

I swear I once saw several flies feasting on a small brown sugary treat no more than six inches away from Ted. He sat there completely immobile, fixated on his model-making, not noticing a thing. The buzzing of excited flies' wings, the incessant noise, Ted didn't bat an eyelid, he was so still. However if you looked closely you could see tiny movements of fingers operating tweezers with the deftness of a micro surgeon.

When in the zone, Ted was completely impervious to the world around him. In this state he seemed to emit a kind of dampening field that appeared to make time slow down. In art college I made a short surreal film based on this called 'The Fly and The Chocolate.' In it, the main protagonist, my father, sits making small raffia birds. Over the weeks nothing appears to change – the light, the furniture, the music on the radio, even the clothes the figure is dressed in all remain the same apart from two things – a piece of chocolate that gets smaller and a fly that gets bigger. I remember my tutor commenting that "some clever editing and creative narrative had emphasised the true horror of domesticity." I showed it to Johnny who laughed and then called it "some weird shite."

It was hard to picture Ted in any romantic way but in a light-hearted moment Olive did suggest to me that when she first met Ted she thought he looked a little like Frank Sinatra. I saw an old photograph of my dad once in his navy days. He was smart, clean cut and smiling and if I squinted a little I could see what she meant.

None of us really looked like Olive or Ted. Derrick, the eldest, was blond, blue eyed and blind as a bat. Stacey was slim, wide eyed and often legless. Johnny, the middle sibling was a gangly well-groomed good-looking young boy. Belle, the baby of the family, was cherubic, brown eyed and loving. I was the youngest brother: quiet, freckly and scruffy. We used to joke that we had different fathers. Sometimes I wonder if that were true, perhaps that was the source of the tension, the arguments, the resentment. Maybe we did have different fathers. Maybe Frank was one of our fathers. Maybe Michael was our half-brother, Olive could be incredibly flirtatious. I wouldn't put it past her. I once mentioned this to Nawab who found it very interesting and commented that it was "an insightful hypothesis and may be worth pursuing."

TERRY EVANS

Olive gave me an art history book when I was thirteen which she had come across in a jumble sale. With little regard she tossed it to me. "Ere," she said, "You like this arty shit!" It wasn't exactly given with love but it was thoughtful for Olive. I never read it much as the language was too academic and boring. I didn't much care for the pictures either because they were poor reproductions of old masters; again boring for a thirteen year old but a couple did stand out. I found one of them – Peter Breughel's 'Fight between carnival and lent' interesting. I remember studying it attentively, running my fingers over the painted figures tracing their paths and imagining their life story.

I am now with those same figures in the dark enclosed landscape. I look across and see young and old, farmers and labourers, men and women, people from different classes. The whole gamut of human life is on display. But they are not together. Some are celebrating carnival whilst others are toiling away for Lent. They are at odds, pulling in different directions, just like my family.

I look closely at the expressions on the faces of the characterful individuals. They are ruddy and full of personality. I see my brothers, sisters and my parents in that scene. Johnny is there. He is the rogue. So too is Derrick. He is the secretive one, wanting to hide. Belle and Stacey are the youngsters playing innocent games. Ted is the cobbler immersed in his craft. I am there, clearly the dreamer and Olive the irreverent is there arguing with the vicar about who could be the sinner but there in the corner trying to help the poorest is Terry, Terry the saint.

"Terry Evans," I say out loud.

I shake my head and smile. He was young and idealistic and quite religious back then. He was only a few years older than my brother Derrick but a lot thinner. Terry was, and still is, a good man and is the conscience of my story. He is still here, still around, not quite the missionary he was then but still a believer. Terry my old youth club leader was one of those people who would do anything for anybody, even give somebody the coat off his back. I know this to be true because he did it once. I was there...

"That's a nice coat," said the scruffy bearded figure, "Can I 'ave it? "

I could see an apprehensive look descend on Terry's callow features. He desperately wanted to do the Christian thing and give Bob the tramp his coat but he hesitated. It wasn't that he'd be terribly inconvenienced (in his own mind he could easily get another coat) it's just that if Olive got to know, he would never hear the last of it. Nevertheless, after a moment's deliberation, he unsheathed his coat and handed it over.

"Ta," said the scruffy figure who took his own shabby fleece off and put on Terry's brand new jacket.

"A bit big," said the tramp in a slightly irritated tone. Terry nearly choked but managed to get a reply out.

"I will try to wear one your size next time," he said in a slightly sarcastic tone. I looked on incredulously.

"Terry, what the hell are you doing?"

For a moment Terry couldn't answer. He was caught slightly unaware by the abrupt manner of my question and then he gathered himself together.

"Jesus said unto his disciples that if anybody asks you for your shirt, give him your coat also."

"You do know 'es got about ten of those coats at home," said Ray, one of the lads from our gang.

It was true, Bob the tramp was notorious for trying to blag stuff off people. His stock phrase of "Can I 'ave it?" was asked of everybody that passed him by, over any item that he quite fancied. Nobody paid a blind bit of notice except Terry who was glad to oblige although I am sure I detected a grimace when he peeled off his outer garment in the cold and dank Manchester air.

"Happy now Terry?" said Ray accusingly. Terry frowned for a second but then smiled which slightly irritated us.

"Well 'e is doin' God's work," said one of the lads sarcastically. "Isn't that right Terry?"

"Fraid so," said Terry and the inane smile widened. I swear it was done deliberately to wind us up.

"Easy meat for Olive," said Owen, one of the older more cynical members of the group.

"Not if you don't tell her," said Terry firmly.

"She'll find out anyway," I said, "Even though my lips are sealed." And then it occurred to me.

"Terry you do know it's Thursday. I take it you will be calling in the shop tonight for your cat meat," I said with a hint of warning in my voice. "I'm telling you now, Olive will know. She's got spies everywhere."

It was a genuine concern. He'd been stupidly idealistic and it always wound Olive up. Although our scrawny youth club leader could infuriate us we still looked out for him.

"Am I supposed to be scared?" said Terry shaking his knees and trying to be humorous.

There was a large collective intake of breath. Wrong attitude.

"Okay, okay, I get the message," said Terry, "maybe if I try and charm…"

"NO!" I cried. I've seen people try that before and it hasn't ended well. Just brace yourself. If you're lucky she might not have heard yet or she will go easy on you."

"Right," came a nervous reply.

Terry was now clearly more than a little concerned. I could see that he was considering buying the pet food elsewhere but Olive was the only shop in the area that supplied Spot's favourite meal.

"Okay. I'm going to go home to have a think," said Terry awkwardly.

As he strode off a collective, "good luck" from the gang hung in the air followed by a lone voice echoing down the road. "You'll need it."

Later that day, as soon as Terry walked into the shop, Olive couldn't wait.

"Why don't you bloody dress him in a three-piece suit as well, you dozy bastard."

"What?" said Terry.

"Bob. The coat. You know," Olive said accusingly. And then she looked more closely and scrutinised Terry's arms which were protruding from a shabby coat clearly a size or two too small.

"Don't tell me you've got his on. Christ all bloody mighty you have...Terry it doesn't even fit you."

"Bob's needs were greater than mine, Mrs Smith," replied Terry who laughed hoping that Olive would see the funny side.

"Ok, Terry very funny. Now take the bloody thing off. It smells like the inside of my arse'ole," said Olive.

"Sorry about that Mrs Smith," said Terry meekly and duly took off the offending garment now that he was inside the warmth of the shop.

Terry's strategy had worked. Olive smiled even though she was trying not to. It wasn't just the absurd state of Terry's dress sense, Olive quite liked the fact that Terry still used the formality of Mrs Smith even though they'd known each other for a quite a few years. It showed respect. It was very clear that Olive did have a soft spot for Terry but she wasn't going to let him get away with his stupidity that easily and his positivity positively irritated her.

"I believe it's going to piss down in a minute. That fleece will be about as dry as a Turkish wrestlers arm pit. I do hope you don't get too wet," she said sarcastically.

And then Olive remembered.

"Oh and by the way I think you left a ten bob note in one of the pockets. Bob came in the shop earlier today wafting it around singing "Joy to the Lord." He thanked you and Jesus, bought a crateful of pale ale and then danced off down the street."

Terry frantically searched the pockets of his trousers. He knew he had one on him. Surely it wasn't in the coat he gave Bob, surely even he wasn't that stupid. He searched his trousers again and then much to his dismay he realised that Olive was right.

"Damn!" There was irritation in Terry's voice and in his manner.

"Does Jesus still want you for a sunbeam?" Olive asked in mock positivity. Terry never answered.

It was at this point that Stacey walked in, head bowed. She was still upset by Olive's go at her.

"What's up with Stacey?" Terry asked as she moped around the shop and then sloped out of the front door.

"Leave her Terry. She'll be alright soon," said Olive hopefully.

There was a brief silence before Olive changed the subject and looked thoughtfully at Terry.

"How are you, really?" she asked. Suddenly the mocking tone was gone and Olive appeared genuinely concerned. Her face also changed slightly – she appeared kinder and softer. Terry thought for a second and then replied gently.

"Fine Olive, fine."

Olive seemed reasonably content with his answer. She then turned round and opened the till draw. From inside one of the compartments she pulled out some coins.

"I short changed the dozy bastard. There's about six shilling there. I guessed Bob's little windfall was from your coat pocket. For God's sake Terry, look after yourself!" And with that she thrust the money into his hand and then slapped a tin of Spot's favourite cat food in the other. "Now go on, piss off."

As a startled Terry tried to say something, Olive practically pushed him out of the door. There was a slim chance she might change her mind. It was quite a tender exchange. I'd come to realise that, unlikely as it seemed, they did have respect for each other. From Olive's point of view, Terry was the closest she'd come to seeing a Christian who wasn't hypocritical or didn't try to shove God down her throat all the bloody time, even if he was "a simple sod."

From Terry's point of view he admired Olive's brashness and her willingness to take a stand against injustice. He recognised that beneath her hardened Mancunian cynicism she was also a voice for some of those children who did not have one. But there was something else besides a mutual respect, something secret, a shared sadness. I always sensed that…in the background. It hung over them both like a damp grey fog.

THE YOUTH CLUB

I need to start the details around the eyes. They will be next. The eyes are important and the most difficult part. I think a little about how I am going to proceed and then without thinking I break a biscuit in half and pop the smaller piece in my mouth and munch away.

Terry quite liked me. Outside my family he and Bill were the ones who encouraged me with my art. I'd often show Terry my drawings, usually of Man United footballers (George Best mainly) or comic super heroes. He was genuinely enthusiastic and praised my efforts whenever he could. He recognised that underneath I was quite a sensitive soul and he did his best to help me. Sometimes we'd have a chat during a break in club activities. On one occasion we were sat relaxed on the tables in the hall when he turned round and looked thoughtfully at me.

"You're not like your Johnny are you?"

It was said optimistically as he passed me a cup of Ribena. I got the idea that my brother gave Terry a hard time.

"Derrick was a lot easier," said Terry who appeared in reflective mood. "Johnny could be difficult but to be fair, very funny."

I knew what he meant. I smiled, said nothing and gulped the juice down. Football could be a thirsty game even in the confines of the small church hall. Terry waited for me to finish my drink and then started back up again.

"A couple of years since they were last here. Your brothers."

I nodded. I continued not to say much. Terry seemed to be thinking out loud and it didn't require a response from me. And then suddenly Terry snapped out of his train of thought, gulped his drink down and then screwed the top back on the Ribena bottle quite purposefully. All went quiet. That last act of Terry's was always a tell-tale sign, a grim realisation of what was about to happen. It was Owen who voiced our fears.

"It's the God slot now," he said dejectedly." The other boys groaned in unison but Terry had, over the past few years, learned to prune the essential Christian message into a quick three-minute homily just as we were cooling down. From bitter experience he had learned that this was the only way.

"Get them when they're knackered," was the sage advice of doughty Mrs Sattersthwaite. Terry was not the most captivating of talkers but that advice really worked. After their exertions the boys had little energy to sabotage his mission. Terry worked out that he had about three minutes before Ray started to make his customary farting sounds. I was however, always intrigued at how Terry brought something quite topical to the God slot. A few weeks ago it was about the split up of the Beatles and how Jesus's disciples sometimes had similar arguments but they learned to get over their issues and stick with each other by prayer and God's help.

"Perhaps," concluded Terry, "Paul McCartney and co might not be in the mess they are now if they had read the bible a little more. Jesus always shows us the way to have a good relationship with each other." I could just imagine my brother Johnny pulling that bag of shit to shreds but at the time I didn't quite dismiss it. But I remember that Terry did give one interesting sermon a few weeks after the business with Jammi had died down. It was about forgiveness.

"It's hard to forgive," he said, "Especially when somebody has done something horrible or bad to you but that is what the bible tells us to do. Jesus was asked how many times we should forgive."

And then he turned to us with his key question. "How many times would you forgive?"

There was a pause.

"It depends if they have done something really bad," said Alex.

"Yeah, that's right," I agreed.

"Well it depends what really bad is," said Terry provocatively.

"What about the babes in the wood?" said Ray in a hushed tone.

It all went quiet. A few of us nodded reverently.

"Babes in the wood" was the name given by the media to some young children found dead in the woods on Lippet Hill in June of that year. It somehow captivated the public in a grotesque way. People listened to the news and read the newspapers with real intent and couldn't wait for the latest updates. It wasn't just in the hope that the killer or killers could be found, some of the papers sensationalised the story so that it fed people's morbid curiosity.

Everybody said how awful it was but would be grimly drawn in, especially us lot. Apollo landings political intrigue, wars, great scientific breakthroughs – forget it. This was the news. Nothing much has changed. But Terry was very quiet and said nothing for a good few seconds. His silence caused us to listen. We became fixed on him for the first time but we could see he was struggling. He could have gone for the trite answer about God's forgiveness being vast but he was wrestling with something within himself which transfixed us.

"I think," he said to himself, "I think I would find some things difficult but the hardest thing of all is to forgive yourself." I remember thinking that, in that moment, he seemed very human and vulnerable and we warmed to him more than usual. Terry didn't elaborate. The room was still for a few more seconds as his mind went to another place. Then Ray let out a proper fart. Terry was quite pleased with the break in his line of thinking. In fact a small smile came to his lips.

"Right then you lot, who's for a game of BRITISH BULLDOG?" he shouted. It whipped everybody up into a frenzy. All of us quickly downed our drinks and then almost in unison slammed the cups down on the table. In the twinkle of an eye that thoughtful and sombre moment was forgotten, consigned to a small fragment of history as everybody went completely mad.

Later on that day (perhaps buoyed by that last exciting game} Terry wrote a report about the progress of the youth club for the parish magazine;

St Luke's youth club report, June 1970

Having started the boys club up this year after an absence of two years, I am pleased to see that numbers are rising. We now have nine boys ranging from 11 to 13. Many thanks to Mrs Sattersthwaite for helping out with squash and biscuits on club nights.

The recent jumble sale raised over £15 and will go towards sports equipment. Many thanks to Olive Smith for donating some tins of Irish stew and helping to set it up.

We are hoping to arrange a day trip to Southport for the boys and organise a football tournament in the summer. We will be joining in with the scouts, any help will be greatly appreciated.

A reminder that in order to be able to attend boys club, you will need to attend church one Sunday in the month.
Terry Evans

It was the first youth club report he had written for the church since Michael's death two years previously.

Eyes are the windows to the soul. I have to get them right. A portrait can be won or lost on this basis. A smaller brush, some burnt umber and a more careful application but it's not working. It's a struggle.

It was Moira, Michael's mum who asked Terry to take Michael along to the youth club. She was worried about her son. She never stopped worrying about anything. She was always yabbin' away.

"'E spends too much time on 'is own. God knows what 'e does in 'is room all day long. Don't answer that Terry, but 'e needs to mix with other lads. You will look after him won't you? 'E can be a bit strange but 'es a nice lad. Why 'e doesn't want to go out I don't know."

"Don't worry," said Terry firmly. His interruption had the desired effect as Moira stopped her nervous ramblings. "He will be fine."

But he was an odd lad, Michael. He never really fitted in with the rougher stuff. Instead he used to enjoy watching from the sides. He would stand there impishly laughing at the other boys' antics. Michael loved watching. He was quite the voyeur. Strangely enough Johnny got on well with Michael. They were an unusual combination but they laughed at the same things. Michael himself was an odd mix of personality traits – he was quite sensitive but he did have a mean streak. Like Johnny he could put someone down but whereas Johnny's humour was more banter, Michael's could be vicious. Johnny would sometimes call him a bitch. That was about right.

Terry always kept an eye out for Michael. He knew that boys like him could be picked on but he wasn't. Maybe the other boys were slightly wary as he was scarily good with words. It was Michael's origami that impressed Terry. He was a bloody master. Terry always goes on about the day he brought some in for a skills talk. The lads loved it. Michael showed them how to make one – a lotus flower or something like that. Terry couldn't quite recall. But what he and all of the boys did remember was that Michael was a really good teacher. Everybody agreed, Michael would have made a splendid teacher. Terry kept his "masterpiece" and tucked it away in a draw for safe keeping.

One day Terry brought it along to the youth club. He called me over, "Have a look at this," he said as he opened the palm of his hand. There, resting on his bony fingers, was a delicate piece of paper sculpture that vaguely resembled something floral.

"Michael told me not to give up even though I was making a pig's ear of it," said Terry. "He told me not to worry as he did just as badly first time." Terry looked wistfully at his pride and joy. "What do you think of my lotus flower?" he said smiling. Terry knew that it wasn't great but felt the need for my artistic opinion.

"Well, it's interesting."

Terry smiled again and then he continued to recall the episode. "What made it worse was that everybody else did brilliantly. The other boys loved the fact that they'd succeeded where their leader, me, had failed. They laughed, I laughed with them but more out of embarrassment and still Michael continued to encourage me." There was a pause.

"'Orrible origami," added Terry, "That's what he called it but his wasn't much better."

"Who's that?" I said.

"Frank. Your lodger. He joined in with the boys laughin' at my terrible attempt, that's what 'e said, 'orrible origami. The phrase stuck with me. But his was just as bad. In fact it was bloody awful."

I still really didn't know much about Frank so I probed a little more.

"What was Frank like?"

"Frank?" said Terry and then he paused. "Frank." He was thinking carefully about what to say.

"He was a good help at the club. He'd originally come down to take a few stints on first aid but ended up doing a little more. It was your mum that encouraged him to come down in the first place. I was quite happy because I was looking for a volunteer to take a few skills sessions. The boys took to him well, particularly Michael." And then Terry stopped as though he had said something he shouldn't have.

"What do you mean?" I asked.

"Well, Michael didn't usually take to others. He was okay with your Johnny but I noticed he wasn't great with adults. Frank seemed to have a way with him." Terry paused. "Anyway, talking of origami and all things arty, how's your art these days?"

It was skilfully done but he didn't need to change the subject. I wouldn't have persisted, I could see Terry was grimacing slightly. Maybe it was the subject of Michael but Terry looked upset and a bit guilty. Terry could feel guilty at the drop of a hat. He didn't need the tragedy to make him feel that way. But he was the one who coaxed Michael into attending the club though he couldn't predict what would happen there. He told Moira he'd be fine and he wasn't.

And there was something about Frank. Terry seemed to hesitate when I asked about him. He was hiding something. Terry didn't tell me everything. Why would he? I was just a young boy. He didn't tell anybody else either, not even the police about what he saw. The only person he told was Olive.

I dip my brush into the small jar of turps. I watch as the dye seeps out from the bristles of the paint brush. The blueish purple spreads quickly; a writhing mass of unfurling diffusion. Very soon it dominates the native clear liquid, taking over, stopping only at the glass boundary of the container.

As if in defiance, a darker plume of blue purple suddenly materialises from the mass and spirals upwards. Liquid becomes air and the soft swirling dye becomes a tendril of smoke feeling its way through the twilight air like a snake slowly unfolding its coils. The dark silhouette of St Luke's Church punctuates a yellow grey sky and as the purple smoke slowly drifts across the spire, echoes of some old gothic horror movie seem to chill the air.

THE GREAT FIRE

The huge fire that had engulfed the large warehouse had just been extinguished but smouldering embers still left a wispy scar across the horizon. The Cheetham Hill district was now fairly sedate and was in the process of coming to rest after the excitement of the earlier full-scale blaze. Me, Ray and Alex stood there for hours watching the fire, fascinated by the red and yellow spectacle.

Nobody knew how it had started but the real excitement wasn't so much the blaze as the frenzied activity that took place afterwards. Although the large pre-fabricated shell was burnt to a cinder, much of its contents remained relatively intact. This wasn't obvious to the uneducated eye but if you looked beyond the surface and scraped away the ash, there was salvage to be had. To the seasoned scavenger this was an opportunity that was too good to miss.

As the light began to fade and late afternoon became evening, Alex and Ray told me that the Manchester Mafia would soon be out. They were not wrong. The timing was perfect. The strange greyness that had engulfed the scene acted as a camouflage but if you looked closely, it wasn't the earth that was moving. They were like ninjas – an army of human ants kitted out in homemade fireproof clothing scuttling along the glowing detritus armed with makeshift sacks. Every so often they would leap into the air or execute some deft side step to dodge the pockets of noxious yellow gas that spat out of the steaming mounds of melted earth. It was ballet on cinders.

We just laughed as the police cordons and makeshift barricades that were erected to keep everybody out were swatted away with contempt by the Manchester Mafia. It was an insult to think that these obstacles could ever be a deterrent. It was a real skill....to be able to sift through red hot coals without getting burnt but these shadowy figures had it off to an art. The reward was great. Everybody knew that the Macdonough brothers who owned the buildings around the area were dodgy to say the least. The toiletries and small domestic appliances that they purported to sell were just a front for some of their more lucrative dealings. The Cheetham Hill grapevine had it that there were quite a few gold watches there to be had and large quantities of expensive booze to be pilfered.

To many, the booze seemed the more appetizing proposition. It was also a well-known secret that the police had got in there first taking the cream off the top of the pile. Fortunately they were unwilling to get their hands dirty which still left a great deal for the rest of us. For a couple of days it was very much like the set of Whisky Galore. A frenzied excitement gripped the community and shady dealings became an open secret.

Me, Ray and Alex were the last in line. We were the street urchins, the play out all day kids waiting our turn patiently, obeying the laws of the urban jungle, hovering over the smouldering wreck, waiting for those higher up the food chain to have their pickings, waiting with gleeful anticipation, waiting for the evening to end and the morning to begin, waiting for our chance.

"Are you ready?" said Alex.

"Check," said Ray in ridiculous military fashion.

"What about you Smiffy?"

"Yep," I said confidently.

"You're supposed to say check," said Alex.

"Ok, check," I added and tried not to laugh as Alex was taking it quite seriously. I paused for a second and looked at them both. They were my fellow brothers in arms. I'd shared a great deal with them over the past year. I looked at their faces and I knew that I could depend on them. Suddenly Ray decided that it was too serious and broke ranks. "What's that smell?" he said, looking over in my direction. We both laughed. It was an old joke and reminded me of the first time we met. I was involved in a fight!

Jamie Wray (Ray)

"Course' 'e can fuckin' take 'im," Johnny stated confidently to the boy standing next to him. My brother looked at me.

"You'll be okay, won't you?" I said nothing. Johnny could tell I was hesitant. He put his arms around my shoulder and tried to encourage me.

"He's just a little fart. Just do what I've taught you."

"What's that?" I said.

"Oh fuck, we're in trouble," said Johnny and then laughed. It was supposed to be a joke to lighten my mood but it didn't work. Suddenly my brother became aware of another presence.

"And what are you lookin' at?" Johnny said aggressively. The kid said nothing. He'd been following us for some time obviously gripped by the unfolding melodrama. My brother didn't like the way he was staring at us.

"Go on, bugger off you scruffy bastard." But the boy didn't go. Just as Johnny was about to do something, a pissy kind of voice distracted him.

"Is there gonna be a fight or what?" said a mean-looking, red-headed gangly figure who was getting impatient, "and is there gonna be a bet?" he added.

"The bet is simply that my little bro' can beat your twatty bro," Johnny declared.

In the stillness of the pre battle I remember looking intently at my brother. It was as though I was seeing him for the first time and I was envious. He was self-assured whereas I was shy. He was growing up to be a good looking lad and he had the good fortune of being gifted with the looks of a young Paul McCartney. I could see how the girls took to him. He had a lot of attention from the opposite sex which he loved and encouraged. He was obviously funny and it was clear that he had also inherited Olive's gift of the gab and quick wit. He was a lucky bastard.

In my early and middle teens I would look on my brother with begrudging jealousy. Yes I had my own interests and saw things differently but I hated the fact that secretly, for a time, he was who I wanted to be. I confessed this to Johnny years later "It's funny," he said, "I spent some time thinking I wanted to be more like you. I'm thick. I never wanted to learn but you went to college, you got an education, you did something with your life. Look at you, you're a teacher." He then paused. "Does an art teacher count? That's not real teaching is it?" I laughed and realised that I had received the praise from my older brother that I had always craved but he still made a joke of it, like it wasn't serious!

Suddenly it was as though a director called action. Me and this other lad quickly took a kind of wrestler's stance and even pawed each other's shoulders like Olympic competitors. I looked into his eyes which gave nothing away. I couldn't tell whether his heart was in it or not. Mine gave everything away, nervous anxious and scared. My heart was definitely not in it.

I had remonstrated with my brother, pleaded with him. He came back with some nonsense about upholding the Smith name. "WE'RE NOT FUCKING DUELISTS IN SOME HISTORICAL FRENCH FUCKING NOVEL." I wish I had said that. But I didn't. In truth I argued little and, in simpering fashion, I reluctantly went along with his resolve.

David Ureghy, a new boy in school whose dad had recently taken over the management of the Polish Club, made the first direct move and went for a strangle hold. I tried to fend him off with a pointed elbow aimed towards his neck. This stalled his initial surge as his head went back but his arms and hands somehow made a pincer movement around my neck. My efforts had only delayed his plan.

Fairly quickly he had me in a head lock. It wasn't quite secure as I had managed to slide one of my arms between my head and his arms. In a second we had both slipped and were writhing about on the floor. Each had the other in some kind of hold. Mine was the weaker and I could feel my leverage disappearing as David began to exert his slightly superior strength.

"Right, honours even then," said my brother who could sense my weakening position. He then promptly separated us and completely ignored any protestations from David's brother that the fight had ended prematurely. "Well done, our kid, "Johnny said as though I really was the victor. "Don't worry. You'll 'ave him next time," he quietly whispered and then gave me a reassuring wink. I could feel the tears of anger and frustration building up as Johnny strode off still arguing a point with his friend and completely ignoring the forlorn figure left behind that was me.

Alone in my bubble of self-pity, I suddenly became aware of smirking laughter: the sort that was trying not to laugh but couldn't contain itself. I turned round to see "the scruffy bastard," the one that Johnny told off. He was laughing so hard that he began to cough. I was like Stacey in that I never usually swore but this time it came out in guttural fashion as my mood suddenly changed.

"What are you fuckin' laughin' at you fuckin' twat?" which made him laugh even more.

"Look at you," he said.

I said nothing as my fists started to clench. I was ready for this fight.

"You've got dog shit in your hair."

I suddenly became aware of a deep, acrid and foul-smelling odour. I must have bashed my head in it during the fight. The flow of adrenalin had made the smell sink into the background but now like a developing photograph it came into focus. I instantly reached up to check my head and in doing so plunged my fingers into a lump of offensive ooze. I didn't need to smell it…a visual inspection was enough. "Shit, shit, shit, shit" rattled from my tongue in machine gun fashion.

Still chuckling and completely ignoring my rage, the scruffy kid got a rag from the tip and started to extricate the dark matter from my hair. It was almost as though he was used to cleaning up shit. The smell didn't seem to bother him that much.

Me and Ray became friends after that but he never let me forget that incident. Every so often he would slip back a pace or two when we were walking. He used to wait for me to stop and turn round and look at him, which I duly did. I would then catch sight of him sniffing the air with his nose pointing towards the sky. I used to fall for it every time.

"What are you doing?" I would ask quizzically. And, with a mischievous smile, the response would come in the form of a question.

"Can you smell dog shit?"

Ray was like that, a real scally and very cheeky but in a charming kind of way. He had a rough edge and didn't really care for any of the social niceties that would gain acceptance in groups. He seemed to have little need for that kind of validation as he had little ego. He was happy enough in his own company and was used to being left to his own devices. There was something quite vulnerable about him. He was often a bit dirty with unwashed clothes but his face and demeanour had not yet hardened through the brutality of street life. He was neglected but had little anger towards other adults (except his mum) as long as they did not try to order him about.

Because of his lack of inhibition, Ray would often do the most outrageous things such as walking close by an adult and then farting or burping knowing full well he would get a reaction. He could also project a thin stream of spit through the gap in his front teeth a good ten feet or more. He was very accurate and, with little time taken to aim, could easily hit the face of some passer by without them having the slightest idea where the spit had come from.

Ray's mum was a sad figure who was seldom around. Poor Nellie, as she was known, was less than five feet tall and was all of about six stone wet through. She really was just skin and bone. She had small rotten stumps where her front teeth should have been. Her hair was greasy and dank and her face was drawn and grey through years of alcohol abuse. She also smoked heavily and gave off a rather unpleasant smell. I could sometimes smell the same on Ray. When he called round, Olive would sometimes run a hot bath and give him some of my clothes whilst she washed his. She also fed him. Many's the time I wished for Johnny to see this and other episodes where Olive championed the cause of the impoverished and showed a real generosity of spirit, but either he wasn't there or he chose not to look.

Ray took no offence at Olive's maternal fussing. He simply accepted it. Her wishes and her motherly insistence were not easily brushed aside anyway. I think he knew that resistance was futile. Likewise you got the feeling that Nellie had given up on being maternal a long time ago. But Ray could be cruel to Nellie. One warm Sunday afternoon Nellie staggered in from the Temple Arms pissed as a fart after a fair old drinking session. We were in the back kitchen but the moment she opened the door I could smell her. The unmistakable waft of Holts Pale Ale drowned out the stale and rancid odour that normally permeated the flat. She slumped down into one of the tatty second-hand chairs that occupied the centre of the room and called for her son.

"Jaaamie."

It wasn't so much a shout, more of a drone. She couldn't see where Jamie was but she knew he was there.

"Jaaamie," she called out again. Ray did not reply. Instead he beckoned me to hide with him behind the kitchen door.

"Jaamie." The tone was similar but more insistent; again no answer. She was so pissed that she didn't have the energy to get up.

"Answer her for God's sake," I said.

"Wait," said Ray hardly able to contain himself.

Nellie could hear her son's stifled giggles which caused her pleas to become more impassioned and elongated.

"Jaaaaaammieeeee. I neeeeed yooouuuu."

"Listen to her. She's like some fuckin' banshee," sneered Ray.

I laughed and immediately felt guilty.

"She's not finished yet," he said laughing with me and revelling in his mother's distress.

And sure enough there was more. Nellie howled Ray's name for a good few minutes. Just as I was about to step in Ray looked at me.

"Watch this," he said and grinned with anticipation as he calmly popped out from behind the kitchen door. He looked casually at Nellie strewn across the beer-stained armchair. She looked back with pleading eyes hoping for some sympathy. Instead Ray laughed. It was mocking and scornful and it hit its mark.

In an instance Nellie's limp and pathetic demeanour changed. She stood up sharply, her eyes a well of fury. She started to hit Ray or rather swipe her arms across his shoulders. The blows were completely ineffectual as there was no substance to their force. Ray laughed even more which made Nellie lose it completely.

"You bastard, bastard, fuckin' bloody fuckin' bloody bastard," she proclaimed in utter rage, each expletive punctuated by more blows. Ray did cover his face with his arms but was in hysterics at the same time. Eventually Nellie stopped, her energy spent, her frame exhausted and her whole face sobbing. This didn't faze Ray. The sadistic glint in his eye told me he was loving it. When Ray felt that this well-orchestrated act had come to an end he stopped laughing, straightened his body and calmly told her to "Fuck off, you old bat." He then took her purse from her pocket and robbed her of the few coppers she had.

This scene was played out many times. It used to be excruciating watching the pain he would inflict on his mother. I would try to persuade him to ease up on many occasions but my protestations had little effect, he loved it too much.

When I look back I shudder at the thought of Ray having to clean up his mother's mess after being so pissed she was unable to get to the toilet. I realised then why it didn't particularly bother him when he had to clean the shit off my head that time at Barney's tip. He was used to it. I guess there was lots he had to do as a child that no child should have to go through.

In my heart I sensed this and was therefore tolerant of his cruel actions. I was tolerant to a point. There was no mistaking the odour of stale urine emanating from the soft stained cushioned chairs. I never sat on them. I only ever used to sit on one of the two hard chairs that were tucked under the small table by the kitchen where Ray and I used to play cards.

Something's not right. I rework the eyes with cobalt blue, a touch of titanium white and a sweep of cadmium orange just above the eye lid. I'm much happier now. They're not quite finished but the intensity is there. I remember the night her eyes were fiery. They had not been that way for some time.

I've taught many boys like Ray. In school they often present as surly, aggressive and unwilling to co-operate but I've done well with them. I've often wondered whether my upbringing has given me some added understanding. It might have done but I just try to see the funny side and I try to have a laugh. There's got to be something in it for me! And besides, I quite like these scallies in the same way that I liked Ray. Maybe, deep down, I see Ray there in the classroom staring back at me and it makes me smile.

And when my class think that my back is turned, I see a few of them messing about. Out of the corner of my eye I see one of them spitting through the gap in his teeth just like Ray used to do. I go up to him and say "That's not very far. I knew a lad who could spit twenty feet or more and hit a bull's eye." I make the kid clean it up and pretend that I am disgusted. I should be but I'm not.

NELLIE'S SAD DEMISE

It wasn't a total surprise when Nellie was found dead but it was a surprise that she had managed to survive for as long as she did. It was an unceremonious and unnoticed death. She was found crumpled up with a bottle of something alcoholic by her side in the ginnel beside the Temple Arms. Me and Ray were about twelve at the time. I can't remember how he took it but I can remember the funeral. Along with Olive, we were the only ones there. Olive was so good that day. A real comfort for Ray.

Ray told me the news of his mum's death quite casually and then just as casually asked if I would like to go to the funeral. I had never been to one before so I thought that I would attend. As well as being supportive, I was curious. I thought there would be more people there, people who knew Nellie, friends relatives, anybody but instead it was horribly empty apart from me, my mum, Ray and the vicar.

I wanted to get away from there as quickly as possible. What shocked me was Ray, who wept uncontrollably for a mother he hated and a woman he rarely saw. Maybe he wept for what should have been. I avoided all funerals after that. I never even went to my father's funeral. It was only when Olive died some forty years later that I attended one.

Shortly after Nellie's death social services intervened and Ray was shipped off to Rose Hill, a boys' home that catered for youngsters in Ray's position. Olive fought to try and have him stay with us as she feared for his wellbeing in that place. She'd heard a few unpleasant stories. Olive knew what Rose Hill was like and she shed more than a tear at Ray's departure. She loved that boy.

Why couldn't she have been like that with Johnny?

I saw Ray intermittently for a year or two after that but he was never quite the same. I couldn't put my finger on it but he was different. Olive seemed to understand why. Ray joined the army at fifteen and that was the last I saw of him.

Alex

Alex Cordwell was the other member of our trio of brothers in arms. A lot of folk quite liked Alex and he quite liked himself. Even then he carried an air of being destined for slightly better things than being an inhabitant of run down north Manchester. He moved into the house round the corner shortly after I met Ray. He was thin with straight black hair cut in a fashion that suggested someone had put a basin around his head. He was a wily character though, good for a laugh and street wise.

He came from an extremely dysfunctional family. When you looked at his siblings they appeared to exhibit a wide range of strange symptoms. In today's society I am quite sure that they would have had a variety of initials and labels against their name. They appeared at odds with the world around them and looked as though they were the product of an abnormal gene pool. Alex was clearly a mutation. He looked aware and his brain was sharp.

Alex was quite good at competitions. He was a master at split the kipper which was a hazardous game that involved throwing a knife with pinpoint precision into a target circled in the dirt. Sometimes that target would be a small area of ground which happened to be in between the legs of the opponent. When throwing the knife we had complete trust in Alex not to dismember us. The same could not be said for me or Ray.

Alex adapted well to any given situation. He was a handy person to have in a crisis and was well suited to the demands of the street scavenger. He and Ray made good counterpoints to my relatively innocent and naïve outlook. Alex had a kind heart to those close to him but given half a chance he would quite easily rob and thieve from strangers and other children with little remorse. He once boasted that he had stolen from a dead man. At the time we all scoffed but I now know that this was true. Alex was an opportunist. It was on one Saturday morning that he pulled out his special black gloves and proceeded to slip them over his hands with easy assurance.

"What are you doing?" I asked.

"What does it look like?" replied Alex.

I knew straight away but still couldn't quite believe what Alex was about to do. A few minutes earlier I'd climbed over the back yard door to retrieve my football and in doing so I fell over and clattered into the bins. It made a terrible racket but nobody came out even though the back door to the house was wide open. I told Alex who became very animated.

"There's nobody at home and the back door's wide open." He then winked at Ray.

"Say no more," Ray added suggestively. And with that Alex flew into action leaving me in his wake.

"You and Ray keep look out."

He then clambered over the back yard gate, went through the open door and disappeared into the empty house. Within five minutes he was back clutching nothing more than an alarm clock.

"Is that it? Is that all you've got?" said Ray disdainfully. "Not worth puttin' your special gloves on for."

"That's all there was," replied Alex. "It's the Pakis 'ouse. They never 'ave much." He seemed to state this from experience.

"Mattresses and alarm clocks," he muttered to himself. "Loads of 'em but that's all there was."

"I wonder why nobody's in?" Ray enquired.

"Probably all at the mosque," said the very sweet and quiet voice of a girl sat on the wall. It was Bill Tanner's daughter Jenny. We were supposed to be looking after her for an hour but had completely forgotten she was there.

"Shit!" said Alex.

"She's just seen us rob a house and her dad's a copper," added Ray

"We're done for," I said, shaking my head.

Ray suddenly lost it and shouted in her face.

"WHERE WERE YOU?"

"I'd just wondered round the corner," said Jenny apologetically. "Don't worry. I won't tell."

"You'd better not," said Ray menacingly.

"She's fine," said Alex confidently, "She won't tell." It was amazing how Alex seemed to add an air of calm to a potentially disastrous situation but he was right. We had no come back from Bill or my mum. I didn't see Jenny again till many years later.

Strangely Alex appeared more upset that the pickings were not juicier than he was about Jenny being a potential witness to our crime. However, he still kept the clock and named it 'Jock the clock.' He used to take it out with him when we were playing football and set the alarm to go off for half time. "It will save any arguments," he used to say but we could never take the second half seriously with the sight of Jock the Clock's alarm rattling away in the middle of our game.

Back to the great fire

So there we were, me Ray and Alex waiting patiently over the dying embers of the 'great fire' ready for the big adventure. Nervous and excited at the same time. We waited till the coast was clear and surreptitiously started to scramble up to where we thought would be a good place to start. We came armed as a result of our planning the previous night. I had procured for us three large hessian sacks. (left over packaging from mum and dad's trip to the local cash and carry). Alex had his special leather gloves but he also had more pairs for us.

"Don't fuckin' damage these. They're Joey's best," said Alex as he handed out his brother's finest leather thieving gloves. Robbing was obviously a family affair.

And then it occurred to Ray.

"Your brother's not called Jumbo Joey is he?"

"Don't fuckin' say that. He hates that name," said Alex quickly.

"Right," said Ray.

"He's an absolute loony tune Joey is. So Ray, don't mess his gloves up."

"Right," said Ray.

"I've also got these," I said as I proudly whipped out a couple of toy spades courtesy of a trip to Southport. Ray laughed and mumbled something about building sandcastles out of shit.

There was no strategy as such. We just dug using hands, spades and other abandoned tools to forage, scrape and hack through the grey and black ash. It wasn't easy. The water from the fire engines and overnight rain had turned the ash to mud. We were soon up to our eyeballs in shit (as Olive would say) trying desperately to find some treasure. Alex was the first to strike. He had superior foraging skills helped by gloves that were a good fit.

"Over here," he shouted.

We all scurried over expectantly to see that Alex had unearthed a charred and sodden box. The lid came away easily.

"What the bloody 'ell. Felt tips. Shit!" said Ray. It wasn't quite what he was expecting. Alex was also a little disappointed but I was quite happy. I liked drawing.

Undeterred, we continued to work through the morning in the hope that we would find something a little more lucrative. Unfortunately all we unearthed were more felt tips. We soon realised that others saw little value in these cheap products as they had clearly been discarded and lay scattered all around. Still it represented some reward for our efforts as each of us put a little store of them in our sacks.

Later on, Alex found a couple of watches and Ray found some charred leather handbags that could be cleaned up but I found a bottle of champagne! It was after we'd been digging for about four hours that we hit on what we all thought was our best find…a large deposit of Brut aftershave and grooming products. We quickly stuffed as much as we could into our sacks and decided to head back home.

"You know the MacBride's are gonna be waiting," stated Alex.

"Yeah. I bet they've got look outs posted all along Smedley flats," added Ray. He knew more about them than we did. He had dealt with two of the brothers before. "They are not to be trifled with," said Alex with an air of menace.

After some thought, we decided to take the route through Queens Road and up through Johnson Street where our old house used to be. Lots of old terraces around this area were being demolished and offered perfect cover should we come up against any problems. Satisfied with this plan we hauled the sacks over our shoulders and in determined mood began the mile-long journey home.

Coming down off the slag heap with those heavy bags was difficult. After a short time our arms, shoulders and legs began to ache. It affected our balance. Ray was the first to go. He stumbled awkwardly and gashed his knee. I followed shortly afterwards but picked myself up quickly. We were all getting pissed off. What started as a great adventure had turned into a trial of pain and endurance. To make things worse it began to rain, lightly at first and then gradually heavier. I could hear Ray swearing. Even Alex who was fairly self-controlled started to mutter. I started to laugh, I couldn't help myself. Alex and Ray stopped and chucked the bags down and confronted me. Their faces were stern but within a matter of seconds they too started to laugh.

"What the bloody 'ell," was all any of us could say. We were a sight. The ash and mud from the remnants of the fire were all over us. We were in parts as black as the ace of spades, in other parts we were a molten grey. Deposits of sludge were embedded in our hair, in our ears and smeared thickly down our t-shirts. All you could see of our faces were two white eyes.

The rain had of course made things worse. Small miniature ski tracks of water ran down our cheeks and through the rest of our pathetic looking figures. But that wasn't all. Some of the containers of shampoo had leaked. The contents of the great smell of Brut had gathered to form nests of foam that sat proudly on top of our heads like surreal ice cream turbans. Small masses of soap suds formed living organisms that slithered and oozed their way slowly down our bodies. A close inspection would see the suds change direction and speed up as they followed the contours of our bedraggled clothing.

On top of this some of the cheap felt tips had broken away from their packaging and had clearly mixed with the rain and grooming products. The result was that, interspersed with all the monochromatic mayhem, was a cacophony of coloured crap! The soap suds were in places crimson red and lemon yellow. There was also what can only be described as a diffused seepage. Some of the colours from the felt tips had mixed with light grey ash and black soot to give the widest array of hues and tints imaginable. In art terms we were a mixture between the abstract expressionism of the late fifties and the psychedelic op art of the sixties. As my old art tutor used to say in his gritty northern accent "We 'ave mayd concrete that which wuz abstract to form a true marridge of consepshun and persepshun."

"Hey Smithy man you look as though you've been trippin' man," said Alex in this hippy-like drawl. He then waved his two fingers in a peace sign and rocked his head from side to side in some groovy fashion. Ray followed suit and said that he "digged this crazy vibe man."

"C..R..A.YZEEE," I said and smoked a fake spliff. Funnily enough, we did kind of trip as we all got the giggles, unable to stop for ages. Eventually the laughter died down and, urged on by Alex, we quickly got back into business mode. However funny it all was, we needed to sort things out. Fortunately by this time, we were in amongst the ruins of some of the old terraces that were being knocked down so we had a place to hide our booty and a convenient place for shelter.

We eventually stopped at what was no more than a shell of a house. The roof had been stripped and much of the timber had gone to reveal crumbling chunks of the old lath and plaster. The side of one wall no longer existed and it was strange to see fractured brick work and hanging wall paper so exposed. There was a savage beauty to the strewn and brutalised container that was once a family home.

Looking back, these about-to-be demolished carcases were like vast uncharted playgrounds for the likes of us. People left all sorts and you could easily build up a picture of the inhabitants from the scraps they left behind. We were detectives. Wray, Caldwell and Smith on a voyeuristic mission to look into the windows of people's lives and piece together a social history of life in sixties Manchester. In other words we were nosey buggers.

Inside the wreckage Alex and Ray stood transfixed by my attentiveness to a girl's book. It was my sister's old Bunty annual with her initials still visible on the inside cover. I'd stumbled across it clambering over the debris of the old fireplace that looked quite familiar. Was I standing in the remains of our old living room? Maybe. Whatever the case, I didn't notice them looking at me but I guess they were dying to say something.

Ray was first. "You big fuckin' cissy."

Alex interjected soon after. "Jesus Smiffy I didn't realize you liked reading that shit."

Chastened by their remarks, I was forced to confess my secret love of teenage girls' comic books and magazines. "It's the Bunty," I exclaimed. "I just love The Four Marys." Alex laughed a little and then it occurred to Ray...

"Is this your old house?"

I was a bit embarrassed. "Maybe. I dunno."

"It doesn't matter," intervened Alex, "We need to move quickly before the MacBrides spot us."

So we rapidly hid our booty in the bowels of the old terrace and agreed to come back early the next morning. But the next morning and for a few days after it threw it down; buckets of good old Manchester rain. When we did eventually come back to reclaim our stash the whole street had been levelled and our prize was crushed under ten feet of rubble. To say that we were disappointed was an understatement.

Alex had always felt uneasy about leaving his stash in that way. I could see it in his eyes as we left the scene. That's why he secretly went back later on that evening. I guess he found the hessian bags easily. It would have been dark but the mound of earth and rubble that hid all from the naked eye still formed a tell-tale heap in the corner. It was no problem for Alex. He had the experience and keen eyes of the seasoned burglar.

Years later he told me about his covert operation and confessed that he just had a "few insecurity issues." He was very protective of his merchandise so he just needed to get it, to store it and hoard it. But he found something else in the rubble of our old house; something unexpected. It was too much of a temptation for a magpie like Alex. It wasn't his to take but he took it anyway. He gave it to me years later. Unlikely as it may have seemed, it set in motion a chain of events that finally led me to the truth. It was extraordinary really because I'd given up trying to solve the puzzle years ago.

I do that thing again. Of putting the end of the brush in my mouth. It is a bad habit but it helps me to think, to mull over things, to find solutions to problems. Painting a portrait is like that but to overcome a problem and find a solution you just have to ask yourself the right questions.

CHANGES

Looking back over that episode, I now know why Alex didn't appear quite as disappointed as me and Ray. But that feeling of dissatisfaction soon faded as further adventures and escapades filled the remainder of that summer. I loved those long school holidays. They were a time when me, Ray and Alex came together. We just played out. The weather was great and I was away from all the stupid stuff that was going on at home.

But after the holidays we had school. Alex and Ray went to the one down the road – The High School of Art. It was close to Strangeways Prison and used the same style Victorian brick. In the grey Mancunian atmosphere it was hard to tell the difference between the two. The school did attract students with a certain artistic leaning but also provided sanctuary for students with low aspirations and damp ambitions.

Stacey, Johnny and Derrick also attended. It was the nearest school but none of them were any good at art. To all intents and purposes, life at the school was easy and undemanding, perhaps that was the attraction. They just didn't want to be pushed. Ray and Alex fell into the same bracket as my siblings. Olive was determined that I should not follow the same route. She saw me as the academic. In her eyes I was never going to achieve anything by attending that "shit 'ole of a school" down the road so I didn't go there.

The irony was that I probably would have thrived at that school of art because I loved drawing and I was good at it. So I went to Central High School for Boys. I hated it. The only things that I remember from my time there were;

a) Swimming with cockroaches at a deathly cold Victoria Baths
b) Forging bus passes for the school bullies which kept me out of trouble
c) Thanking the lord for my artistic skills
d) Being punched when I broke somebody's conker by mistake
e) The emergence of Mohican haircuts in the 6th form in 1976

Fancying Mrs Rowen, the art teacher who I later learnt had an affair with a student
f) Only getting a D at art 'A' level.
g) Watching the numerous fights which were the result of simmering racial tensions between Asians, blacks and whites.

I was however happy enough outside of school but before I knew it all that changed. Ray was forcibly moved to the boy's home at Rose Hill after his mother's death. Shortly after that Alex and his family were shipped back to Glasgow. I saw nothing of Nawab and, one by one, my older siblings moved out. Derrick was the first to go. It was only to the flats across the road but he couldn't wait. He was seventeen at the time.

MY SPORTING HERO

When I say that I didn't really know Derrick, strictly speaking that wasn't true. I got some insight into his psyche in the sports arena. Occasionally he'd take me along to golf or football or some other sport. It was in these moments that I became aware of a more Walter Mittyish aspect to my brother's personality and a more aggressive side to his character, particularly where golf was concerned.

I know he brought me along mainly to act as a lookout to see where his golf ball went, only I was never any good. On this particular day he asked me a question that he nearly always asked after he hit a bad drive.

"Where did that one go our kid?"

And I gave him pretty much the same nervous reply, "I, I don't really kn...know."

I stammered because I knew what was coming next and sure enough, kapow! Slightly more than a cuff but less than a full smack, right across the side of my head. It happened to me countless times. I never seemed to learn but it didn't really hurt, not as much as Johnny's.

"Bloody look next time!" came the cry.

At least he didn't call me a gormless bastard I thought to myself as I picked up his golf clubs and trudged a yard behind my older brother who had stormed ahead annoyed that I hadn't got the faintest clue where the ball had gone. I was his lookout because he was as blind as a bat. His round-rimmed NHS specs seemed to be of little use. What made matters worse was that they would often get steamed up in the Manchester rain.

It also didn't help that I lost concentration too easily. My mind would wonder and half the time I was bored. I would find myself engrossed in the minutia of the golf course, a leaf fluttering in the wind, a bird pecking on the ground nearby. I would hear the smack of club against ball and I would know straight away that I had missed it. I was so wrapped up in my own world. My brothers never understood that side of me.

We looked for a few minutes in the deep rough that lay on the right hand side of the ninth. I swear that the long thick, wet strands of rye grass fluttered with delight as they wrapped themselves around my brother's prize Tony Jacklin golf shoes.

"Bloody 'ell," said Derrick stamping his feet trying to get the shit off his spikes, "this is your fault!"

I said nothing as Derrick extricated himself from the rough.

"Right. Watch where this one goes. I'm going to reload," he said menacingly.

Derrick then withdrew a large-headed club from the bag and in deliberate fashion removed the woolly head cover. He was like a gun fighter slowly drawing the pistol from the holster. The unsheathed club stood proud and upright in Derrick's small hands. He looked at me and then patted the club carefully as though it were a dangerous pet. "It's Big Bertha," Derrick uttered in a hushed tone. He then slowly turned his head and looked out to the broad fairways of Heaton Park Golf course. And then for good effect he squinted his eyes like a top marksman taking aim. It was as though he were about to strike terror into the golf course and expected me to step back in awe. I tried my best to oblige.

"Right, our kid. I know you're gonna rip this up," I said in determined fashion trying to gee him up but it was said with no great conviction. It wasn't just that I was a poor actor, Derrick rarely made good connection with this club and would often send a piece of hacked turf further than the ball. I waited for this to happen and sure enough it did.

"Unlucky," I said as a brown sod of earth spat up from the ground courtesy of big Bertha. Derrick paid no attention to my hollow attempt at sympathy, instead he cussed and cursed.

"Twat, twat, twat tw..."

"There!" I shouted interrupting his self-loathing.

"What?" said Derrick.

"There. There's the ball," I said (just about stifling my giggles) "Just there, about five yards ahead." Derrick didn't see the funny side, I was lucky I didn't get a second smack.

Despite my travails on the course with my older brother, I did quite like those times even though I was his sporting bitch. Mostly we had a laugh and it was the only time I really got to know Derrick. He used to let me take a few shots and took time to teach me. On his day he was pretty good. And he chatted a lot more away from the rest of the family.

Football was slightly more enjoyable and more interactive. I was more a provider than a caddy, I used to cross the ball so that he could practice his finishing. "YYEESSS" would be my brother's elated cry as he would strike the ball into the imaginary goal. He would raise his hand aloft and point his finger upwards towards the heavens just like his idol Denis Law. Giddy with imaginary success, he would wheel round and acknowledge the imaginary crowd. Like the golf, I felt obliged to stroke his ego and would congratulate him on his outstanding aerial prowess. "Leapt like a salmon," I would say and then, once out of earshot, mumble to myself, "More like a tin of salmon."

Sometimes he would insist that I give him marks out of ten. I never gave him less than eight and when it was a nine or ten his confidence was high enough to try more acrobatic responses to my crosses. Flying headers, bicycle kicks. You name it, he tried it but all missing by a mile. Occasionally when he did connect he would order me to go and get the ball which I duly did so like an obedient dog retrieving a stick for its master. Johnny didn't join in with me and Derrick. Occasionally he would hang out with me but I can't remember a time when me, Johnny and Derrick played together.

I tilt my head to one side and view my painting from a different angle. It is a way of seeing things differently. I then turn it upside down and the features become abstract shapes. I leave it like that for a minute or two in the hope that it will give me a fresh perspective. It's like that with people, especially the ones you know well. You have to try to see things from a different point of view.

As the ball plopped into the hole on the last green, Derrick turned to me. "Right," he said. "Fancy coming to see the flat?"

"Why not," I replied in chirpy fashion. He'd been dying to show me ever since he moved out. My brother lived in one of the flats just across the road from us. They were grotty to say the least but they were dirt cheap. They looked quite grand from the outside but on closer inspection the crumbling brickwork and general decay of the exterior left a lot to be desired. It didn't bother Derrick too much as he knew that he wouldn't be staying there long. His recent employment as a shoe salesman at Timpson's was just a stepping stone.

"Welcome to my palace," said Derrick with a mixture of pride and irony as he turned the key and flung open the front door.

"Blimey, Derrick," I stuttered.

"You no like?" said Derrick trying to be funny by mimicking the accent of Chinese Vera from round the corner.

In truth, I didn't quite know. First of all the room was quite small but the black and purple ceiling made it appear even smaller. The daylight that shone through some flimsy bright orange curtains bathed the interior in a strange amber glow. But it was the gold and orange polystyrene tiles on the main wall that made me gasp. I couldn't stop looking at them, transfixed by their hideous beauty.

"Dad helped me put those up," said Derrick proudly.

"Why?" I answered flippantly.

Derrick ignored me and switched on the oil lamp. He stood there waiting for the first oil globules to heat up in the red and yellow liquid. Once they were on the move he stepped a couple of paces to his right and drew the curtain that sealed off the red and cream Formica-styled kitchen. He switched on another lamp that had an orange and purple shade and it felt remarkably cosy.

"It's a bit daring for you isn't it?" I said. In fact I was stunned as Derrick was usually quite conservative. Buoyed by what he thought was my approval, he went over to the record collection that lay neatly stacked up against the wall, sifted through the pile and selected a single. He then carefully placed the disc on the turntable and gently lowered the stylus. After a few seconds of slight crackling out piped the Jackson Five and Derrick did a little Motown-style jig. It was a well-crafted move that involved a rhythmic clap of hands, a jump in the air and precise twirl on landing.

"I've used it in Tiffany's," said Derrick proudly. He could see that I looked quizzical so he elaborated. "The night club down the road…the move…the girls love it." I nearly said "why" again but I didn't want to prick my brother's bubble.

Suddenly he burst into song. "As long as that apple don't spoil the whole bunch girl." He then turned to me and spoke loudly over the music. "I know it's not much but I'm a lot happier here." I couldn't help agreeing. It was as though a part of a large weight had been lifted from his shoulders. We all knew how difficult it had been but I still asked the question.

"What makes you say that?" My brother got up turned the sound down and then sat on the bed opposite. "It got too much. I'm better off on my own," he said. Derrick didn't elaborate, he didn't need to. I didn't ask more questions on the topic, even as an eleven year old I knew when to leave it. Derrick then got up to get me a drink and some biscuits. It gave me a chance to have a further look at my surroundings.

Behind me was a poster of a semi-clad Raquel Welch from the movie 1 million years BC. It was that iconic one where she's looking slightly ravaged, bold and vulnerable at the same time. Every young pubescent male had it on their wall. There was also an eclectic mix of smaller posters featuring David Bowie, The Jackson 5 and Jimi Hendrix all crudely stuck around a small silver framed mirror. But draped over the chair in the corner was Derricks pride and joy…a hell's angel jacket hand made by Ted for his sixteenth birthday.

"Johnny says that you put that on when you ride your tricycle." And for a second I wish I hadn't said it but Derrick just smiled and said nothing. He was used to it.

"Johnny puts out all kinds of stories about me and my jacket. He's just jealous."

"Johnny's movin' out too," I said. "He's joinin' the army. They'll be no more arguments with mum, thank God."

"Well, that's good," said Derrick feigning interest.

"Johnny's packed his suitcase for real this time."

After some of the worst quarrels with Olive, Johnny would often pack a suitcase ready to leave home and Olive wouldn't try to stop him. She would even open the door and wish him good luck as he stomped out. "Do me a favour," he would say to anybody listening, "tell her she's a shit mother." In reply, Olive would stick up one finger of a two-fingered gesture and shout out that he was "Not worth the other half." And then the silent treatment; both of them not talking to each other. There was no easy reconciliation. Sometimes it would last for weeks.

I never fell foul of Olive's combustible northern abrasiveness and so avoided the silent treatment. Me and Belle...we just didn't. It used to piss Johnny off. He could understand it with Belle but not with me.

A younger version of Johnny suddenly appears and starts to argue with me. It disrupts my flow but he doesn't care...

You did stuff. You were just as bad.

Not really. I wasn't as bad as you and I didn't let her get to me.

So it was my fault?

No. It was just in our natures. I tried to avoid the confrontation but you rose up to meet it.

You talk a load of shit.

Maybe I do. Anyway, I did get the treatment.

Once.

Utterly fucking ridiculous it was too.

I agree.

Then Johnny smiles as his anger disappears. My brush hits the canvas with renewed vigour and the whole incident comes flooding back. I am fifteen years old.

It started as a slight disagreement. It might have been vaguely political. I am not quite sure but it got a little heated. At this stage I would usually have stepped back and considered giving way. Alternatively I would have begged to differ but I would have always accepted that she had a valid point even if it appeared ridiculous. It was a useful tactic with Olive. In fact I was pretty good at diffusing most clashes with her. I'd witnessed many of the mistakes other members of my family had made and I was not going to follow in their footsteps.

Perhaps it was a growing confidence in my ability to debate. Perhaps I just wanted to test the waters but I needed to experience what it would be like to argue back, to properly argue, just once. So I did. It was a small point but I argued the toss. I thought my argument had conviction, I was forceful and I was eloquent in making my point. I think Olive laughed sarcastically and found it amusing to see the son who was vaguely educated answer back in such a way, and then in a millisecond her face changed and she snarled.

"Who the bloody 'ell do you think you are?" She then reeled off a verbal assassination of me. Her outburst concluded with these stinging words.

"'Ave 'ad bigger men than you. Shut up you little shit before I put you between the cheeks of my arse and spit you out like the little fart you are."

I couldn't resist a come back and said that "It was a shame that she had to resort to such base language but I suppose ignorance is bliss."

It wasn't particularly funny but it hit the mark. It derided her for her lack of education and there was a certain aloofness in the latter part of my comment. If there were two things that got Olive going more than anything else, one was the idea that someone could think and act as though they were better than her. The other would be to highlight her lack of schooling. (Her father frowned on girls receiving any kind of academic education) And I did both. I could tell it hit the mark and awaited the response. Her eyes squinted menacingly and her lips curled back to reveal smallish teeth clamped together. In an instant her arm drew back cocked and ready to fire. I knew what was about to come.

It's amazing how time slows down when violence is about to engulf you. I seemed to have time to think, I knew that Olive would not hold back – a fierce slap was about to smack the side of my head. Options: one, I could take it. The pain would be severe and the shock would make me wince or even cry but then it would be over; or two, I could duck. I would have no pain but I would be uncertain as to what would happen next. I could get more slaps for ducking or she would call in Ted. The punishment he would deliver would be more severe than a slap (to appease Olive). Probably the belt and dad would hate doing it.

There was a third alternative – a block. I'd just come back from seeing a Bruce Lee movie and had taken note of some of the Kung Fu moves. Interestingly enough, I'd just been practising the block which was a move that involved bringing the forearm out from the body to protect the side of the face. I believed that I could successfully use it now but I was unsure of what the consequences would be.

I never went into too much detail on that option as Olive's slap was about to make contact around my cheek. Instinct took over as my arm launched itself out from the side of my body to form a guard that was sturdy and firm. The force of the slap was in an instant repelled. It was the perfect block. At the same time I let out a small "yaaah" sound similar to that employed by Bruce Lee himself.

Before I had time to congratulate myself, Olive had begun a swing with her other arm. This time there was a slight difference in her countenance. Whereas before there was controlled aggression, now something a little more terrifying took over. Her eyes began to bulge and the drawn lips became wider to reveal more teeth. The flared nostrils now emitted a quiet but extremely menacing hiss, and most intimidating of all, the open hand had now become a fist.

BLOCK!

Exactly the same result as my arm stopped her attempted punch dead in its tracks. There was even another "yaaaah" to accompany it.

Silence.

What next? I let out a little laugh. It was sheepish and nervous but came out all superior.

Olive lost it completely. She gripped the first thing that she could put her hands on which happened to be a knitting needle. I could see the knuckles of her right hand turn white as Olive's small chubby fingers clenched tightly round the pointed weapon. The initial thrust came at me quickly and directly. Fortunately the needle still had some intricate crochet work attached to it which hindered the move and I managed to dodge the first stab easily which infuriated her even more.

Her face was now manic. All semblance of reason had gone. Her rage was such that the delicate crochet which took hours of dedication to make was, in an instant, torn off and unravelling like ribbons in the wind as it flew across the room. It added a sense of theatre to the ensuing mayhem as I became the matador dodging the horns of the raging bull that was Olive. The second and third thrusts were quicker. I dodged each one …just… and then ran. I didn't return for some time. All this and I was her favourite son!

I can't remember how long I stayed out or how I managed to calm her down. Perhaps the neighbours helped. I think I might have blocked that part out but I never laughed at my mother in an argument again.   All happy families are alike, but all ridiculous families are ridiculous in their own way. Not quite the opening lines to Anna Karenina but close.

I don't remember Derrick having that big an argument with Olive. I know he had them but they were small compared with Johnny as it was all happening below the surface. I can see that now. He just withdrew. I remember those last few looks around at my brother's flat before I left, I remember smiling at that jarring psychedelic décor.

"Not bad," I said, "But I don't think I will ever get used to the gold and orange tiles."

"You don't have to," he said.

We both laughed and as Derrick showed me to the door he looked at me earnestly. "Look after yourself." I nodded. He seemed genuinely concerned for me and then he smiled. It was a broad smile that meant well. I remember thinking that it was the happiest I had seen my brother in a while. It was a long time before I saw him quite that happy again.

It was a few days after my visit to Derrick's place. I remember lying awake one night unable to sleep. I can still feel the bump of the coil that had sprung from the steel-sprung mattress. The bed was just starting to go. We'd jumped up and down on it for years. But it wasn't that that was keeping me awake. My brother was leaving home. He was joining the army and his train was leaving early tomorrow morning. I looked over. I could sense Johnny was as wide awake as I was.

"I can't sleep," I said.

Johnny sighed as he pulled the sheets back a little. Our beds were directly opposite and I could see part of his face lit by a shaft of moonlight. His eyes were wide open. I guessed that he was thinking about the challenges that lay ahead.

"Are you excited?" I asked.

Before Johnny could answer a muffled cry was heard from the street below. Somebody had stumbled and fallen over the bins, probably drunk. Johnny immediately shot up and leapt towards the window with a gleeful smile spread across his face. We both knew who it would be at this time of night and we were right as a flat-capped aging figure called Chick bounced along the wall. He was a well-known character in the neighbourhood. Johnny saw his chance to have some fun.

"Give us a song, Chick," he shouted.

Chick looked up and immediately straightened his posture and cleared his throat. He then took his cap off and carefully stroked back the few strands of hair left on his balding bulbous head. Next he coughed a little and in a very dramatic move pulled his cap close to his chest.

"You watch. He's gonna go down on one knee," said Johnny. "Al Johnson. You watch."

And sure enough Chick did. "Mammy, how I love ya, how I love ya."

And the more he sang the more his whole posture became one of extreme pathos. It was as though he was performing to some long lost love.

"It's proper style old bleedin' music hall," said Johnny under his breath.

I couldn't help it, I howled with laughter at his sincere and earnest attempts and pretty soon Johnny joined in. I am sure Chick could hear us but it didn't deter him, he simply carried on, occasionally pausing to take a large gulp of something from a dark green bottle.

"Chick, shut your bleedin' cake 'ole," bellowed an angry voice from an open window opposite. The cry reverberated through the black and gloomy streets of an empty Cheetham Hill. It had the desired effect as all fell silent and then he started up again. This time piss pots and old boots were hurled out of various windows in his direction but again after a brief period of silence, he continued. And if it looked as though Chick really had stopped, Johnny made sure that the entertainment continued by loudly whispering those immortal lines "Chick, give us another song" and off he would go again. Nobody heard Johnny, thank God, otherwise Olive and the rest of the neighbourhood would have gone ballistic.

The performance went on for ages and we loved it. Nobody had the heart to do anything physical to move him on. He was a war veteran with clear symptoms of shell shock and, somewhere in his past, (so the story goes) his wife and children had left him.

The song was really meant for them. We never gave his history a second thought; we just took the piss. Kids are like that. In the end he was quietly escorted away by the local bobby, Bill Tanner at about three o'clock in the morning.

Afterwards me and Johnny were exhausted through laughing so much. We sat there crouched beneath the window panting and sighing at the same time. Slowly we regained some control. And then something quite eerie happened…a rhythmic undercurrent took over that controlled and synchronised our breathing. The silver glow of the moonlit bedroom ebbed and flowed with the same pulse and the quiet flutter of the lace curtains danced in time to a soft beat on a warm summer breeze.

I tell my students, "It's not just your eyes that you use when you draw. You are not just a recording device. You have to sense it, feel your medium, absorb your surroundings and when you do then something magical will happen.

I saw the moon dance over the silver grey slates of north Manchester and all was beautifully quiet. An age seemed to pass before I turned to my brother.

"I bet you're glad to be going," I said in hushed tones not wanting to break the spell.

"Yeah, too right" said Johnny as he smiled to himself. And then he repeated it quietly, "Too bloody right." There was a pause and then Johnny asked me something odd.

"What do you make of our old lodger Frank?"

It was a surprising question and one that seemed out of context. And before I could think I suddenly blurted out.

"Did he kill Michael?"

Johnny just burst out laughing

"Kill Michael. Jesus no chance. What fuckin' planet are you on?"

I suddenly felt stupid.

"I just thought…"

"Thought!" interrupted Johnny. "What kind of thought is that? Christ!"

I shook my head and mumbled, "Bloody Nawab."

We laughed and then I asked him why he'd asked me about Frank.

Johnny just shook his head. "No reason."

I felt even more stupid. He was going to say something. I know he was but my ridiculous reply just put him off. He just shook his head again. Then he said something else which seemed equally strange. And I wasn't sure at the time whether it was connected.

"You know there are some right bastards out there. Don't take any shit our kid."

"No. No, I won't," I replied.

"Good."

And then it was quiet again.

I felt as though my brother was going to say a little more but he never did. It would have made a difference. He should have said something and he knows that now. He just never liked being too serious, perhaps it would make him appear vulnerable. So that night he ducked it. He said nothing and instead told me a joke that was the crudest I had ever heard involving two nuns, a ham shank and four candles. It was pretty disgusting but I couldn't help laughing. I am quite sure that my brother could even make dying appear hilarious. In fact, he did once.

"C'mon, let's get some sleep," said Johnny. "Don't worry. I will wake you up in the morning before I go," he added, sensing my anxiety.

The next morning my brother was true to his word. A gentle prod in the ribs woke me just as the sun was rising. He stood over me, smiling gently and then gave me a hug. Before I knew it, he was gone. Of all the people – brothers, sisters, friends who moved away, he was the one I missed most.

PHOTOGRAPHS

It wasn't just me who lost something when my brothers moved out. Stacey felt it just as keenly. She missed Johnny's antics but she missed Derrick. Perhaps it was something to do with him being the eldest. She naturally looked up to him. Derrick had a quiet assurance with Stacey that often calmed her down. She could get emotional and sometimes easily upset. (Particularly where Olive was concerned.) It was good for Derrick too. Stacey's reliance on him must have made him feel good. They should have kept in touch more.

Poor Stacey, Olive wasn't easy to live with. Looking back, things were never the same after the Jammi debacle. Even I could sense that. So Stacey was always looking for a way out and she found it in the arms of a dashing young German and in June 1974 they got married. It wasn't so much the wedding itself, it was the plane journey home. Something interesting cropped up, something important. But the wedding. Oh lordy! How could I ever forget?

The wedding
Olive was in combative mood as she looked over at the unyielding figure across the room. She had her arms folded and stood in exactly the same provocative manner as Olive with a face just as stern. What's more she was giving Olive the eye. Tension was in the air.

"Look at 'er," Olive proclaimed. "Christ all bloody mighty she thinks she owns the bleedin' place… frau bleedin' Führer,"

"She probably does own the place mum," I chirped up. "She is going to be Stacey's mother in law and this is her house."

"You know what I mean," snarled Olive, her frustration building up. "What's 'er name…Gerta?"

"Yeah. Gerta, the granite goblin," said Johnny chuckling away.

"Don't start anything mum," I quickly interjected sensing that Johnny had inadvertently wound her up. "You are in Germany so you have to do as the Germans do. Don't forget it's Stacey's time."

"And Peter's" chirped Belle who had a little crush on Stacey's husband to be.

Olive just shook her head. "A pissin' German. My daughter's married a German. Jesus."

But the old lady heeded her children's advice and much to our relief did nothing for the time being. She was also away from her patch and not being on home territory made her wary. I was nervous. I was praying that my mother would not cause an incident. If she kicked off I could envisage us all moving out, suitcases in hand to some hotel that we couldn't afford led by a bustling Olive Smith. Thankfully that never happened. To be fair to Olive, she did have reason to be annoyed. At the beginning there was a certain amount of disdain in the way that we were treated. Gerta was particularly dismissive.

It was our arrival that triggered it but Johnny didn't help matters. As we all piled out of the car he shouted. "Shnell, shnell, schell, verboten. Gott in Himmel" which were the only German words he knew. As he did so he pushed me out of the car with my suitcase. I stuttered forward and tripped. The suitcase hit the floor spilling the contents (undies and all) across the path.

"Shit," I muttered.

Johnny translated suddenly remembering another German word.

"Scheizer." He looked up and gleefully proclaimed, "scheizer ya?"

Johnny thought it was hilarious and started laughing. Peter's older relatives who were there to greet us did not find it in the slightest bit funny although Peter's younger brothers, Bernt and Hans smirked. They soon stopped however when Gerta sent them a withering look.

Olive came out of the car last of all puffing away at a cigarette. "'Ello everybody," she said in good northern warm-hearted fashion. It was met with a subdued nod of the head. I could sense my mother's awkwardness at such a formal greeting. I think she felt it would be impolite to be received fag in hand so she quickly dropped it and stubbed it out with her black high-heeled shoe. Only it was on Gerta's beautifully immaculate and well-swept path. In response, Gerta rolled her eyes, marched back inside the house and left her dutiful husband to help with the luggage. The look of utter contempt that was on Gerta's face did not go unnoticed by Olive.

Gerta wasn't looking forward to meeting our family anyway. The idea that her son wanted to get married, and to an English girl, had come as a complete shock. And she was so young! It had been a whirlwind romance ending in a proposal six months after they'd met.

Stacey had clearly been swept off her feet by the handsome 23 year old. As I saw her there with Peter she was clearly in love, but Gerta didn't look too happy. In complete contrast Olive was unconcerned as Stacey was now off her hands.

Despite the initial difficulties, it turned out to be a real hoot. We couldn't speak a word of each other's language (apart from Peter) but no words were needed. We communicated none verbally. Toilet humour seemed to be a unifying factor. They ate a tremendous amount of bratwurst and salami as part of their diet which created some strong smells in the throne room. There were always various signals given to others, who were unfortunate to be in the vicinity when the door to the chamber of smells was being opened. These signals usually included fingers pinching one's nose or the wafting of one's hands in the air.

"Ppooh" or "eeghew" would accompany the actions. This was particularly embarrassing for those who were seen leaving this stinking room. Some of the young lads laughed it off but a couple of the old dears failed to see the funny side especially if they were the perpetrators of the big stink.

An extension of the toilet humour and a way of gaining a laugh would be to mimic the face you would pull when having a shit. Johnny called his imitation 'the parachute'. For this enactment his arms and elbows were tucked into his body and his fists were clenched under his chin. He would then say "parachute" through clenched teeth and scrunched face. This act was so good you could be forgiven for thinking he really did have constipation. The Germans found this hilarious.

When Peter's brothers were around, Johnny took particular delight in exclaiming loudly "Bernt Hans!" He would then hold his hands out over an imaginary fire. "Ouch, ouch" he would exclaim but I don't think that Hans and Bernt got the joke. They just laughed at Johnny's comic expressions.

My brother was happy to take centre stage wooing the German women in the process. The only people who weren't laughing were Olive and Gerta who continued to stand across either side of the room arms folded eyeing each other up.

For a time it was like some Mexican stand-off but whether it was the drink or they simply got bored, the granite goblin and Olive the destroyer called a ceasefire. Nothing was said. It was just a nod of the head. The frosty barrier they put up thawed slightly as the two matriarchs joined in festivities.

As much as Olive could be an agitator, she also knew how to party and there ensued a competition between Olive and Johnny as to who could be the most outrageously funny. In that place and in that atmosphere they put aside their differences and had a ball. Nothing was resolved but oh my word they had some fun, particularly Olive.

"Get an eyeful of this," she shouted to a host of elderly German men as she hoisted up her skirt to reveal the shapeliest legs for dancing. Her head went back as she laughed heartily. Anybody that didn't join in was forcibly dragged up by Olive.

"C'mon Fritz or whatever your name is," she said invitingly as she tugged on the ear of Gerta's brother not letting go until he was up trotting around with her and loving every minute of it. She completely beguiled her hosts. She could be like that. She had real charisma.

Johnny meanwhile had initiated the balloon game which involved passing a balloon to each other without using hands to the tune of oom pa pa played by Uncle Willem on the accordion. Needless to say my brother positioned himself between two shapely blond frauleins, Romy and Nova.

"Ich liebe dich," he proclaimed loudly (he'd learnt this from Hans and Bernt) as he rolled the balloon along the curvatious lines between neck and bosom of these two lovelies. I am sure that Johnny hooked up with one or even both of them. I can't quite remember and neither can he. I think I had my first Bavarian lager and that was it. Everything became a bit of a blur.

I pick up the photograph that I have been working from. I hold it firmly in the palm of my hand and scrutinise it. I don't usually like working solely from photographs, I usually do some preliminary sketches of the person I am about to paint first and in the process have a conversation. I try to establish a relationship with my subject and get them to reveal aspects of their personality which I then try to incorporate into my final piece. Usually I need to see the real person in the flesh but this time I only have a photograph but photographs are still hugely important.

It was on the flight home from the wedding that I became a little bored.

"Have you still got those photographs mum?"

"What now? Bloody 'ell!" spluttered Olive. Unfortunately I'd disturbed her just as she was about to nod off. Olive was still recovering from all the drink and festivities the night before. She was now paying the price as was Johnny who, once on the plane, didn't wake up until we arrived back in Manchester. Nevertheless she reached into her coat, pocket plucked out an envelope and through the gap in the seats thrust it into my hand.

"Don't bloody lose them!" she stated firmly. I'd become accustomed to Olive's swearing but other people in the airplane were a little shocked not just at her language but at her coarse manner. They were mainly Germans. Olive had taken "enough shit" from Gerta. She wasn't taking any more, especially from these foreigners.

"WHAT?" she rasped as she looked directly at the shocked faces staring at her. Olive's grimace was confrontational and her statement uncompromising. It had the desired effect. Those who were gawking at her looked away. Olive turned her attention back to me.

"What do you want them for anyway?" asked Olive. Her tone was a little more relaxed but still contained irritation at my request. "You've seen them all at the wedding."

"Just curious," I replied. In truth I wanted to look at them all by myself. To ruminate on them. It was a nice touch by Olive (first suggested by Belle) that we bring some photographs of our friends and family back in Cheetham Hill for our new German friends to see. After all Ted and Derrick couldn't make it. (I think Ted was scared of flying)

They provided a good talking point, particularly the ones of Stacey as a toddler. Everybody laughed at her as a little girl, all dressed up for the whit walk. What made it even funnier and more embarrassing for Stacey was that her furrowed eyebrows and pouted lips gave away the fact that she was clearly disgruntled at being made to wear an outfit that she hated. Stacey said that she felt like a "trussed up bloody turkey." It was clear that she had revisited an uncomfortable memory.

But Peter loved it. I can still hear him cooing "Aah my puppe" (doll) and I can still hear the thunderous laughs from Bernt and Hans in response to their brother's unbridled adoration of his new bride. I singled out the picture and studied it more carefully. Stacey was clutching a little white handbag and was standing in the middle of the cobbled street. In the left corner the remnants of a game of hopscotch lay chalked on slabs of pavement. Mum's friend Elsie couldn't get out of the way and her head and shawl were a blur escaping off the right hand side off the picture. Part of her seemed to be in quite a few of those early photos. Elsie was the original photo bomber.

Belle who had been quietly reading her Bunty annual started to become quite interested.

"Can I see that one of dad? "She asked thoughtfully.

"Sure," I said and sifted through until I found it. "You like this one, don't you?" I said smiling and I could understand why. It was a great picture of Ted with a few of his navy buddies just before he met Olive. He looked happy and appeared to be sharing a joke with those around him. He was as relaxed as I had ever seen him. He and his friends were all shirtless. It looked as though they had put in a shift with glistening sweat trickling down bronzed torsos. Judging by the large palm tree leaves that surrounded the group, the climate was hot and sticky. I think they were somewhere in the Pacific.

Their laughs were caused by the ridiculous way in which they wore their navy hats. They were tilted at the most irreverent and jaunty angle. Olive liked this picture of Ted and his friends and said that she found it quite sexy. She confessed this to me one night after downing two sherries and a Bailey's in fairly quick succession.

Belle wanted a few more photos to look at so I handed her some. As she viewed them attentively, I looked closely at her face and realised that her little girl features had started to change. Her face looked less rounded, the puppy fat was starting to disappear. Her eyes also seemed to be more prominent. Perhaps it was the eyeliner that she'd been using recently. She looked more grown up.

Despite this, Belle still had a quality of innocence. There was no side to her; no guile and she was fiercely loyal. She doted on Ted and would often stick up for him when he was being ridiculed. Once Belle had said "that's enough", then even Johnny would stop taking the piss out of the old man. My sister's goodness exerted a real power in the family dynamic. Ted would often call her his little ray of sunshine. And indeed she was.

After Belle had finished, she handed the photos back to me. There was one in particular that I wanted to see…an old black and white one and it was there on the top of the pile. I picked it up and looked at it closely. There were a few figures in the shot but one person in particular had a presence that towered above the others. His face was quite stern as he looked uncompromisingly at the camera. He was probably in his fifties then but he still appeared stocky and powerful. There was no mistaking Ernest Harold Jones – my grandad. There and then I sensed the importance of pictures and photographs not just as a reminder of lineage but of heritage. He was my past as well as my future.

Ernie as he was known was a proud man. Some would say too proud. You could see by the defiant way that he stood that he would not suffer fools gladly. Beside him stood Annie Jones his dutiful wife. She was looking kindly at the camera. Her eyes were small and dark. Her hair was a mass of straggly black that was slowly being taken over by an invading silvery grey. She was swarthy in complexion and quite large having born seven children.

Holding hands with Annie was a small boy with straw white hair struggling to hold on to a melting ice cream. He was their grandson, Derrick Smith. Just in the background, a step or two behind, was their daughter, a trim, good looking blonde woman. A young Olive Smith. You couldn't see much of her. She was largely hidden by the imposing figure of Ernie. They were strolling along the sands at Southport.

Even though the picture was monochrome, the deep shadows and bright light suggested a clear blue sky. It also appeared to be one of those typical windy and blustery English seaside days. If you looked closely you could see parts of Annie's hair trailing off in the breeze. Her arms were down by her side. I suspect that they were holding down a long flapping dress. Little Derrick Smith was squinting in the sunlight. He was also frowning as some of his thin wispy hair had become entangled in the ice cream. He appeared uncomfortable and ill at ease whilst in complete contrast Ernie appeared steadfast and unaffected by the swirling gusts of wind. I turned the picture over and could just about make out "Southport 1959" scribbled faintly on the back in pencil.

I don't remember much of grandad Ernie. He was an enigmatic figure. The only time we saw him was on his birthday in his flat in Kersal. When I do try to think of him, I remember a more portly character with a slightly softer and rounder face than the one in the photograph but I liked that old black and white image. It captured the man he was rather than the faded memory that I have now.

Olive told me that he once worked as a bouncer at some of the toughest pubs and bars around Salford and it wasn't hard to see why. Mum sometimes described him as "a bit of a bruiser" but more often than not as a "hard bastard." Ernie openly admitted that it didn't matter whether it was a boy or girl he never held back on giving any of his children a slap or two, or three in Olive's case. He stated on many occasions, that he had "no favourites. They would all get a slap equally as hard."

Olive hated Ernie. She was quite open about it. Not only was he a bully but, according to her, he crushed any dreams she had of going on the stage. (She was a great singer!) Olive told us that he was scornful of any of her ideas and that he thought women generally were "a contemptuous breed." He had a particular disregard for his daughter who often had ideas above her station. Olive once confessed to me that she cried herself to sleep with tears of anger and frustration because of her father.

His uncompromising approach and her rebellious nature were always going to end in tears; usually for Olive. Her frustration was often at boiling point. It was no surprise that Olive tried to get away from her father as soon as she could. That's when she met Ted and reeled him in. I've often imagined that first meeting. I can picture it now like some excerpt from an old 1950s film noir – Olive the predatory femme fatal, Ted the poor unfortunate victim.

A handsome man

It was on her nineteenth birthday one Saturday night down at the local palais that Olive spied a shy and relatively handsome man. He was older than her and she quite liked that. She had spurned the advances of youths her age who wanted nothing more than a furtive grope. She was at times happy to oblige but certainly didn't want anything serious. It was still a temptation however, to succumb to something more permanent just to get away from her oppressive and bullying father.

Lately, that desire to escape had begun to gnaw away at her. It was on her mind in the heady smoke-filled atmosphere of the local dance hall as she surveyed the livestock. The tall stranger she had been eying up for the last five minutes appeared happy enough. He was smoking quite nonchalantly and talking to friends. It was strange that he didn't appear too concerned with all the dressed up females around him but, most importantly, he didn't appear to be anything like her father.

Olive was not shy and decided to test the waters. She walked over with a slow deliberate walk and asked the young man for a light. She cocked her hand gracefully to one side and let her fingers embrace the cigarette with a feminine touch. She looked confident but slightly vulnerable. It was a well-managed move. She didn't want to scare him off. He looked a little startled and paused before stammering, "Er. Yeah. S...sure." The man nervously patted several pockets before finding the right one. He took out the book of matches and paused.

"Well, aren't you going to light me?" she asked provocatively.

The warning bells were beginning to sound in the young man's head. He tended to avoid the female species. Women like this one were dangerous. The stranger was in danger of losing his equilibrium but he gathered his wits enough to strike the match...just. Olive revelled in his befuddlement. She was most definitely in charge. She loved this. She loved his reaction so much that she played him even more.

She slowly clasped her hands over his. Her touch was smooth and gentle. The man's hands began to tremble. Olive laughed inside as she brought his hands up to where her mouth was. The stranger noticed how poised the cigarette was in that sensual mouth. Olive inhaled showing a hint of pleasure as the hit of nicotine instantly began to take effect. For a second she closed her eyes and then gradually refocused back to where his eyes were staring back at her.

When she had sucked in enough of the intoxicating fumes she paused slightly and then blew out a long stream of grey smoke. To ensure that nothing went in Ted's face, Olive pursed her red ruby lips at an angle. Whilst doing this her face tilted to one side but all the time her eyes were firmly fixed on the stranger's gaze. This deft operation did not go unnoticed by the stranger who muttered that "She was thoughtful." It was also quite sexy. Ted Smith was bewitched and Olive knew it. And so it began.

Ted, bless him, never knew what hit him, he must have been quite smitten, and Olive used this power to manoeuvre him into any place that she wanted. He was like putty in her hands. She wore the trousers from day one. All he had to do was say yes and do as he was told and life would be easy. Ted didn't mind a bossy woman. Olive told me that dad's own mother, who he was quite fond of, could be quite forceful. Ted didn't need to say it but implicit in his manner was the need for a dominant female figure in his life. He admitted it. He liked Olive telling him what to do. It probably gave him security and a strange kind of comfort.

They married quickly. To the outside world they were an unlikely and ill-matched couple but I can see how it worked for Olive. Although she felt affection for her husband that was only part of the reason she married him. She determined, particularly after her tumultuous relationship with her father that no man was ever going to rule over her. No man was ever going to control her or ever tell her what to do. No man was ever going to be her boss or bully her in the way that Ernie did.

Ted wouldn't dream of being anything like Ernie and so at the beginning of their marriage Olive was free. She was free to be herself knowing full well that she would never be challenged by her husband. She was free to say anything she wanted to anybody she pleased. All the bottled up emotions of that awful father-daughter relationship spilled out into any confrontation she could get.

Every argument she had was subconsciously an argument with Ernie and strangely enough she began to enjoy the battle as much as she enjoyed flirting. We could all sense that. Life with her husband must have become a little boring anyway. She needed some outside interests. But Ted knew what he had married and decided to settle for his lot. So long as he didn't know he didn't care and gradually, bit by bit, he retired into his own little world of model making and macramé.

I love painting portraits but I like them to be different. I couldn't paint the same face over and over again. I often ask myself why Rembrandt painted his own face so many times. Beautiful as they are, did he not get bored of painting his own image all the time?

Meanwhile back on the aircraft returning from Germany, Belle had found something quite interesting.

"Why is this one cut?" she said inquisitively.

I looked at my sister. She was staring intently at a photo of mum and dad that had been taken a number of years ago. They looked happy enough. It appeared as though they were on a night out and sitting round a small round table smiling at the camera. Both of them had a cigarette in hand. The unmistakable clear golden pallor of a pint of Boddington's lay half drunk in the centre along with the custard yellow of a snowball.

"Maybe there was a coffee stain or something," I replied, "and it was just cut off."

"Maybe," said Belle, "but I just wander whose hand that is."

I looked more closely and sure enough someone else's hand was there – just on the edge. He or she was in the picture before it was snipped. It was one of those things you realised you'd seen but never really noticed. The hand was resting on the table and was close enough to Olive's to suggest that whoever it belonged to was sat with them. But before I could study it more closely, Belle stretched over the seat that was in front of me, operated her arm in crane-like fashion and planted the photo in Olive's eye line.

"Who was that in the photo?" she blurted out. It woke Olive up with a start. Poor old Belle got a right mouthful. Fortunately the sudden roar of the aircraft drowned out most of the expletives. My sister went white as she had never suffered one of Olive's outbursts before. It wasn't just because she was the youngest, there was something about Belle, an innocence, even Olive couldn't bring herself to inflict her wrath on one so untarnished. She was always very protective of her daughter anyway. Poor Belle. I could see the tears well up immediately. Amazingly enough Olive apologised and then proceeded to blame me for not having the foresight to warn my younger sister. Olive then picked up the picture that had fallen to the floor. I saw her look at it, intently concentrating on the hand.

"It's no one," she said. There was a pause and, as she handed it back to Belle, she repeated softly, "No one." That wasn't true. Olive clearly knew who it was and didn't want to say and didn't want to remember but she did. I know she did. It was Frank.

1968

As the figure walked up to the door and rang the bell Olive could almost feel Ted's heart beat a little quicker. She could see a difference in his demeanour as he visibly became lighter as though some imaginary shackles had been lifted. In that moment Olive had to acknowledge to herself that Ted looked different, a little more alive. She watched as her husband greeted the smartly dressed man with a firm and manly handshake. They both smiled and patted each other on the shoulder. It was a warm and friendly exchange.

"How are you? It's been…"

"Fine. Fine," said Ted interrupting Frank in his excitement. "Absolutely fine. And you?"

"Yeah. Good thanks."

Suddenly Ted threw an imaginary punch which Frank dodged in exaggerated fashion. They laughed. Whilst Ted's laugh was generous, Frank's was slightly uncomfortable but still warm. He wasn't quite prepared for Ted's ebullience. For once Olive was happy to take a back seat as she looked surprised and happy at seeing a new and rejuvenated Ted Smith. "There's life in the old dog yet," she mused.

Ted's face had lit up when he heard that it was Frank, his old navy chum who was asking about the spare room. Since marrying Olive and leaving the navy Ted had lost contact with many of his old friends and found it difficult to make new ones. He did have his brother Phillip but they didn't get on. Olive didn't like him either. It was for no reason other than she never trusted a man with soft hands.

Olive knew that Ted was in some respects quite unhappy. He was not a party goer like her and he was uncomfortable with the odd friendships with the police that she had started to cultivate. (aside from Bill) She could sense that a part of Ted longed for the camaraderie that his old navy buddies gave him. Still, he chose his bed, thought Olive. He knew what it would be like. "I still want Ted to be happy though," Olive said to herself and then the thought came to her that maybe Frank could help. Olive was therefore pleased when Frank accepted the room.

"Are you sure you won't mind the kids?" Olive added.

"No. That's fine. That attic room is well out of the way," replied Frank. A big smile beamed across Ted's face so Frank felt the need to put things in perspective.

"Look, I won't be staying long, six weeks tops. I'm just down to sort out some stuff at the bus depot on Queen's Road. I'll probably go back up to Preston at the weekends so you won't see much of me."

"That's a pity," said Olive unashamedly.

Frank just smiled. "Look, I'm happy to pay full whack even if I am not here at weeke…"

"No you bloody well won't!" Ted interrupted.

Again Olive was quite stunned at her husband's new found forcefulness.

"I insist," said Frank quietly and so the deal was settled.

Olive watched as Ted helped Johnny up to his room. She was curious about what the next few weeks would hold. Frank was not Olive's usual type. She liked men who were a little more dangerous even if they were players. She was very careful but suspected that Ted knew about her flings. But Olive was drawn to Frank in quite a different way. He was not overly handsome nor was he tall but there was something oddly attractive about him. It wasn't so much about how he looked but was more his manner. He was thoughtful, attentive and very considerate. He had a quiet charm.

At first Olive ignored her attraction to him. She saw very little of him anyway. He went out with Ted for the odd drink. God knows what they talked about and usually after tea he retired up to his room but as the weeks passed, Frank began to come down from his attic room for the odd chat usually after the kids had gone to bed. Sometimes when Ted was on a night shift just the two of them would talk a lot about all sorts of things.

She was happy that Frank's initial stay of a few weeks turned into a few months. "There's more to deal with at the depot than I first thought," said Frank matter of factly. Olive knew that it was just an excuse to stay. They were both growing quite fond of each other. She was also pleased to find out that he wasn't married. Frank had had a few girlfriends but things never worked out. Olive couldn't understand why. "Maybe you're hiding something," she would say teasingly. Whatever the case, she was intrigued and wanted to know more about him.

Olive was only too pleased to invite Frank out to the Beech Hill Club on Ted's birthday. It was an invite that he gratefully accepted. They were joined by Bill Tanner and his wife Margaret. Bill had just finished his shift and was complaining about his sore feet.

"A policeman's lot is not a happy one," he said, bending his aching joints but Olive wasn't really listening. Pat Gill or Patricia (as she liked to be known) had just walked in. She was well dressed and paraded what looked like a brand new fur coat that hugged a well-rounded figure. Olive took a short drag of her cigarette and then exhaled through pursed lips.

"Now then Olive," said Ted sensing his wife's unease.

It was clear that there was bad blood between her and Pat. For Olive it was the way that Pat and her little toadies appeared to look down their noses at her. Jibes were often made in her direction about some of the "riff raff" that frequented the club. Although Olive's name was never mentioned, it was clear that she was the target. In Pat's eyes Olive was simply coarse and vulgar. It was an alpha female rivalry which led to some classic verbal jousting. On one occasion, as Pat walked past Olive with her little entourage, she complained that there was a "bad smell in the room." The blow that Pat had intended fell way short of its mark as Olive simply replied that Pat's nose was "too close to her arse." They nearly came to blows that time and they got even closer to fisticuffs when Olive brazenly flirted with Pat's husband Keith. Unfortunately, he quite liked the attention.

Right now Pat was doing her best to wind Olive up. She was doing that thing of glancing at Olive and then whispering to her little posse of women gathered around who in turn looked at Olive and started laughing. Olive was bristling.

"That was a great potato hash you cooked the other night," said Frank who sensed that Olive was distracted.

Olive didn't answer. She was too busy eying up Pat. She took another drag of her cigarette, a deeper one that calmed her a little. She had to be careful, any more fights and she would be barred from the club. As Olive sat there plotting, she observed the plumes of grey smoke that she had exhaled drift slowly along to where Pat and her acolytes were sitting and then linger contentedly amongst hats, hair and coats. Olive smiled a wicked smile. She inhaled again. This time she took a deeper drag and exhaled with more force. She then watched as the thick grey clouds deposited their noxious contents over the fur coat that her enemy was wearing.

"Silly bitch," said Olive to herself, "She should've put it in the cloakroom straight away. Too busy showin' the bleedin' thing off."

Pat looked on with dismay as her pride and joy had become enveloped by the grey gaseous matter. She looked across to where Olive sat smiling. Pat somehow held it together and simply tutted disdainfully whilst wafting away the smoke in a remarkably controlled and regal fashion.

"Oh dear, bad smell," was all she said. She was determined not to be put off her stride by Olive.

Olive smiled back but through gritted teeth. Pat's reaction had effectively countered her offensive. Olive bristled some more.

"Who the bloody hell does she think is?"

"Olive ...c'mon don't do anything," said Ted, "it's my birthd..."

"Oh shut up!" Olive interrupted. And then she continued in irate fashion.

"That posh arse'ole wafting away my smoke in that way. I'll bloody well show 'er." And then the smile evaporated and was replaced by a snarl. Her back teeth were showing. Ted knew this was a bad sign.

"Now then Olive, don't do anything stupid," he pleaded but it had little effect.

Olive didn't have much lung capacity but she filled every cubic centimetre with the most enormous drag of her cigarette. Frank looked on with astonishment as he could see the fag end light up with a fierce red, grey and yellow glow. The force of Olive's suction sounded like a hoover getting a piece of cloth stuck in its nozzle. The whole act was fuelled by a surge of rage. Olive hung onto the poisonous noxious fumes for as long as she could before let out the most chilling exhalation of breath.

"PPHHHOOOOWWTH!"

The smoke that escaped spat out like the fizz from an uncorked bottle of champagne. It was laser like in its precision. Within a second it hit Pat full on. Then miraculously the propulsion stopped and there followed a slow diffusion of the contents on Pat's startled entourage. Cries of anguish rang out. "Jesus Christ all bloody mighty."

Pat stopped her conversation and started to splutter and then wretched. She wafted away the smoke but this time, much to Olive's glee, it was not a queens's wave but rather a desperate flapping of arms that tried to push the fumes away. As the air started to thin and the greyness started to part, there appeared a hideous visage. It was Olive stood upright, her face staring right back at Pat, defiant and menacing like some hideous gremlin with a satanic smile. No words were said. The bent and gasping figure that was Pat was led away by her husband who tried to give Olive a withering look.

"Do you mind," came the indignant voice of husband Keith.

"No, not really," said Olive who was positively ecstatic. In the melée, Pat had spilt a glass of burgundy over her new fur coat.

"Oh my God, Olive," said Frank, astonished.

"I forgot to warn you about Olive," said Ted apologetically.

"No, that's absolutely fine," said Frank. "She's a queen, a warrior queen" he laughed. "Queen Boudicca." Frank's admiration for Olive surprised Ted and it also surprised Olive. It wasn't so much what he said but it was the way he said it. He seemed so alive, so wonderfully dramatic. Ted simply frowned.

"Aren't you just a bit embarrassed?" he whispered to Frank.

"Absolutely not!" said Frank with a real verve, "Absolutely not."

Suddenly a large figure pushed its way through the crowd,

"'Ave I missed something?" said Bill who had been busy getting the drinks.

"Just another day at the office for Olive," said Ted despairingly. It was an unintentional joke but suddenly everybody was laughing. And even Ted began to smile as he reached for his beloved pint of Boddington's.

"Cheers, Bill," said Ted who gulped half of his drink down quickly…a nervous response to the previous altercations.

"Yep, cheers Bill," echoed Frank as he took up his seat beside Queen Boudicca. The Queen took a sip of her snowball.

"It's good 'ere innit?" she said triumphantly. Everybody smiled and then Margaret took a quick picture with her new camera.

As Olive looked at the photo, I could see that she couldn't help smiling at some memory. "Patricia bloody Gill," she chuckled to herself. She looked at me. "That was a good night. We laughed so much." And then Olive's gaze wandered to the part of the photo that she'd snipped off, to where Frank's hand was just about showing. She frowned and then tucked it away in her handbag out of sight and out of mind.

1978. THE AABEN

I take a break and slump down in the easy chair opposite. I allow myself to sink slowly into the soft scruffy paint-stained cushions. I look long and hard to assess what I have done. As I stare at my painting, demons come and I doubt myself. They are not right – the tones, there is no depth, I cannot paint and then I realise that for all her bravado, Olive too had her doubts.

She acquired the shop on an impulse, I got the impression that Ted just went along with his wife. It was quite a drastic move because what little savings they had went into the venture, but after a couple of years she had misgivings. The shop wasn't doing as well as she'd hoped and the demons that caused her to take such a course of action never went away.

So Olive's Offy began to fail. It wasn't because of Olive as she was a great host. It was more a case of the shop being in the wrong place at the wrong time. That stretch of Cheetham Hill Road was becoming desolate as surrounding businesses and houses were being knocked down. People started to travel further up the road to the new precinct and the growing Asian community went elsewhere to buy their kind of food. Fresh bread from Warburton's held little sway when pitted against a tasty spicy nan. The grim truth for my parents was that the business was dying. We had to move.

We were relocated to one of the council maisonettes on Bonsall Street, Hulme not far from the notorious Crescents. Sometimes called the bull rings, they were an absolute disaster with old people stuck on top floors, lifts that didn't work and young families trapped behind grey concrete walls. I remember reading that they were 'inspired by Georgian Bath' and promised to 'revolutionise urban living.' They were even named after the main architects Robert Adam, John Nash, Charles Barry and William Kent. I mentioned this to Johnny. "What a load of old bollocks. These people wanna try livin' in these shit 'oles."

Olive likened the circular design of the crescents to "the ring around her arse'ole." We were all in agreement. It wasn't great there. Crime was rife, unemployment had risen sharply and tensions were high due to new controversial police enforcement laws being used in the area and neighbouring Moss Side. It didn't help that it tended to discriminate against young black men. There was a deep resentment in the black community and who could blame them? I knew then that something would kick off.

And for all my liberal attitudes and growing political awareness I was fearful of the black youths who hung around on street corners and who looked on my fresh-faced art college image with suspicion. I could see it in their eyes. Not only was I easy meat but I was part of the white male privileged majority that was part of the problem. I wanted to scream "It's not my fault. I'm not some snotty-nosed kid from Surrey with rich parents and I am not Alf Garnett!"

Despite some fear, there was something quite surreal about walking through parts of that neighbourhood, particularly the area around Jackson Crescent. Some of the residents would think nothing of tipping their unwanted furniture over the balcony of their flats. I once walked by as a fridge came crashing down several feet in front of me followed by a settee from another flat. They fell and landed in such odd positions. I thought they looked quite sculptural so I photographed them. I even stood around for hours hoping that I would catch a cooker or an arm chair in mid-flight but I never did get the 'money shot'. Still, I have an interesting record of my time there. And I managed to display them in a small exhibition in Hulme library. I took my parents to see it.

Olive frowned when she saw them "It's just a load of old rubbish," she said disdainfully.

"Yes," I said proudly. She wasn't amused.

I saw Ted move his head to a horizontal position in the hope that seeing it from a different angle would help him to get it.

"Er, hmmm. No. I'm not sure. Hmm, er," Ted sounded constipated. I loved it.

"And you say you've sold one?" said Olive in disbelief.

"Well, the library woman said that someone made enquiries."

"Well you'd 'ave to pay me to take one away." And with that she swanned over to the Mills and Boon section in the second isle. Meanwhile Ted had given up on trying to see the merits of my art and seemed more taken with a stack full of some old Man, Myth and Magic periodicals that lay enticingly on the table nearby.

But there was another side to Hulme that had less tension and bizarrely the deposits of unwanted furniture helped. Sometimes people would sit on and around the settees and light up a spliff. It got to be quite communal and a home from home for some. For others it seemed a perfect place to finalise a drug transaction, sitting on a manky old armchair on the croft, open air, nice and relaxed weighing out the dope.

Faces became familiar and squatters would saunter down from the rent-free flats, can of beer in hand and say hello with not a care in the world. And there was reggae. Who could ever get annoyed about the state of the rubbish-strewn crofts when that was belting out? There was definitely something appealing about this unconformist slightly anarchic way of life.

Hulme, the dirty old town that housed the slums of the fifties and sixties had been reborn into a dirty new town of the seventies. It was apart and didn't quite fit in. Tony Wilson, the TV presenter and champion of punk, summed it up perfectly saying that "it was like something that history had spat out."

It was not what my parents were used to but thankfully they were only there for a couple of years. In that time Olive made various complaints to the council and was a constant thorn in their side. She also headed up a residents' association to fight for better conditions. The old battle axe was still a force to be reckoned with and had lost none of her bite.

But there were bright spots – the Russell Club just across the road was a really dingy place that saw bands such as Joy Division and Echo and the Bunnymen appear there. Looking back I wish I had seen them as they were right opposite me. I definitely heard them on a Friday or Saturday night through my open window. I cursed the fact that they kept me awake and on that basis refused to see them. It is a shameful confession and one I only reveal after a few strong ales.

Another bright spot was the Aaben Cinema. It was slightly alternative and very community based. It had a really interesting interior, very arty and way ahead of its time. It paved the way for art-house cinema long before The Cornerhouse was established. I once took Ted and Olive there for their anniversary to see a film called Erazerhead by David Lynch. What a big mistake! It was advertised as a 'feast of visual entertainment' and a 'tour de force' by the critics. It sounded great and much to my surprise I managed to persuade them to come. But, oh my God, I wish I had researched the film a little more. If only I had known what the story was about.

After fifteen minutes of painful viewing where one of the residents, a disfigured lady gets lost in a radiator, Olive inhaled her cigarette, blew hard and came straight to the point.

"What on earth is this shit?"

I was panicking but decided to play it cool.

"Give it time," I said, "Hopefully it might get better."

"Better!" exclaimed Olive incredulously. "Jesus! Ted, can you believe it?"

My father took his glasses off and rubbed his eyes which was always a sign that he wasn't happy.

"Look son, I know you mean well, but, oh no! WHATS THAT? Is she giving birth to a lizard?"

Ted turned away from the screen and looked at me.

"Your mum's right son. It's shit."

I sighed as Ted and Olive got up to leave. I must say that I wasn't particularly enjoying it either but I stayed put out of stubbornness. As Olive bustled down the aisle with Ted in tow she turned to the other six people in the cinema and told them in no uncertain terms that they "must be bleedin' mad to sit through this pile of shite." After watching the whole film I returned home. As I walked in through the front door Olive looked at me.

"You didn't sit through it, did you?" she asked whilst laughing at the same time.

"Well I thought it had some interesting points to make about loneliness and…"

"'Arse'oles," interrupted Olive. She then turned to her husband. Ted can you believe it. He's tryin' to justify shit. Is that what they do at art college son? Get you to try and justify shit?" They both laughed. Ted shook his head. He saw the deflated look on my face. He knew I'd tried hard to get them both to go and succeeded only for it to end in failure. He smiled warmly.

"Never mind son. Maybe another time."

It always makes me smile when I think of that episode and similar ones where my world and their world collided. They just didn't get modern art. Much of it is pretentious anyway but I always felt that they were proud of me. I'd gone to college. It was a big thing in those days.

I leave the brushes to soak and put lids on paints. It's enough for today. At the end of the night I lie in bed and replay my father's words in my head. "Maybe another time son" but I realised that there never was. For the next few years I was having the time of my life at Manchester Poly. Then I was off travelling and all the troubles and woes surrounding my family were forgotten and all my suspicions began to fade away.

The time passed quickly but me and my father never made another cinema date and before I knew it, Ted was gone.

I am suddenly quite tired and drift off. In my slumber I dream about my father.

1983. TED'S LAST STAND

It wasn't really that unexpected. Ted had been suffering from angina for years and coupled with his stomach ulcers had not been in a good way for some time. A bad smoking habit and sedentary lifestyle hadn't helped but there didn't seem to be a problem that day.

Johnny felt OK about leaving him to babysit his daughter for a couple of hours. Dad jumped at the chance as his son had just bought a new video player. They had started to become popular at the time and the good news for Ted was that Johnny had a few pirate copies of the most popular films. Ted knew exactly what he was going to watch, Conan the Barbarian, the Arnold Schwarzenegger classic. Perhaps it was the excitement of the semi-clad women or Arnie's dashing sword play that triggered the heart attack but towards the end of the film Ted was feeling rough and complaining of chest pains. As Johnny came in he saw Ted collapse and in Johnny's words "that was it."

Whenever he recounts the episode, he usually paints a vivid picture of dad's false teeth juddering whilst trying desperately to give him mouth-to-mouth resuscitation. Johnny's impression is, as usual, wonderfully slapstick. I don't know how he does it but he could even make our father's death appear funny.

I was working abroad when I got that message to ring my brother urgently. I will never forget that phone call. It has stayed with me all my life. When I think back I can still feel that awful numbness. It wasn't just the news of my father. Ever since I attended Nellie's funeral all those years ago I couldn't face up to anything to do with death. When Johnny rang he did most of the talking, thank God.

"I did everything I could," he said, "I even gave him the kiss of life. Christ that was difficult. I slammed his chest. C'mon ya bastard I said but that was it. Gone."

"Shit," I replied.

"I had to tell the family," continued Johnny, "that was a bloody fiasco. Stacey was the first to go. It wasn't just a cry, it was fuckin' biblical, talk about wailing and gnashing of teeth. Poor Belle, she was already sobbing, shoulders bobbing up and down but when she heard Stacey, that was it. They were like a bleedin' hoard of banshees. AAggghhhheeeee," cried Johnny in mock imitation.

I actually laughed a little and then Johnny continued.

"You could see Olive getting angrier by the minute. I mean I could understand it. It was fuckin' hysterical. As soon as the squinted eyes came and that bloody grimace I knew what was going to happen. Someone was going to get a slap. Do you know what was so bloody incredible?"

"What," I replied.

"She couldn't decide which one to slap. Honestly. I could see it in her face. She was almost counting on her fingers – eeny meeny miny mo. In the end it was poor Stacey who copped it. SLAP right across the side of her face. To be fair it did the trick."

"Did the dragon's nostrils flare?" I asked inquisitively.

"Not this time," said Johnny, "not this time."

"What about Derrick?" I asked.

"He came later. He was pretty upset. He loved Ted."

"Did he say much?"

"No, not really. You know what he's like. He never does."

Comic tragedy

In the service that followed, Olive tried to soften the grief by saying poignantly to all who would listen, "At least Ted got to watch one of his favourite films before he died," as if that somehow eased the pain. Poor Ted.

Whenever I think of my father, those two words always come up. And in the aftermath of his funeral the same words sprang to mind as we toasted the old man and tried to give him a decent send off. Poor Ted. No matter how hard we tried to revere him or how sympathetic we were, everybody was in agreement that his life was, in many respects, a comic tragedy. I don't think I am being unkind because Ted really didn't help himself. He was such an easy target. And inevitably, as the drink flowed, the stories started to surface.

"What about Ted's sneeze?" said Belle shaking her head.

Suddenly Johnny felt prompted to mimic the grunting build up.

"AAGH, AUGH AGHH ooohhh."

Stacey laughed. "I thought he was having a bloody orgasm,"

"Chance would be a fine thing," muttered Olive.

"It was bloody inhuman," stated Derrick.

My family's description was no exaggeration and if the build-up promised something spectacular the final explosive sneeze did not disappoint. It was brutal in its involuntary execution. WHHOOOOFFFTHH. The crumpled handkerchief would often billow and creak with the force expelled from mouth and nostrils. If there was no protective cloth or hand in the way then his false teeth would often fly out chattering away with a life of their own.

On one occasion his dentures were spewed forth with such venom that it was frightening. I can still hear the awful clunk of plastic hitting brick and I can still see the writhing pair of gums hipping and hopping against the spiral patterned carpet as they dropped to the living room floor. The amazing thing was that when it occurred, Ted simply popped them back in and went about his business as though nothing had happened.

"Guy Fawkes would have succeeded if Ted was there leading the gun powder plot," said Belle sarcastically. "No need for gun powder – just get Ted to sneeze underneath the Houses of Parliament and then BOOM!"

"Christ, he could have altered British history!" exclaimed Johnny in mock awe.

Everybody laughed. Even Olive allowed herself a little chuckle in the middle of her grief.

But we were on a roll now and it was inevitable that Ted's chameleon impression would be remembered.

The chameleon impression

Ted quite liked natural history and one day he tried to explain to us all about the chameleon. We were listening to him (for a change) crouched round the gas fire one Sunday evening after bath time. Belle even asked Ted a question about the creature's feeding habits. We all groaned as we knew that Ted would be flattered by his young daughter's interest and would then go on for ages. There was a tremor in Ted's voice as he was clearly excited that at least one of his offspring was listening. He was as animated as I have ever seen him when he exclaimed that, "The chameleon's tongue leaps out to catch insects," and then added, "A bit like this!"

Ted then arched his neck and spat his tongue out and made a "phthh" sound but as he did this, his glasses flew off and some unintentional phlegm came out at the same time which unfortunately hit his young daughter in the eye. Such were the howls of laughter and ridicule from everyone, Ted never ever added any drama into his explanations again. I looked over to Belle who was still laughing at the recall of that episode. And then she managed to stop. "He was only trying to be helpful.

Bless him," she said in defence of her father's actions. Belle could be like that. She wasn't afraid to stick up for the outsider or those who were much maligned. She was always protective of Ted.

Despite the sadness of the day Belle looked good. It was only a few months ago that she had celebrated her twenty-first birthday. In her self she hadn't changed that much since she was a little girl. She still had that same caring outlook, the sort that would stop and help those in need or tend to a stray dog. Her fair and honest complexion matched her nature. The budding flower had bloomed. She was a bonny lass as my grandma would say.

"Hey, you," I called over to Belle, "How's the nursing training going?"

"Fine, just fine" she replied. She then smiled at me and added, "It's hard work, but enjoyable."

"I believe you are going out with an older man," I added.

"Yes, yes." she spluttered. He's ok. I...we've been going out for quite a few months." She hesitated and then continued, "I think we might get engaged."

"Blimey that was quick."

Belle did not respond but simply went on to her next sentence.

"I believe you have already met. You won't remember." She paused which had an unintentional dramatic effect "He was the young policeman who came in the shop with Bill when dad had his car bashed in by the lorry."

"Really," I said surprised. "I obviously haven't got a clue who you are talking about but I remember the incident."

Belle then felt that she had to justify the age gap. "He's only 38." she said. You'd like him, Gary. He's not in the police any more. He's a hospital administrator. It's where we met. He's a big united fan."

"That's OK," I said. Belle's face was blushing slightly. She didn't like to talk about herself too much and was easily embarrassed if she had to do so. We often teased her about it but she didn't seem to mind and in the end she laughed at her own vulnerability. I could see how people could find her attractive.

I looked over and there was Derrick with his wife Janice sipping a glass of wine. It was only about the fourth time I'd seen her. They got married in some posh place in Cheshire a year or two back. I hadn't seen him since, nobody had. He hadn't changed much. The glasses were better (only just) and his hair was tidier but he was still quiet. All that stuff with him and Johnny seemed such a long time ago but seeing them all together for the first time in ages brought back those memories. They seemed okay now they were chatting. Maybe I exaggerated it all. Maybe I saw things differently as a child and tended to remember the most painful things more vividly.

Suddenly Stacey's voice rang out. "Hey, our kid, tell us the one about the night time shenanigans."

Belle looked at me and smiled. "Go on, go on. You know you want to."

Suddenly all went quiet with anticipation as I could feel that all eyes were on me. They'd heard it all before…many times but they still loved it.

Night time shenanigans

I was about nineteen at the time and had just started college. Although I had my own bedsit, on this particular night I needed to stay over at my parent's place. It was quite late and I was in my bedroom reading when I heard Olive's voice cry out from her bedroom.

"Turn the light off!"

"What?" I said, surprised at her abruptness.

"I said TURN the bloody light OUT!" said Olive re-issuing the command.

"What are you on about?"

"It's nearly midnight," said Olive irritated by the dim glow emanating from under my door.

"What difference does that make?" I replied.

"Just turn the bloody light out."

"Mum, I'm reading," I protested.

"Yes but you're burning electricity."

"Mum please I'm nineteen years old and anyway a light bulb hardly burns any electricity."

"It burns enough. Now turn the bloody light out."

"No," I said defiantly.

"What did you say?" piped Olive.

"No," I repeated.

Indignant at my refusal, she turned to her husband who was lying peacefully under the bed covers just about to nod off.

"Ted. He's said no! Tell him!" The old man sighed and then did as he was told.

"Son, turn the light off." He paused and then added wearily, "Just do as your mum says."

There was a point of principal here.

"No dad," I said, "This is ridiculous." There was another pause.

"Olive he's not doin' it," said Ted soulfully.

"Tell him again Ted," Olive ordered and Ted complied.

"C'mon son, you know what your mum's like."

I could hear another Ted sigh – a world weary sigh. He didn't need this. He had already had a difficult night. Their Jack Russell had become increasingly aggressive towards him and earlier on had bitten him on the arse as he tried to get into bed. It was Ted's fault as he forgot to check under the bed covers where Kimmy sometimes lay snuggled up by Olive's feet. Besides marking out his territory, Kimmy clearly wanted to protect his mistress, the great and powerful Olive Smith. Any attempt by an intruder to remove Kimmy from his self-appointed position would often be met with a vicious riposte.

Usually Ted was prepared and had an old broom by his side of the bed ready to fend off the yappy little bastard when the time came to pull the blankets back. Dressed in vest and baggy white undies, nearly every evening Ted could be seen poking timidly at the small snarling Jack Russell that simply refused to vacate his position. The look of fear etched on Ted's sweaty face was like a lion tamer fearful of being eaten alive.

The scene would often play out for a good few minutes and would end with Kimmy eventually being swept off the bed with a forceful swipe of the broom by a relieved Ted Smith. This particular time Ted was tired. It was as though the sly little bastard had sensed a moment of weakness in his victim. He crouched down low making himself undetectable, operating in stealth mode and waiting silently. All it took was the slightest pressure from Ted's arse on the bed and without warning the little bugger shot out from under the blankets, fangs at the ready and bit into the irresistible flesh of Ted's rump. According to Olive, the strike was a "thing of beauty like a cobra seizing its prey." I heard Ted's howl of anguish and came running in to see Ted hopping about clutching a bum cheek and cursing the dog who was licking his lips waiting for more! Olive looked on with little sympathy as Ted examined his bruised and bloody arse.

"Why didn't you use the broom?" she asked a bemused Ted. The thing was, the question wasn't asked with any tenderness. No, that was saved for her favourite little pet who bless him was quite distressed by Ted's howling. Olive patted Kimmy's head, called him a good boy and then gave him a little doggy treat to calm him down. Olive then suggested that Ted should try to be a little quieter next time Kimmy nips him. Ted muttered to himself as he patted away the last drops of blood with a bit of San Izal toilet paper. My reluctance to switch the light off later that evening simply fuelled Ted's world-weary view of life. I had some sympathy with the old man but I was not going to give in.

"No dad" I said. "I'm not switchin' the light off. I'm not a little kid," I protested.

Olive quickly interceded with another command. "Ted, go in his room and turn his bloody light off."

Ted groaned and got up out of bed, put his slippers on and slowly walked over to the door but couldn't open it.

"He's locked it," said Ted, thinking that would be the end of it.

"What? He's bloody locked it?" Olive couldn't believe it.

"Affirmative," said Ted.

Olive was not going to be beaten and after a momentary pause sounded the trumpet call.

"Well break the bloody door down!"

"What?"

"Ted! Break it down!" decreed Olive.

"C'mon son, open the door," Ted pleaded.

"No dad, this is ridiculous."

There was another pause.

"Ted!"

Olive's voice rang out and with that last order Ted realised what he had to do. The first charge was just a low thud which had little effect. I heard the stifled cries of my father, however, as he realised that the impact of the solid pine door upon his shoulder actually hurt.

"C'mon Ted, give it some bloody oomph," Olive cried.

With that encouragement, Ted's second charge carried more weight and I could see the framing around the door buckle ever so slightly. Again I heard the muffled cry of pain as bone and flabby muscle connected with hard wood.

"OK, OK, you win." I said.

I would have been happy to have maintained my resolve and kept the door locked because I really couldn't see my father having the strength to break the door down but I relented because I felt sorry for Ted. As I opened the door to switch the light out I caught sight of him tenderly rubbing his shoulder and wincing with pain. He was limping slowly away with what appeared to be a blood stained piece of toilet paper peeping out from sagging underpants courtesy of Kimmy's bite. Ted was not happy but he had done his duty.

After the telling of the story I looked to the heavens and pleaded with whatever deity was listening. "Please lord, don't let this be my abiding memory of my father."

Everybody was in hysterics, even Derrick, and when the laughter had died down Johnny looked at me.

"Scarred for life. You poor bastard."

"Yes," I agreed, "I have had trouble forming relationships ever since. My father is to blame for everything."

We all laughed again. Despite our collective scorn we loved him really.

In my dream I see a forlorn figure weeping in the corner. It is my mother who is beside herself. She didn't want anybody to see but I did. I wanted to go over and comfort her with the advantage of knowing what I know now but I could never quite get to her. I call out to her and say I know what he did. I know the price he paid but she doesn't hear. I awake to feel the pain of her loss. Ted, the calm stillness in the centre of her storm, had gone.

PHOENIX FROM THE ASHES

A week after Ted's funeral Thatcher won another election by an absolute landslide. Given that we were all in mourning anyway, Johnny summed it up perfectly as a "dirty great fuckin' kick in the nuts." And he normally didn't give a shit about politics. It was hard to believe that it was only a couple of years earlier that we had such unrest. People in the north were well and truly pissed off with the government. There were fights and protests all over the place. You could feel the sense of anger and betrayal. I remember that time well. It was the time that the Moss Side Riots took place…and I was there.

I was at my friend's house near the Harp lager brewery when it all kicked off. We were just outside the main action but we could see and hear the commotion. Just down the way, Princess Street had suddenly become a mass of belching black smoke. The sound was incredible…loud shouts, blaring sirens and smashed windows. It was complete and utter bedlam. I remember thinking "Yes! Something's gonna change."

It was destructive and anarchic but it was exciting. The fight back had started. We were not going to take this shit any more but obviously I was wrong because ultimately nothing did change. I couldn't understand how or why many people from our working class backgrounds helped keep her in power. Most people I knew in and around Manchester hated Thatcher but somehow a number of them allowed themselves to be persuaded that any alternative to her was a liability. Perhaps I was stupid to believe that something was going to change.

History is repeating itself.

The general despondency around the place and Ted's sad passing didn't help my sister Stacey who was having a hard time anyway. Her life story over the past few years did not make for a great read.

After she got married to Peter, Stacey settled down for a few years in Germany. With little money they had to live with Peter's parents which meant living with Gerta. It was hard work and my sister was never really happy. It turned out that her mother in law was in many ways more oppressive than Olive could ever be. Olive was never controlling yet she wanted things done in her own way. If you put up much resistance there was a slap and that was the end of it. There was no subtlety. She never tried to influence what you did. She just needed you to acknowledge that she was the boss.

Gerta got her own way by quiet oppression. Her subtle put downs and smiling criticism of Stacey undermined the young English usurper at every opportunity. Gerta had a suffocating love for her son and she made sure that she had an influence over every aspect of his life including his marriage. Her son's wife was never going to be able to take away her mother's love.

Poor Stacey was devoid of any standing, and any happiness she tried to have was slowly smothered by the domineering Gerta. Unfortunately Peter never supported his wife enough and almost inevitably Stacey met a new man, Donald Kay from Wigan. It happened so quickly. Stacey originally planned a short trip back to the UK to attend her nephew's baptism but in the end didn't return. At the do after the baptism Stacey met Don and before we all knew it, she was permanently back in England shacked up with this new man.

Apparently the deal clincher for Stacey's choice in Don was that, according to her, he looked like Sean Connery. He did have a balding head with some hair just above his ears but the comparison ended there. In truth Don was quite a gnarly old guy with a thick Lancashire accent but in Stacey's mind he was there for her at the right time and provided an escape route from Gerta, the granite goblin. That relationship lasted about five years before ending in an acrimonious split. Deep down Stacey knew that they could never really be happy together. She couldn't see anything long term and he wasn't the brightest spark. It probably didn't help that Don Kay sounded too much like donkey and in the end, according to Stacey, he was one.

One thing that did seem to make Stacey happy was the Manchester music scene – she and others were "mad for it!" According to Belle, she was a little bit on the old side for the new wave stuff and she hadn't tried drugs before but she found both to be an interesting mix. When questioned about it she was quite open and confessed that "she needed to have a bit of fun, life was too short anyway." But the highs never lasted long. Stacey was really pretty depressed.

An old friend

It was on one rainy Manchester evening whilst she on her way to the Hacienda Club that life took an unexpected turn for the better. Stacey was just looking to have a good time but as usual there was a large queue. In the middle of the queue there was a commotion as a few of the youngsters were laughing at an older figure slightly hidden from view. Stacey was curious, something about one of the voices seemed vaguely familiar so she asked her friend to keep her place whilst she stepped forward to investigate.

"You daft twat," said one of the younger men laughing. "I don't think they'll let you in."

"I am fucking mad for it," said the figure in the middle. "I am not shitting you."

The others, who were gathered round, laughed again.

"Is that a fuckin' tank top you're wearing?" came an incredulous cry from the crowd.

"It fuckin' well is," the man stated proudly. The others laughed again and the small brown-skinned figure in the terribly styled seventies leisurewear laughed with them. There was clearly no trouble. In fact it was a great comedy spectacle. In common Mancunian parlance everybody was loving it, especially when the odd figure offered them some of his sweets.

"Here, fucking have some. They are so twatting delicious. So shitting good."

Then a slim smartly dressed woman emerged from the crowd and took one of the sweets. Jammi watched transfixed as she delicately popped a wine gum in her mouth and smiled. She looked at him and spoke.

"I see you have increased your repertoire of swear words."

Jammi took a second or maybe five. He was unsure and then it clicked...

"Stacey?" said Jammi excitedly.

When Stacey nodded they both laughed and embraced. Stacey gripped Jammi's hand and pulled him out of the queue. It was comical what was happening but they were taking the piss out of Jammi, Stacey didn't want that...that wasn't right. They needed to get away so she gripped Jammi's arm tightly and Jammi let himself be guided by her hand as she frog marched him away from the scene. He wasn't sure where they were going and neither was she.

"This feels bloody lovely," shouted Jammi deliriously.

Stacey took no notice as she spotted a little pub just off Whitworth Street and sat him down whilst she got them both a drink. Jammi's face lit up as she came towards him clutching two glasses of amber nectar. As soon as Stacey placed them down Jammi gripped one and took a huge slurp.

"I thought you lot didn't drink," said Stacey.

"Just a little bit. Now and then," replied Jammi smiling inanely at his long lost sweetheart.

Well, don't go mad," said Stacey sternly as she tried to deflect Jammi's gaze. She was also aware that beads of sweat were collecting around her eye brows after their quick walk from the Hacienda. She gently mopped them away with her scarf and in doing so hoped it would somehow distract Jammi from looking at her in that way. It was no use. Throughout their conversation Jammi continued to peer into Stacey's eyes like some love-struck teenager. Stacey told him to stop it a few times but the funny thing was, she quite liked it. They sat talking for hours. Jammi told Stacey that his arranged marriage hadn't worked out. His wife went back to Bangladesh to be with "someone she loved." They had no children so it was easy to use that as the main reason for their separation. In truth Jammi was relieved. He was never happy being with Samira. According to Jammi, "she was NOT bloody lovely."

"I was an unambitious simpleton," said Jammi repeating his wife's scornful words.

Stacey frowned when she heard that.

"That must have hurt."

Jammi nodded. "I still tried my fucking best. I shit you not."

"I know you did."

"My mother has not forgiven me," said Jammi soulfully.

"Oh dear." Stacey could see real sadness in Jammi's eyes.

"My life is a fucking crash of a shitting car."

Stacey couldn't help laughing.

"You mean a car crash." And then she confessed that her life was similar. And then she couldn't help repeating Jammi's words loudly.

"You're right. My life is a fuckin' crash of a shitting car!"

Jammi chuckled but all of a sudden Stacey snapped back,

"What the fuck were you doing there? The Hacienda?"

"I was shitting mad for it," said Jammi innocently.

"Of course you were," said Stacey. She then laughed again and Jammi joined in. It was uninhibited as hearty laughter often is. And when the laughter had died down Jammi reached over and gave Stacey a kiss. It was tender and kind. For a second Stacey was reminded of their date in Heaton Park. She resisted then but now was different. She let Jammi press his lips on hers without resistance. She had the smallest of tears in her eyes as she drew back and smiled.

"Bloody lovely."

Was it Olive or Jammi that caused change? Jammi was the catalyst that's for sure but Olive always had the capacity to produce the unexpected.

I make a mistake and overwork an area. There is too much paint there. As I scratch away at the dark purple, I realise that all is not lost. It's part of the struggle; an important part because when success comes it is all the more rewarding.

Stacey and Jammi soon shacked up together in Jammi's one bedroomed flat in Rusholme. Jammi got a job as a postman. He loved it. He loved the people he met and the people loved him. He tried desperately to moderate his swearing but many people preferred that he didn't. He became a real character in the area. As for Stacey, she continued with her hairdressing business and became content with her lot.

A year after they met they did go to the Hacienda. Stacey made sure that Jammi was suitably dressed and they had a good time. Stacey didn't need the drugs. She and Jammi were perfectly happy without them. They had both decided that they were not going to marry. Given their situations, especially Jammi's, it would have been too complicated. Instead, they decided to have a gathering of friends and family to celebrate their union in their newly-acquired terraced house in the centre of Rusholme. It was pretty run down when they bought it but in no time at all with a little bit of renovation and a good lick of paint they made it quite presentable. They were ready for some guests and a party! Jammi's mother was coming which was a miracle. And even more of a miracle was that Olive made it happen.

A good deed

Mrs Haider had more or less ostracised Jammi once she had learnt that her son was living with Stacey. She had barely talked to him in the last couple of years anyway and certainly did not want to see him with this woman who had caused such a stir all those years ago. In the beginning Olive also wasn't happy with the idea of those two being together. It was another one of her daughter's "ridiculous flings" but over time she grew to quite like Jammi. She found herself being seduced by his innocent charm and she had to admit, the two of them were good together. When she heard that Jammi's mother would not be attending the blessing, Olive decided that she had to do something about it.

She called round at Mrs Haider's and, despite her protestations, wouldn't leave until they talked. Whatever Olive said worked because an hour into the celebrations a knock at the door heralded the entrance of Mrs Haider. She was hesitant about stepping in but then after a pause she marched forward and handed over a large bowl of Jammi's favourite vegetable curry to Stacey who accepted it and then stood back in shock. Jammi raced past Stacey and gave his mum a great big hug. Mrs Haider scolded her son for being so effusive in his welcome but secretly smiled. Stacey turned to Olive.

"Was this you?"

"We had a word," was all Olive would say. As somebody grabbed Stacey's attention she turned back and mouthed thank you across the room to her mother but Olive didn't notice. She was too busy scoffing Mrs Haider's vegetable curry. "Bloody lovely."

It wasn't quite a party, rather a small but cosy gathering of people. Some of Stacey's old friends, one or two of Jammi's, the next door neighbours, me, Belle, Olive and Mrs Haider. But there were enough to make it an occasion. As we were gathered around sitting on the floor in the sparse but brightly decorated front room Jammi decided to play DJ with his new CD player. Before we knew it a medley of Manchester's finest belted out much to the annoyance of our parents. Jammi had to turn it down immediately but it was still peculiar to see Mrs Haider, her sister and Olive sat on the floor eating curry to the beat of the Happy Mondays, Inspiral Carpets, Joy division and The Fall.

The conversation was stilted but became very interesting when Jammi put on a new CD just as Stacey went upstairs. It was sneaky – waiting till she was out of the way – he knew that she surely would have censored it. He was so excited, I could see that he so desperately wanted others to appreciate this next artist as much as he did.

"This is John Cooper Clark," he announced proudly and then pressed play.

As the lyrics of "Twat" bellowed out there was laughter from all, except Olive and Mrs Haider.

"I am sorry, Mrs Smith," said Mrs Haider trying to make herself heard. "My Jammi. No matter how hard I have tried he has always been swearing."

"I have noticed," said Olive.

"This Cooper Clark," said Mrs Haider. "I do not like his humour."

"I agree," said Olive. "I never use the f word. A bit of shit and arse now and then never 'urt anyone but fucking or twat...no! I draw the line at that. That's out of order." And with that they both nodded reverently to each other in complete accord.

They were never going to become best buddies...Olive and Mrs Haider but there was a small bond that had been forged between them. They seldom met over the next few years but when they did it was quite warm and friendly. As for my old friend Nawab – our paths didn't cross until a number of years later. In the meantime I found out that he had become a doctor and was practising somewhere in Africa. His mother was very proud of him. He always was a decent chap.

As the eighties drew to a close, Stacey and Jammi's love blossomed. Olive was moved enough to observe that the two of them were as "happy as pigs in shit." In a moment of rare poetic vision Stacey once turned to me and stated that "Me and Jammi, we're like two petunias sprouting up from an onion field." She had just downed a bottle of Tesco's finest Sicilian red but I couldn't help agreeing with her. She deserved some happiness.

And with that thought the day is done. I leave the brushes to soak and put the lids back on the paints. I will finish the painting tomorrow. The best part is yet to come. The early struggles seem a long time ago but they are not forgotten. I sleep and dream again.

A nurse tends to a broken man and gently rubs his forehead. He grips her arm.

"I can't remember," he says. Why can I not remember?"

"It's not good to remember," says the nurse gently, "some things are better left buried and forgotten."

"But you know, don't you?"

The nurse says nothing but smiles. It is a soothing smile and calms the man down but it doesn't stop him from asking more questions.

"Will I always be like this...not remembering?"

"Some would hope so."

"What do you mean? Have I done something bad?"

The nurse says nothing but lovingly strokes his arm.
The man looks closely at her serene face. There is something
familiar.

A BLAST FROM THE PAST

I wake up and immediately go to my painting. I see something. I have to make an adjustment. I will have breakfast and organise myself but first I just need to change that one small thing. It will not take long but it does. I lose myself as a memory of the past begins to unfold.

Saturday 15th June 1996. I remembered feeling quite positive. There was a sense of optimism in the air. You could feel it in the city, in the country. A young labour leader was sounding the drumbeat of change to the chorus of 'Things can only get better.' And the lowly inhabitants of Manchester started to believe that things really could be different. That aside, this day was a day pretty much like any other. I was shopping.

I'd just been to pick up my Pentax from the camera shop on Deansgate. Whilst there I got quite a thrill to see an old Kodak in the shop window. It was similar to the one Bill Tanner gave me all those years ago. It was now a piece of retro display. I always thought the one he gave me was knocked off. It seemed to be quite a gift for a young boy to receive back then. I remember that I had to keep it secret so that I didn't make my brothers jealous. I always said it was Ted's and my father was happy to play along.

But right now I was content with life. I was a successful photography/art teacher in a steady relationship and had one glorious claim to fame – I taught Ryan Giggs or Ryan Wilson as he was then. I tried to cash in on my association with young master Giggs at every opportunity. As soon as I met someone new or important I mentioned my connection with him within the first few sentences. I couldn't wait to blurt it out in the hope that it would give me kudos. I even learnt how to say, "I taught Ryan Giggs" in several languages so that I could appear equally as impressive abroad.

My thoughts and reflections on life, however, were interrupted by the noise of the crowds being ushered away from their intended route by men in uniform. As I looked on I could see that all transport was being asked to turn round and head away from the city centre. Cordons were being erected and there seemed to be a lot of police in and around the area. I didn't pay too much attention to what was going on. I remember thinking about my family before it happened.

Johnny was now a foreman at an industrial plant in Trafford Park. The job was in his own words OK and was reasonably well paid. He also quite liked telling others what to do but it wasn't exactly the love of his life. The money however did allow him to indulge in his passion for women, cars and sex. He never hid this from me. In fact he enjoyed telling me about his various sexual adventures. It was never boastful but it was colourful. There was always an attempt to make the stories amusing and he often succeeded. I tried not to laugh too much as I didn't want to indulge him but I am ashamed to say I did. *Lustful, vicious and acerbic. I've always liked Johnny.*

But then I remember, we did fall out once – big time – over something stupid. It was a list my brother made about Olive's use of the word arse'ole. He made it when we were younger. I remember us both laughing as we read it out loud several times. Johnny was quite proud of it and was a bit miffed when he lost it. I found it a few years later scrumpled up in the pages of my old art books. I looked at it and it still made me chuckle but I believed I could improve on it so I made a few alterations and showed Johnny the new list.

Olive's use of an arse'ole

Arse'ole: pronounced ar-sowl not to be confused with arsehole. (The opening at the end of the anal passage)

Arse'ole slang: noun, most commonly used in the north.

Arse'ole: a person full of shit....he/she is being an arse'ole.

Arse'ole: a place for unwanted items or items that are deemed useless. These can be metaphorically stuck up an arse'ole at any time.

An arse 'ole: a place where ridiculous ideas and pretentious crap may be housed. "in my arse'ole."

An arse'ole: can in many instances be used to describe a person who is either stupid, selfish or simply a dozy bastard. However, in certain areas of Manchester can be used affectionately...usually preceded by a complimentary adjective eg "you lovely little arse'ole" but this is rare.

Arse'oles: a collective group of individuals with a mob mentality that cannot think for themselves. These can be a mixture of dozy bastards, selfish twats and people full of shit.

Arse'ole: a derogatory word for any politician.

Arse'oles: can be used to stop an argument that you are losing. When said firmly and at the right time- can be highly effective – "it's a load of old arse'oles!"

I thought it was funny and that what I had done had made it better, but instead of laughing he got pissed off with me. I can see him now scrutinising the list. "That was my list," he said "You think by puttin' in some fancy fuckin' words. What are they?" And he looked at the list: "metaphorical... derog... derog...I can't even fucking say it."

And then he came out with it. "You think you know it all now you're at fuckin' college."

"Well, I know more than you," I interrupted.

The moment I said it I wished that I hadn't. I'd betrayed my arrogance and highlighted his ignorance. He was angry and I thought he was going to swing for me. And then he went icy cold, "I'll tell you what," he said. "I will let you take the first fucking punch," and with that he held out his chin, "But when I get up you won't know what's fucking hit you."

And this snotty nosed college kid that was me backed off quickly. I'd seen that look in Olive's eyes. There was no way I was going to take him on. Absolutely no way. So I walked out. For a time it left a frosty atmosphere. But my brother had a point and I realised that all those early childhood resentments of my position as the favourite were never far away. He also hated college kids who "didn't know what real work was." I was one of them.

Remarkably we came together after that. It took some time and it was never any one single event but like my parents, underneath it all (much deeper in his case) he was actually proud of me.

I remember. I was annoyed that my thoughts were constantly being interrupted by crowds of noisy people.

But my other brother Derrick was a bit of an enigma at that time. He wasn't around much and rarely made contact with any of us at all. I certainly hadn't seen him much since Ted died. Olive and Derrick had not seen or talked with each other for the last five years. At the time I couldn't get to the bottom of what caused the rift. Somehow it always seemed inevitable. It was sort of heading that way since Derrick left home. It was sort of natural for him to withdraw in this way.

Although we had little information about Derrick, we had heard that he had started up his own business selling and delivering incontinence pads. By all accounts he was pretty successful even if it was "a shit job" as Johnny used to say.

Belle was happy – she had definitely found her soulmate in Gary. They loved each other. He was a good man. He was there when it happened.

The deafening roar that heralded the percussive shock wave of shattered glass took us all by surprise. The immediate aftermath was just as shocking – an eerie silence that seemed to take an age to be broken. Without any self-realisation, my body had collapsed onto the floor where my arm had instinctively formed a protective shield over my head. I was vaguely aware of lying motionless along with other figures strewn across the road by the side of Kendall's.

There was an incessant ringing. I can feel it now. And something else. A low disconcerting hum but no other sound. Masses of shredded paper falling quietly to the ground like confetti making small spirals in the sunlit sky. A terrible beauty.

CLUMP!!

A mass of blasted matter hits the ground.

And suddenly it was as if someone had turned the sound back on. Sirens and alarms quickly filled the air with a discordant bullying presence. People awoke from their millisecond slumbers to see that not one window was left unscathed as shards of glass and debris lay all around. Some were shocked to see their own pierced limbs and blood stained clothing. Children started to cry followed by some of their parents as people found it hard to comprehend what had just happened. Slowly but surely those that were able and alert began to comfort those who were upset. Parents found their children and threw a protective arm around them. From nowhere a number of blankets arrived to be gently draped around shocked figures perched on pavements.

I looked up to see thick white and black plumes of smoke billowing out from the mass of urban structures. Gripped by a strange curiosity I walked towards what I believed to be the heart of the explosion. And there through the smoke-filled vista I could dimly make out the severed structures of the former shopping mall known as the Arndale Centre.

Suddenly I was a boy back in Cheetham Hill playing amongst the burning heaps of rubble of the freshly demolished terraces. I wanted to go up to the wreckage that lay before me and prod and poke with it with a stick as little boys do. That unmistakable smell of smoke and plaster that now invaded my lungs brought back memories of my playground; of my time amongst the crofts with Ray and Alex.

Maybe it was through some unconscious associations with my nostalgic daydreams but there was something vaguely familiar about a figure standing on a mound of debris who was carefully surveying the scene. His unruffled demeanour seemed at odds with the shock and disorder that lay all around. I eyed him more closely. His build was slim but quite muscular. He stood tilted to one side, his weight slightly to the right and he was stroking his chin thoughtfully. His thick black hair was definitely more shaped than the last time I had seen him but I could recognise that individual even with his back to me. I'd seen that person in that stance with his special gloves on some twenty odd years earlier. Now though he was a lot smarter. His tidy, well-groomed appearance stood out like a sore thumb. I was quite sure, there was no mistake.

I called out his name. The figure wheeled round and tried to see where the shout had come from. My voice was unfamiliar as it had deepened since last we saw each other. "It's me. Smiffy," I shouted and waved my hand frantically. He caught sight of me and smiled. It took a second or two to register and then a big broad grin enveloped his face. I was surprised at how quickly he recognised me but in truth I hadn't changed that much in the last twenty years but he had. He looked good.

The Alex Caldwell I knew was still there but he was altogether more polished with tanned skin and well-groomed hair. The drawn sallow face of an undernourished street urchin had become the strong chiselled features of a handsome man. He clambered down from the shattered glass rise, strode towards me and gave me a hearty embrace.

"Shit. Bloody hell! What the fuck!" I shouted.

"I know," said Alex who smiled warmly. For a brief moment the chaos that was all around was forgotten.

"What the hell! What's going on?" My comments seemed to bring the scene back into focus. The sirens which were a dull background noise became loud and intrusive again. Alex could see that I was still a little disorientated.

"Come on, let's get away from here. The medics are picking this up. We're just in the way," he said. I agreed and followed him away from the carnage. We didn't say an awful lot. It wouldn't have been right to be reminiscing over old times, laughing and joking at a time like this. It was a short but solemn journey to the hotel. Alex occupied a very smart apartment near the top floor. It wasn't the penthouse but it was a step up from the usual hotel room and there appeared to be a more spacious and luxurious feel to the place. We walked quietly through to the main living area where he immediately switched on the TV to find out more.

He poured us a drink from the bar and then we both slumped down in the soft chairs pulling them closer to the TV as we did so. "You do drink whisky, don't you?" I nodded. It wasn't so much a question than a statement. It was as though Alex was saying we are thieves and scavengers from the streets of Cheetham Hill. We are made of northern grit, of course we drink whisky. He then took his tie off and undid the top buttons of his shirt. He still looked smart.

Details

Apparently there was a van armed with explosives left on Corporation Street outside the Arndale Centre. There was a phone call earlier to the police alerting them to this fact and at about 9.40am the bomb went off. As yet there were no fatalities but a number of injuries. The number being treated was still rising.

"Shit."

Silence.

"Shit. Bloody hell," I gasped as Alex poured me another whisky form the hotel bar. Our utterances were sporadic as reports unfolded. Gradually the conversation became more joined up. About an hour after we first stepped into Alex's room we decided to switch off the TV and talk about something else without feeling guilty. There was much to catch up on.

I looked at Alex more closely. It wasn't just that he was smart and well-dressed, there was a calm assurance to his demeanour. It was there to a certain extent when we were kids but now it had matured. Even during the news reports, it was me who sounded the expletives and expressed my shock. Alex was, I am sure, just as shocked but he appeared to be very much in control of his emotions. Alex could see that I was impressed with him.

"C'mon, Alex," I said. "What happened to you, what's the story?"

Alex smiled and calmly took a drink before shaking his head and smiling again.

"It began," he said, "where we left off. You probably won't recall my leaving Cheetham Hill but I can tell you it was sudden. Dad had many debts, he drank a lot, we hadn't paid the rent…the bailiffs were round and before I knew it I was off to Glasgow. I think the term used is rehoused." I smiled in ironic acknowledgement.

"It was a real shit hole in those tenements." Alex seemed to wince at the memory and then continued. "For a couple of years I was doing pretty much what I was doing at Cheetham Hill but on a much larger scale. I suppose I was becoming a full time robber. I was in with a bad crowd and I mean bad. It makes me sound noble but part of the reason I was doing this was to support the rest of my clan. You remember them, don't you?" he said, looking at me waiting for my response.

"Yes, vaguely," I said and then added that "They were interesting."

"Interesting. Yes, they were." Alex paused and smiled a weary smile as uncomfortable memories were retrieved. "They've had a rough time," he said softly, "but they are OK now." Alex wouldn't expand on this and it was quite clear that he didn't want to talk about his family too much. At that point a memory came flooding back about me and Ray taunting Julie, his younger sister. Her gormless demeanour and terrible stammer were easy targets. Alex looked at me intently and could see that I had a guilty look on my face. I needed to confess.

"Look, Alex I need to…"

"Don't worry," he said. "I used to do the same thing though I was probably crueller than you were. I was angry with them because they were so stupid." It was clearly a painful admission, one that Alex did not dwell on.

"It was gonna be a light touch – a quick in and out," said Alex changing the subject. "I'd cased the joint and sussed its weak points. I was an expert thief by that time. I never noticed the body lying there," he said as though he was reading the start of a murder mystery novel. "I certainly never noticed the pool of blood that I had stepped in leaving my bloody footprints stamped all over the expensive carpet." Alex made a mistake I thought to myself. Never!

"It was only after I tripped over him and pointed my torch in front of my feet that I realised that I'd got a problem. Blood everywhere and obviously the big question." He paused waiting for me to interject. It took me a second or two but eventually I blurted out.

"How did this happen? Was this an accident?"

"That's two questions," Alex said wryly, "but you are right. I'll be honest" he said. "Part of me wanted to run. After all the killer, if there was a killer, could still be around but as you well know I have a pretty cool head. So I decided to stop and have a little think." As if to mimic the scene, Alex paused and took a slow deliberate sip of whisky. He had me. I was right there hanging on his every word. He then continued. "I heard a groan and shone my torch at the figure. The old guy was still alive…just. And here's the dilemma. I could leave him, make a quick exit and be free or stay and help and suffer the consequences. Alex stroked his chin and continued to re-enact his thought processes from that night.

"What would you have done?" he asked mischievously. I hesitated, amazed by his question and before I could answer, Alex carried on. "I surprised myself at how easily I arrived at the decision. I didn't really hesitate, unlike you," he laughed. "Anyway, given that I could find myself in prison and my future was at stake I simply switched on the light, shouted for help and went over to see to the old guy." Alex slowly poured another whisky and offered me a top up.

"The family came running down the stairs to find me knelt over granddad with blood all over the place." Alex laughed wryly and shook his head "It was absolute bedlam with lots of screaming and shouting. Anyway, it turned out that the old man had wandered down the stairs for a midnight snack. He'd moved in with his eldest daughter a week or two ago and was a little disorientated. He was unsure of which room he was in and couldn't find the light switch. In his bewilderment he stumbled and cracked his head against the side board." Alex paused again waiting for me to ask another question and I didn't disappoint…

"Did anyone call the police? Did you get into trouble?" I asked.

"Yes" said Alex, "the police were called and no I didn't get into trouble. Mainly due to her."

"Go on," I said, clearly intrigued by what he had just said.

"Well, she took charge. She was his daughter but she was definitely in charge; no doubt. She was calm and confident and very attractive."

Alex didn't try to hide his admiration for this woman as she figured prominently in the rest of his account. She was the one who questioned him intently before the police got there. She allowed him time and space to explain what had happened. He admitted that he was pleased that he was "unerring and precise" in his report back to her. I could imagine Alex stating his intentions to rob her home. It would be said in a manner that was neither brash nor apologetic. It would be said in exactly the same way as all the other facts. The conversation played into Alex's hands. I knew from my own experience my friend's gift for clarity and a clear head under pressure. I sensed that this would impress her and by all accounts it did.

"That day changed my life," Alex said in an understated way. "As you've probably gathered she was impressed with me. She liked what she saw and took me under her wing. She got me a job in one of her companies. It was only minor but I was given a chance. I worked bloody hard and within a few years I had risen up through the ranks. All the while I sensed that she was keeping an eye out for me. She was very helpful."

The way that Alex uttered that last sentence made it clear that their relationship was a little more than friendship. It was also clear that I shouldn't go there. My friend had a subtle way of putting a full stop to a subject. He never once mentioned her name. She was private. He then briefly told me about some of the other things that he was involved in but didn't dwell on anything. He placed his empty glass down on the table and appeared in reflective mode.

"I suppose I am a successful businessman now," he said, "but I know that I have had some luck and one or two angels by my side because you and I both know the direction I was headed." I had to admit to myself that it was a humble account. Alex had somehow reached his potential despite his upbringing. A few more whiskies and we were soon talking about our times in Cheetham Hill back in the day. Alex confessed that he had a soft spot for Olive. "She fought for us all," he proclaimed. He then reminded me about the time she found a cockroach in one of the pockets of his jacket. I remembered.

The wee beasties

The boy Alex was embarrassed and didn't want to talk about it but under the stress of Olive's interrogation he confessed that the council flats where they were staying were infested with them. "Well, what 'ave you done about it?" she demanded. Alex looked downbeat and explained to Olive that they had complained to the council a number of times but they hadn't done anything.

"'Aven't they?" she said, "Leave this to me."

A few weeks later she marched down to the council offices with me and Alex in tow. She gave no indication of what was to come. To all the officials that she came across, she was sweetness and light. During her appointment with a large middle-aged woman, Olive began to explain the plight of poor Alex and his family. The woman was polite but had a hint of condescension in her tone. She explained to Olive that the services were stretched and that everybody would have to take their turn. Then Olive's tone began to change and her eyes squinted just a little. I knew then that something bad was going to happen.

"'Ave you ever 'ad cockroaches?" Olive asked.

"No, I can't say that I have," said the large woman mildly offended that Olive would even think such a thing. The woman's voice was posh, I think she was from Prestwich.

"Well, I found this in this lad's jacket pocket." Olive pulled out a massive cockroach from her own pocket. The woman recoiled in horror.

"It's OK love, it's dead."

As she said this, Olive looked at her menacingly and talked slowly "in his bloody pocket." She paused for dramatic effect and then looked at the lady accusingly.

"Really Mrs Smith, there's no need for this. I don't think bringing in vermin will get you anywhere. Now if you will be good enough to leave and take that creature with you."

Olive looked into the woman's eyes and although her little piece of theatre had elicited some shock, it was not enough. Olive knew that this woman was not going to do anything more than she had already done, despite Olive's intimidation. More direct action was clearly needed. Olive further opened the palm of her hand where the black cockroach lay framed against her white chubby skin.

"I'm sorry love, 'a can see that this can be construed as quite offensive and puts you ill at ease but it is dead." There was another dramatic pause.

"BUT THESE LITTLE BASTARDS AREN'T!"

With that, Olive drew out a large jam jar that had been hidden underneath her coat, unscrewed the cap and chucked the contents full of black twitchy little beasties all over the woman's lap.

"Aaaghh!" The large woman gasped in shock, disgust and revulsion all at the same time.

Excited by their freedom, hundreds of cockroaches and other writhing creepy crawlies scurried and hopped with gay abandon, not just over the woman's lap but all over the grey office floors, across people's shoes and up the odd leg or two. Olive had obviously hatched a plan and this was to spend every minute of every day collecting all the vermin she could to put in a glass jar ready for use if she did not get satisfaction. In her mind it was a logical and perfectly acceptable course of action…to unleash them if she was not being taken seriously. Only then would they fully appreciate how such an infestation would feel. For as long as I live, I will never forget the screams of horror and anguish that came from those offices. Within a week the pest control people came round and fumigated the whole block of flats.

There were more stories about Olive that were in Alex's words "priceless" and we must have spent a good hour or two talking about "the good old times." All of them seemed to feature Olive in one form or another. Even if she was peripheral to the story you could still picture her defiant grimace or hear one of her pithy comments in the background. The whiskies were being downed with relish. As a gap appeared in our conversation, Alex stood up and went over to his briefcase. He took out a small pouch and emptied the contents onto the coffee table. As I looked closely I could see several small items of jewellery and coins. They did not appear to be expensive. If anything they appeared to be quite cheap and weathered.

"I couldn't fit the clock in," Alex said with a wry smile." I hadn't a clue what he was on about. And then he explained that the contents were a collection of items from his former life as a robber in Cheetham Hill and Glasgow. The clock that he referred to was of course Jock the Clock, the one he stole from the "Paki's 'ouse", the one he used to take with him to our football matches. Alex quite liked the idea of saving things that he'd stolen as they were mementos of his daring. "After all, thieving wasn't easy," as he used to say.

Alex then confessed that he used to have this romantic idea that he would turn out to be some kind of notorious thief dressed in black like the man from the Milk Tray advert.

"I would not be harming any one, just gently relieving them of their possessions."

"And redistributing wealth," I added.

"Of course," he said and we both laughed.

"Maybe I would have a notorious name. I was thinking of The Magpie," said Alex.

"That's too obvious what about the Falcon?" I chirped. Although it was said in jest I could see that Alex quite liked the name. He stroked his chin in familiar fashion.

"Not quite the Pink Panther but it does have a ring about it."

Alex then took another sip of whisky and looked over the array of baubles.

"For whatever reason I couldn't part with them. They are remnants of another life, they're in my briefcase wherever I go."

"It's a bit Victor Hugo-ish isn't it?" I asked. "Next you'll become mayor of Manchester."

Alex scrunched his eyes and looked at me closely with an 'I am not amused look'. Nevertheless he continued.

"But I have something that may be of interest to you, or rather your mum."

He then handed me a small silver casket.

"You didn't steal from it from Olive?" I asked with a little concern in my voice.

"No, no," said Alex who was quick to reassure me that this was not the case. "I'll explain," he said in answer to the quizzical look on my face.

"You must remember the big fire over at the trading estate."

"Of course," I replied.

"Then you must remember digging through the shit, piling up our sacks full of felt tips, handbags and shampoo. Shampoo that had the great..." He paused deliberately waiting for me to complete the sentence. There was only a second before I got it.

"...smell of brut," I said excitedly. We laughed.

"I went back. I went back that night without you," said Alex forcefully as though he wanted to get to the main point but it only served to illuminate the fact that he had reneged on an agreement made all those years ago. Alex could see the mild look of betrayal on my face.

"I wasn't being disloyal. I went to get my stuff, that's all. I didn't know that the whole block would be demolished the next morning," he said, smiling at my emotional reaction (fuelled by the alcohol).

"I found it all quite easily, even in the dark," he stated proudly.

"Congratulations" I said still smarting at his treachery. Alex ignored my sarcasm and then got serious. "It was there in the rubble of your old house. I couldn't tell you at the time for obvious reasons."

I stared hard at my old friend.

"Honestly, it's true. It's yours now anyway." He then reached over and handed me the small casket.

I took it, opened it and tried to focus on its contents but things were becoming a little fuzzy as an alcoholic stupor began to take over. I just about managed to slip it into my pocket before closing my eyes and gently losing consciousness. The next morning I felt a gentle tap on my shoulder from the tall suited figure of Alex.

"I couldn't wake you. So I just put a blanket over you. I hope that was all right."

"Sure."

"Look I've got to be off. A flight to catch. I've left you my details. Give us a call. Help yourself to anything. Just be out by ten!" And with that I sat up, shook his hand and embraced him and then he was gone.

TERRY EVANS: A BIT OLDER

"Every canvas is a journey all its own. All you need to paint is a few tools, a little instruction and a vision in your mind. If you say it in words, there would be no reason to paint. Painting is just another way of keeping a diary." Pablo Picasso

A few weeks later I developed a roll of film and was surprised to see that I'd taken a few pictures of me and Alex. God knows how I did it. I didn't remember taking them as I was pretty sozzled at the time. They were a diary of the evening that told a story of one out-of-his-skull teacher and a slightly tipsy yuppy. Unfortunately I didn't take any of the Arndale and events surrounding the bombing. In the middle of it all I just forgot but I'm not sure people would have liked me pointing a camera in their faces at such a time anyway.

But I was positive that Terry Evans would like to see the ones of Alex (not necessarily the ones of me pissed). After all he was part of Terry's youth club years. I hadn't seen Terry in ages. He was now a bus driver and lived with his sister in Cardinal Street near The Abraham Moss Sports Centre. I'd kept in touch with him sporadically over the years. He always asked about Olive so I suggested that we go and see her together. I'd call for him first. I had been waiting outside Terry's house for ages. I'd rang the bell a few times. Then I banged hard and rang the bell again with my finger on the buzzer for a good ten seconds. I knew he was in because I could hear noises, strange noises.

"C'mon Terry, hurry up!" I barked impatiently. I listened intently for any reply. I heard something so I pressed my ear against the door to try to find out more. It was then that I could hear what I can only describe as feverish grunts.

"What the bloody 'ell are you doin'?" I shouted through the letterbox. Still no answer and more odd sounds. Then all went quiet as Terry's sister Heather opened the door.

"You'd best come in," she said quietly.

I was a little worried. Heather was shaking. As I stepped into the living room, it was carnage. Padding and clumps of foam were strewn across the living room floor and bits of broken wood lay splintered across the beige coloured carpet. In the centre of the room lay the remnants of a settee. To the side stood a tall slightly balding figure in his mid-forties bloodied and scarred holding a bread knife in his hand. Beads of sweat were rolling down the sides of his forehead.

"What the bloody hell. Terry! Terry, are you all right?" I shrieked.

"It's Mitzi," he said. "She got stuck down the settee and I couldn't get her out."

It was then that I noticed what looked like a ball of fluff in one of his hands clutched close to his chest. It was purring contentedly as Terry and Heather nestled their noses into the mischievous little bugger's fur.

"Oh Mitzi, we love you," exclaimed Heather delightedly.

They were then joined by the rest of the cats who'd all hidden themselves away during Terry's sofa slashing debacle. Their feline steps were nervous at first but as their confidence returned (and it was clear that their owners were not mad) the cats began nudging and pushing their snouts into legs and feet and shoes. They seemed just as relieved as Terry and Heather. I was still astounded by it all.

"For Christ's sake Terry, that sofa was your pride and joy. Surely you could have found another way to get her out. It's gonna cost you a packet to replace it."

"She's worth it," said Heather oblivious to the wreckage and still overjoyed that they'd got their Mitzi back. And with that, she crumpled her face further into the cat's fur, her long straight greying hair wrapping itself tenderly round the body of the ginger moggy. I shook my head at the strange rapture on show. I let them both wallow in their euphoria before I gently interrupted them.

"Well Terry, we'd best get going. The old lady will be wondering where we've got to," I said.

Terry looked blank.

"Olive. Remember we said we'd go and see her."

"Yes," replied Terry, "We can't keep the old dragon waiting. That wouldn't be right."

"Are you ready for this Terry. It's been a few years hasn't it?"

"About five," said Terry.

"Will the old dragon recognise you?"

"I haven't changed that much," Terry said indignantly.

In one respect he wasn't far wrong. His clothes were pretty much the same as when I first met him as an eleven year old. He still seemed to be wearing that old grey anorak accompanied by easy press slacks, pale grey shirt and a v-necked jumper complete with coffee stains down the front. He'd lost most of his hair and put on some weight but he was still the same Terry Evans of twenty five years ago.

Olive heard us coming and opened the door even before we knocked.

"Ello luv," she said and gave me a warm hug and kiss on the side of my cheek. She turned to Terry "I'm not givin' you a hug. I can smell cat piss. 'Ow many bloody cats 'ave you got?"

"Nine," said Terry sheepishly.

"Get some of them put down or something. You smell bloody awful. And for God sake change what you're wearing. You look like a dirty old man."

"Hello, Olive. How are you? I can see you've not changed."

'Ello Terry," Olive replied and grinned in response to Terry's remarks. "Sit down you two. I'll make you a nice cuppa." Olive then shuffled to where the tea making stuff was.

"I've left you a paper to read," said Olive cheerfully. That was strange, I thought, Olive never bought a newspaper let alone leave us one to read and she sounded very jovial. There had to be something in it. The old lady was never that nice and then I realised why. The lead story was about a member of the clergy who succumbed to the temptations of the flesh. Nothing would irk Olive more than a well-loved vicar. They were always too good to be true. Nobody could be that kind. There had to be some angle somewhere. Either they were robbing the charity box or "kiddy fiddling" as she would put it. Even from an early age I would regard the challenge of trying to get my mother to see the good in these people as one of my life's missions. Unfortunately I was thwarted by the very people I tried to uphold.

"Cheating vicar bonks women in his love mobile," was the headline in the News of the World. She wasn't very subtle and proudly left this particular edition on the coffee table in full view for all to see. Her glee was there in the jaunty angle and singular placement of the offensive newspaper, the salacious headlines clearly visible, mocking the bright-eyed optimism of any do-gooding idealist.

"I told you so I never trusted that bastard," stated Olive proudly, her distrust being completely vindicated. What made the story quite distressing was that we all knew the vicar in question. He was a young curate back in Cheetham Hill. Me and Terry got to know him well. Unfortunately the story was true. Before we could get into any arguments the doorbell rang and there was an enthusiastic knock on Olive's door and in walked a gangly figure with a bright mop of bleached spiky hair.

"Ello Olive. It's me, Martin.'Ow are you?"

"Martin!" Olive exclaimed clearly pleased to see him.

"Come in." Olive looked over at me and winked. "You remember Martin?" And then she winked again. Olive then introduced Terry to Martin. "He's one of those born again thingamyjigs." Terry just smiled and nodded.

"Sit on the poof Martin," said Olive with gusto. She then looked over to us and winked very deliberately just in case we didn't get the fact that he was gay the first time. Martin was slightly bemused but Olive made her instructions clear. "MARTIN, SIT ON THE POOF." Martin still looked a little perplexed so she quickened her approach. "Sit on the poof. Martin. MARTIN! Sit on the poof." The last request was said with a little impatience as though a poodle was not doing as it was told. Martin then cottoned on and was happy to play along and sit on the poof. As he did so his long legs splayed awkwardly across the small living room floor and his thin white arms sprang out to act as levers like some giant four-legged spider. All the while his small derrière sank slowly into the old dilapidated poof. Martin was uncomfortable but there was little empathy from Olive as she sought to drive home her point of humour at Martin's expense.

"Are you OK with a poof?" Olive asked in earnest. Martin sighed in grim resignation, rolled his eyes and replied simply.

"Yes Olive. I'm OK with a poof."

Olive had a way of getting away with such comments despite the political incorrectness. It was easier with Martin as she knew him well. He used to live in the maisonette next door to Olive back at Wythenshawe. They had become quite friendly over the years as a sweet but unusual bond developed between the two. It was Martin's first visit since he moved away from their old place a few months back. It was also Martin who gave Olive her first spliff at the age of 65.

"I knew there was something a bit strange," she said to me one day. "He (Martin) was giggling a bit too much when he gave it to me. That roll up smelt funny right from the start. I am sure he was thinkin' about givin' it me for some time. We often gave each other ciggies anyway and I thought what the hell, why not? I'm not getting any younger."

For a minute I let my mind picture the moment of that first hit. I could see Olive inhaling deeply and fearlessly. I could picture Martin's excited look as he anticipated the effects it would have on Olive.

"What do you think, Olive?" I could hear him say.

"Not bad, Martin," would be the understated reply.

There would be a long pause and then I could imagine them both bursting into giggles like little children unable to contain themselves. And between the fits of giggles I could hear Olive mutter. "You little bastard Martin." It would be said with a wicked and devilish grin on her face.

Every so often when I visited Olive, I was sure that I could detect the faint smell of weed. After that first "hit," I remember that there was a marked change in the gadgets that Olive purchased from the shopping channel. They became more frivolous and indulgent. They didn't just cut, dice or whisk, they flickered red and blue and played jaunty little tunes whilst spitting out some sweeties at the same time. The best one was the gnome dressed in grey that drew open its mac and flashed its privates when the doorbell rang. (Let's also not forget le pis manikin)

Terry found Martin's appearance interesting, in particular his highly decorative and indulgent fingernails. They were mini works of art. The strange thing was that Martin was staring at them just as much as everybody else. He was running a critical eye over his mini masterpieces seeing if there were any mistakes in the application of his designs. He could get quite fretful if things weren't quite right.

"For Christ's sake Martin, stop lookin' at your bloody nails otherwise 'am gonna chop the little bastards off," snapped Olive. It shook Terry and Martin out of their trance-like state.

"Sorry Olive," said Martin in a tone which suggested that he had apologised for that same annoying habit a thousand times. As Terry chuckled, Olive berated him for slurping his tea. Terry then found himself apologising in similar fashion. This time they both laughed which broke the ice and before long the conversation flowed. Terry and Martin got on well but Olive loved to be the social detonator.

"So Terry, do you think that there is room for a sexual deviant like Martin in heaven?" she asked innocently. Terry was used to Olive's forthright manner and took her attempt at mild provocation in his stride.

"Well, if there's room for me I am sure that there is room for Martin," replied Terry. We all laughed but at the same time acknowledged the wise and humble reply. Olive was particularly impressed.

"On that note," said Martin, "I'm gonna be off. Sorry I can't stay longer. I was just passing through. The visit's short but sweet"

"Not like you then," said Olive.

"Nice one, Olive," replied Martin who then turned to us. "She's a charming cow isn't she?"

Olive then gave Martin a big hug and a peck on the cheek and told him that he could "piss off now."

"Nice meeting you Terry," said Martin as he glided through the front door.

And in that moment of quiet that followed his departure I remembered something. "Hey Terry, I saw Alex, Alex

Cordwell." I turned to Olive. "You remember Alex?" Olive nodded. I explained the circumstances of our meeting which genuinely shocked both of them. I hadn't told them until now that I was in town when the bomb went off.

"Jesus," was all Olive could say. I didn't reveal how close I was and played it down.

"Anyway, enough of that, Alex has done really well for himself. Look, see for yourself." And with that I pulled out the photograph of Alex. He was clean shaven, beautifully tanned, immaculately dressed and looking good. "You must agree he even looks the part."

"It doesn't surprise me," said Terry, "He was always a cool customer. Destined for greater things." Terry then took a gulp of his tea being careful not to slurp.

"Oh, I nearly forgot," I blurted out, "Alex said he found this in the rubble at Johnson Street, possibly in the remains of our old house!" I took the small casket from my pocket and picked out the small silver crucifix that was inside and laid it down on the coffee table. "There was a note that came with it which simply said "Sorry." Alex said that he could just make out the signature. He said it was from a guy called Frank. Now I've thought about it and the only Frank I can think of and I don't really remember him too well, was our lodger Frank, Frank Tapper."

Olive looked troubled. She looked over to Terry who also looked a little pained.

"What? Have I said something I shouldn't?" I said, alarmed at their reaction.

There was a silence. I looked at Terry who shook his head as if to say "don't go there." I didn't press and then Terry commented on Olive's interesting choice of curtains. It did the trick as Olive bounced back to the present.

"£2 from the charity shop," said Olive proudly. She could never resist boasting about a bargain.

"You were done," said Terry wryly.

We laughed as the previous mini drama was brushed aside. For the remainder of our visit everything was okay again up to a point.

The car journey home

I stepped into Terry's old Ford Cortina, buckled my seat belt and turned to Terry who was inserting his favourite Harry Secombe collection of hymns into the car deck. He always played this when he was worried about something.

"What was all that about?" I asked.

Terry paused for a minute as Harry's rendition of 'How great thou art' wafted through the car's stereo sound system. Then he turned the music down.

"There's a few things you need to know. Where to start?" He took a deep breath and then began. "You remember Michael don't you, Michael Jones from the youth club?"

"Yes. Yes of course," I stated and then added quietly, "who wouldn't?"

"Quite," said Terry. There was a moment's pause and then he continued.

"Something happened with Frank. Frank your lodger and Michael."

"Go on," I said.

"I didn't know Frank that well. He helped out at a few of the youth club sessions. I found out from Olive that he was a first aider and invited him along to talk to the lads and give a few demonstrations. It was Olive that encouraged him to go. After one of his talks the lads played football. That was normal but it was the only time that Michael joined in and you guessed it, he got injured. Not seriously. Some of the boys took him along to Frank because he was after all a qualified first aider. They left him with Frank in the back kitchen. When I walked in and opened the door they were kissing."

"What? Michael and Frank?"

"Snogging really," added Terry.

"Really?"

"Yeah, really," said Terry in a funny kind of tone and then he continued. "I just shut the door quickly. Shock I suppose. I should have said something there and then but I didn't. They both seemed to be...involved." It was clear that Terry was struggling to find the right words.

"But he was only young and Frank..."

"I know, I know!" Terry sighed and shook his head. "Anyway Frank rushed out to see me but some of the other boys came in the hall at the same time. I could see he wanted to talk but I didn't want to, not right then so I kind of mingled with the other lads. I didn't know what to say. I needed more time. In the next five minutes I made sure I didn't move from my position and then when I turned round Frank was gone. And then I realised. Michael, I needed to see him." Terry stopped for a second. "I should have seen Michael earlier, seen if he was okay but I needed those few minutes to digest what I had seen if that makes sense."

"Yes. Yes, it does," I said in affirmation.

"And then when I looked in the back kitchen Michael was gone. Some of the boys saw him walk off and said that he seemed fine but I'm not so sure. But Frank didn't seem the type to prey on people but I suppose given their ages that's what he would be seen as. A predator."

Terry paused and reflected on what he had said. It was obvious that he was struggling but then he tried to continue. "I never would have thought." There was another pause as Terry struggled to finish his sentence. "I dunno," said Terry, "it's the quiet ones." And then he shook his head as though he wanted to shake the past away but he couldn't.

I knew what was coming. I knew what Terry was going to say.

"That time. It was the last time I saw Michael alive. It was only a few days later…"

Terry didn't have to say any more. Everybody who was around at the time knew about the tragedy and I remembered the headlines again.

"On Sunday June 2nd the body of 15 year old Michael Jones was found dead lying near the railway track behind Smedley Fields. A young couple walking their dog spotted the body late on Sunday afternoon. Death was by electrocution. Police are not viewing this as suspicious circumstances."

Manchester Evening News

"You don't blame yourself, do you?" He said nothing. "Terry, there was nothing you could do. How could you have prevented it?"

"If I'd have managed to speak to him. Why did he go down there anyway?" said Terry imploringly.

"Was it because of what I saw happen?"

"Look Terry, from what our Johnny says, Michael was a bit of a daredevil. He probably went down there out of mischief – not because of what happened. We all played down there. We shouldn't have done it but we did. For goodness sake it's not your fault!"

"You don't know that!" said Terry fiercely. For a second I was taken aback by the force of his reply and didn't say anything. Terry then calmed down a little as an uncomfortable smile appeared across his lips. In his own mind it was quite clear. He was responsible. Not just for failing to see Michael at a crucial moment…but in not paying more attention.

"Frank. I should have kept more of an eye on him but I never thought."

As Terry's voice tapered off a thought began to materialise about how Olive was connected to the whole event. But before I could say anything, Terry put into words what was on my mind.

"I think your mum and Frank were involved," he said nervously.

"Yes, you may be right."

Terry looked surprised that I seemed to accept his proposition so easily. "I take it you told her about Frank and Michael," I added.

Terry nodded. "Better it came from me. If she found out from some other source, I would be dead meat."

"I think you're right", I replied sympathetically. "And the silver crucifix in the casket?" I asked, half knowing the answer.

"Probably a parting gift from Frank," suggested Terry. "I saw Olive a few days after he left. She looked devastated."

"I think she cut him out of her photos," I said.

"That's understandable," replied Terry, "Especially if Frank left suddenly."

I wonder if Olive got an explanation. That note. Maybe he didn't want to face her. Maybe he just left.

Terry shook his head again. "The whole thing's still a bloody mess."

And it was. Nothing was resolved. Only questions but even then I had a nagging doubt about Frank, that all was not as it seemed. What confused me is that I remembered Johnny asking me about Frank all those years ago. He asked it in a weird kind of way. Poor Olive. She was on good form that day with Martin and Terry and then it was as though I'd pulled the rug from under her feet. On the surface she recovered well but as we drove off I had my doubts.

*Alone again. She looks at the beautiful silver cross and gently
runs it through her fingers. It was a long time ago. She loved
Frank and he loved her. She found him attractive for sure. He
was different. At the time she told herself that she was never
going to tarnish anything with some tawdry affair but had she
been fooling herself?*

When Terry told her about Frank and Michael. That was
shocking. That Frank could have been attracted to other men,
that was difficult enough to accept; but young boys. And
Michael's death shortly after. Was there a connection? The
thought horrified Olive but then she quickly told herself that it
couldn't be true. Not Frank. Could it?

My paintbrush hovers over the canvas. I am hesitant.
There were so many questions that Olive desperately wanted
answering. Maybe there was a mistake, maybe. But she never
had the chance because he left suddenly. As soon as she saw the
small silver casket that looked so alone on the kitchen table, she
knew. And when she opened it and found his "gift", she
remembers the small tears that formed in the corner of her eye
that day. She would never forget that note saying simply
"Sorry." But sorry for what? Sorry for what he had done to
Michael, sorry for leaving, sorry for not telling her? And all of a
sudden those same feelings of frustration and betrayal sweep
over her, and then she realises that they never really went away.

NINE MONTHS LATER

Olive went into the kitchen and brought in several boxes of all shapes and sizes and placed them on the living room floor. She wouldn't let us help. She insisted that we stayed put. After she carried the last box in, she stood as tall as her five foot and a tea leaf would let her.

"I am decluttering," she pronounced. We looked perplexed.

"Gadgets!" she declared. "I've got too many."

"No. Never," said Stacey in mock astonishment.

Olive ignored her daughter's cheek.

"I've decided to give some away."

This was quite a statement from Olive. She collected gadgets for a hobby, mainly accrued through the Shopping Channel. They were her pets. She was always reluctant to give any away and many lay unopened in the darkest recesses of her cupboards until now.

"Bloody 'ell. Are you getting' soft?" said Johnny sarcastically.

Belle stared hard at her brother. Although his comment appeared to be in jest she recognised that there was still a barb to it. Their animosity towards each other loomed in the background, simmering away. Johnny rarely visited the old lady. It was quite by chance that we were there when he called round.

"Let her be generous," whispered Belle to her brother.

"Why?" he said sharply, "She's never been that before."

Belle stared at her brother again. "Don't!" she said firmly.

Olive simply ignored her son and reached for the first box. There was an air of solemnity that slowly descended upon the gathered clan. A reverence if you like. And then she began. It was like a regal ceremony.

"Stacey, you are my eldest daughter so you shall have the bread mixer. Belle, the youngest of my children, you shall have the most modern of microwaves. Johnny the lippy bastard, treasure this food processor. It will encourage you to cook once in a while." Then Olive looked at me and smile. "This blender will be like a paintbrush in your hands."

And when the old lady passed these most prized of possessions onto us, she gently wafted them first over the tops of our shoulders and then over our heads as though some profound knighthood was taking place. We in turn (perhaps subconsciously) acknowledged a certain gravitas in the scene by allowing ourselves a slight nod of the head like a gesture one may make to the queen when receiving an honour. Olive kept one new food processor and one microwave even though she had one. She then turned to me and handed me an old shoe box.

"Treasure these. I know that you are always looking at them. You've taken most of them yourself anyway.

I opened the lid slowly.

"Mum I can't. These photos...they're precious...I know. I took a lot of them but...."

"I am decluttering," she interrupted.

"You like that word, don't you?" I said. Olive ignored my comment and thought for a minute.

"Well borrow them. Give them back when you have finished. They mean more to you than me."

At first I was not sure why she did this but she certainly knew that I would "have a bloody good ganders" at them.

Olive wasn't wrong. As soon as I got home I couldn't wait to get the box out, yank the lid off and have a proper good look at them. There is something about old photographs. They're a window into people's lives, a visual diary of a personal and social history. In this case it was mine and I was fascinated. I was like a child opening a sweet packet. There were lots that I hadn't seen before. There were some interesting ones of my parents in their younger days. Ted was quite handsome and Olive was quite glamorous. There were also some pictures of people I didn't know that were my parents' friends back in the day. The older the photographs were, the more I loved them.

But the familiar ones were still there looking back at me. There was that great picture of dad with a few of his navy buddies just before he met Olive, the old black and white one of granddad Ernie and Stacey's infamous one of her at the whit walk pulling a face as long as the Mersey Tunnel. I laughed to myself as it brought back memories of Stacey's wedding. There were a few more new ones of Ted. In a rather macabre fashion I lined up these pictures in chronological order to see the deterioration in Ted's physical wellbeing through the ages. The last one was of Ted and Derrick. Ted was quite thin by that time and against Derrick's reasonably well trimmed body he looked quite ill. Poor Ted.

I sorted out all the old Christmas ones tracing the history of Christmas crackers through the ridiculous designs of those stupid paper hats we all had to wear. I saw one of Johnny aged about seven running towards the sea at Southport. He was completely starkers. His trunks lay in a crumpled heap on the sand. Ted's outstretched hand appeared to invade the right-hand side of the picture trying desperately to grab him. In the background a four-year-old Stacey was in a world of her own. Dressed only in vest and navy blue knickers, she was patting sand with her spade.

There was also one of a nine-year-old Derrick blissfully happy with his fort that Ted had made him for Christmas. His smile was wide and uninhibited. Where had that young boy gone? Strangely enough, there were one or two of Frank. Olive hadn't cut him completely out of her life. I found myself looking more closely at the ones with him in trying to work out who he actually was, this strange enigmatic figure from my past

FINDING FRANK

When I eat a meal, a good meal, I usually save the best till last, mostly that's the meat. When I come to that part I eat a little more slowly and savour it. Similarly, with painting, I consume the vegetables first. That is, I establish all the base colours and map out the broad tones. Then I am left with the best part – the meat. This is the top layer, the detail, the final defining brush strokes. I take my time and I savour it.

I have a smaller brush. It is flat shaped but I don't dispense with the bigger one. That will still come in handy if I get too careful. I don't want to lose the energy and become too precise. If I am good the portrait will tell a story. I am at a critical stage. Everything is coming into focus.

"What do you make of Frank?" I always thought that it was a strange question from Johnny at a strange time. He had to have known something, surely.

It was at his house one rainy afternoon that I asked him the question.

"What can you remember about Frank, Frank Tapper?"

Johnny was surprised. "Christ, that's going back a bit. He was okay. Well actually he was quite a nice guy it's just unfortunate that…" And suddenly he stopped short.

"What was unfortunate?" I said sensing that my brother was holding something back. It wasn't like him to be secretive. He didn't like talking about stuff too deep, but he was never in the habit of deliberately withholding anything. Or so I thought.

"Nothing really. It was just unfortunate that he was around when Michael died," said Johnny slightly defensively. I wasn't

187

quite satisfied with the reply and then surprised myself by ordering my brother to tell me what he knew. I would never usually dream of speaking to Johnny like that but it worked and the barrier lifted.

"Where do you want me to start?" asked Johnny submissively.

"Frank and Michael." I replied and just to make sure that he was on track, I gave him a helpful hint.

"You know Terry caught them snoggin'."

"That doesn't surprise me. I knew that it was going to happen," said Johnny in matter-of-fact fashion.

"How?" I asked incredulously.

"Because Michael bloody told me. He told me beforehand that that was what he was gonna do. He was gonna snog Frank. Go on, I said, I dare you. I remember thinking, yeah, this is gonna be funny. And then Michael even told me how he was gonna do it. He was gonna feign an injury and because Frank was a first aider he'd have to treat him, preferably alone. That was his plan. As soon as Michael joined in the game of football, I knew. He never joined in those games. I was even laughing as he hobbled off faking his bloody injury and when I saw him skipping away ten minutes later delighted with himself, I knew it was mission accomplished."

"It sounds as if Frank didn't stand a chance," I said.

"No, no I don't think he did," replied Johnny. "I could see that Olive was upset when Frank went so suddenly." He paused. "And I didn't tell the old lady that Frank had been set up."

"Why not?" I asked.

"Because that would have meant me being kind to her and at the time I didn't want to be. I wanted to leave her not knowing the truth and believing Frank was a twat." Johnny looked at me. "I'm not very nice am I? But she…" his voice trailed off and he just shook his head. It wasn't really like him.

I was shocked.

"I do regret it," he continued. "I regret it now. I would have even told Frank about Michael's plan but he'd left pretty quickly. I tried to tell you on quite a few occasions. I nearly told you when I was about to leave for the army. I knew it would get back to Olive through you and you'd find a way to smooth it over but I bottled it."

Then there was a long silence that Johnny eventually broke. "But Michael, he was one funny fucking fucker." It was the way my brother said those last few words. It was the most sublime alliteration. Me and Johnny just burst out laughing. I didn't want to but it came out.

Only he could do that. Take a serious subject and completely turn it on its head. And then it was as though a dam had burst. Once he felt free to talk about Michael, Johnny spent the next half hour telling stories about him and the other lads. By all accounts Michael was quite anarchic and had little regard for religion. He once got hold of the church's lectern bible and altered some of the words so that cunt, twat and arse'ole appeared all over the sacred text. He was brilliant at calligraphy so that these alterations were almost undetectable. Apparently there was uproar in the Sunday service when the aged Mrs Walmsley, the Girl Guide leader, read in her best church voice that "Jesus wanked on the water." Reverend Powell did not see the funny side and threatened to close the youth club down if that ever happened again. Johnny told the story beautifully and we both creased up. Not just at that story but at many others.

I got the feeling that this was the first time Johnny had talked about Michael. I know he was upset at the time but he never spoke that much about him or what happened until now. It did him good. By the end we were a spent force – pretty much exhausted and before I knew it, it was time for me to go.

"Tell Terry," said Johnny just as I stood up to leave. "He needs to know. I never realised that he felt so responsible. It was a childish prank but I can see how much it may have affected people."

"Will do."

"It's up to you whether you tell Olive," said Johnny "I don't think I can." Then, just as I was about to go, he spoke quietly. "It's not such a daft idea to find out about Frank."

"Perhaps"

As I drove home, I remember thinking about what my brother had said but I never quite got to the bottom of why he had such an intense dislike of Olive. He ducked it again. It was funny all that stuff about Michael but it seemed to stop me from asking any more questions. And then I realised, he's always used humour to deflect away from subjects he doesn't want to talk about. He's clever that way. But one thing was for certain, I had to tell Terry what my brother had told me. My old youth club leader had suffered enough. Telling Olive and revealing the truth of the past would be difficult. It would re-ignite old wounds particularly with Johnny as they had a level of civility with each other at the moment which nobody wanted to undermine.

And what about Frank? He was still a bit of an enigma. Although he looked to be in the clear, I still wasn't absolutely sure. As for finding him…was there a moral argument to try? It could have affected him as much as it did Terry but it was highly unlikely anyone would be able to locate him with nothing to go on and a thirty year gap since anybody last saw him. But even then I knew that there was more to come and that Frank would no doubt play a part, dead or alive. It was all far from over.

Some white and mimosa yellow gives me the colour and tone I need for around the eyes. I look at the portrait. It's definitely her but a side to her that's rarely seen. I can see that. It's honest and that's what counts but sometimes being honest is difficult.

The next day I met Terry in a café in town and we talked over a large hot chocolate. I told him what my brother had said about Frank and Michael and I could see the burden that he had been carrying visibly lift. I still had to repeat "It's not your fault," several times. "Praise be to God!" Terry cried. I used to cringe when he came out with these religious exultations but now I simply smiled, especially when he spluttered, "Well not for Michael's death obviously."

Terry's positivity lasted a minute or two before the old sadness surrounding Michael reappeared. It had always wrapped itself around Terry and even though much of his guilt had been thrown off, he still found it hard to let go. A boy who he had known and looked after had died. He quickly cast his own relief aside as he remembered a young life that had ended all too abruptly.

"It's not just Michael," Terry added, "they're all affected, your brother, Frank. Poor old Frank. And let's not forget Olive. Has anyone told her?"

"No, not yet," I replied. "I'm waiting for the right time."

A NEW MILLENIUM

There never was a right time to tell Olive. I was so scared of what might happen if she found out that Johnny had known the truth all this time. So I kept putting it off. I did, however, come to the conclusion that finding Frank would help. I spent months trying to track him down from one of the old photos that Olive had given me. It featured Frank outside his mum's house in Preston. It must have been one that he gave Olive. He looked good.

Eventually I found the house but nobody remembered him or his mother apart from one elderly resident and she couldn't give me any information. All my leads and investigations came to nothing. Whilst that area of my life proved to be frustrating, other areas were far more uplifting. As a new millennium was about to sweep in there was a buzz around Manchester.

After the bombing of '96 a transformation was taking place and there was a sense of optimism now that Tony Blair was in power. The Arndale was being re-built and new high-rise luxury apartments were sprouting up around the edges of the city making urban living fashionable.

Those glory boys in red (or any number of shirt colours and designs that would help their commercial success) had achieved the unachievable treble one year earlier. Who can forget that wonder goal in the FA cup executed so majestically by my boy Giggs? I was in a pub at the time. It was absolutely heaving with United fans. When Giggsy did his thing I unashamedly shouted at the top of my voice that "I taught Ryan Giggs." I then did the hokey kokey with anybody that would join in.

As a man approaching his forties I am not ashamed to admit that I went to sleep dreaming about that magnificent goal on more than one occasion. Even better...the "noisy neighbours" were yet to be heard as Noel Gallagher's anthemic cry for his beloved blues was no more than a whimper at that time.

It wasn't just the city centre; some of my old haunts like Belleview, Ardwick and Heaton Park, were all being transformed mainly through the successful Commonwealth Games bid. Everything in and around the centre was changing. Except Cheetham Hill!

It all seemed to pass Olive by. She wasn't interested in the larger world outside anyway – it was too wide and vast. She had always been quite parochial. Olive was happy to rule over a small patch but as she aged, her world seemed to shrink even more. Perhaps the scars of all her old battles had left their mark. She'd burned up so much energy in winning them. But a part of her had softened. It was Stacey and Jammi that did it. She never wanted to admit it but she looked forward to her trips down to Rusholme to see them, especially when she managed to baby sit for her "golden brown grandchildren," as she called them. And since they had moved into a bigger house she was able to stay once in a while.

It was Stacey that suggested she move. There were plenty of good one-bedroom council flats close by. Olive's two bedroom council house in Wythenshaw would be easy enough for the authorities to swap which they did. On the day that Olive was due to move Stacey wasn't well and Jammi was working so it was left to me and Belle to sort it out. Olive hated moving. She wasn't in the best of moods and when Belle dropped one of her best kiss-me-quick Blackpool mugs, Olive wasn't best happy.

And here I am back at the beginning or not quite the beginning.

"Arse'oles. It's all a load of arse'oles," muttered Olive as we loaded her stuff into a small removal van minus her favourite mug. We took some of the more fragile items in my car. Belle insisted she take le pis manikin by hand. She sat on the back seat and continued to press the head draining the last of the contents through its shrivelled penis into a plastic cup.

"Play nice," said Olive sarcastically.

"You're not still annoyed at the arse'ole joke are you?" said Belle laughing.

"No, not really, I'm just surprised that you thought that I couldn't hear you," said Olive ruefully.

"Nothing gets past old Jodrell ears," I added but I noticed that Olive wasn't laughing too much so I tried to lighten her mood. "Look it's fine. You will be much closer to Stacey. It makes much more sense. I know it's Rusholme, land of the curries but…"

"I'll be fine!" said Olive abruptly. She hated people fussing over her. Belle sensed that and quickly changed the subject.

"Hey, it's your seventieth in a few weeks' time. Do you want me to get in touch with Derrick?" she asked.

"If you want," said Olive.

"Don't be like that," said Belle who looked at me for solidarity.

I just shook my head, "You know what she's like." And there it was. As soon as I said it, I was my father. I used to hate Ted saying that. It always sounded so feeble. Olive wasn't too pleased with my comment either."

"*She* is sat right here," she stated indignantly.

"Sorry mum." And then I thought I'd get her back on side. I knew that she hated birthday presents so I assured her that we would not be getting her one. Olive could see that Belle was frowning. My sister loved giving presents and no doubt she would be having words with me afterwards. It didn't bother Olive though, as she happily continued my theme.

"No birthday cards either. A bloody waste of money and a waste of time."

"Can we at least wish you happy birthday?" implored Belle.

"If you must," replied Olive disdainfully.

Belle gave a firm knock. Even before Olive got to the door we were both singing happy birthday. Belle thrust some flowers into Olive's hand and then turned to me.

"Don't you dare say anything."

"'Ello you two," said Olive generously. You could see that she was pleased to see us and much to my surprise was pleased with the flowers. Belle turned to me. "I told you so," she hissed. However, Olive's smile quickly turned to a frown as she eyed Belle up and down. Something wasn't quite right.

"What the bloody 'ell 'ave you done to your hair? You look like Worzel bloody Gummidge," said Olive clearly annoyed that her daughter had made a mess of her crowning glory. In a sort of helpful manner Olive quickly made a suggestion.

"Get that bloody sister of yours to cut it. She is a hairdresser for Christ's sake." Olive then shouted down the hallway "Stacey! Cut your bloody sister's hair!" Stacey poked her head round the door. "Yes mum," she said dutifully. Stacey then looked at Belle and rolled her eyes suggesting that Olive was a silly bugger. Belle then turned to me and whispered in rasping fashion.

"It's the latest bloody hair fashion."

"No, it's not. It's like a bloody beehive gone wrong," shouted Olive.

"Christ," said Johnny. "She's not lost it."

"The flat looks nice," I said, changing the conversation. "You've definitely done the right thing. Moving that is." Olive was irritated "Christ son, you've said that about five hundred times. I'm all right. I know I've done the right thing." It was as though that hesitancy and vulnerability she revealed to us a few weeks back when she was about to move, was but a moment's weakness. She was back now. She was her old hardened self.

"But thank you for asking," Olive said wryly. She then reached over to a plate of goodies.

"Who wants an éclair?" asked Olive with a self-satisfied smile.

"Oh God. You know why she's smiling," said Belle.

"Did she put her thumb through one and pretend it was damaged," asked Johnny disgusted at his mother's practice. He turned to Olive. "Did you get money off then, you tight arsed bastard?"

Olive simply smiled and said smugly. "Half price from Tesco."

There was a collective shake of heads. Shopping trips with Olive could be so embarrassing. Always looking for a bargain, mum would deliberately damage fruit and other soft food stuff in the hope that she could get money off. She wasn't subtle and didn't care. "What could they do? I am just a little old lady. These supermarkets are bloody loaded anyway," was her stock reply. Olive never liked the idea of being diddled or ripped off. She once bought a luxury item of soap by mistake, saw the price and immediately asked for a refund citing the fact that she did not want to buy shares in the company.

Out shopping, she would stop to talk to anyone. Her cheeky chatter would very often elicit a few laughs. In later years after talking to Ely, Arnold or whoever, she'd turn round to Belle and either call the guy a pervert or the woman a money-grabbing bitch. It was said with enough venom to be construed as malicious but would lack the potency of her firebrand years.

Sometimes she meant what she said but there was often an element of self-parody about her utterances. In these instances, if you were to laugh (as me and Belle often did) then she would laugh with you. A wholehearted laugh. Laughing not just at how ridiculous her comments were but how much wasted energy there had been in such utterances and arguments in her past. Suddenly there was another knock on the door.

"Hello mum," said Derrick.

"Hello stranger. It's been a few years, hasn't it?" It was a frosty reception.

Derrick kissed his mother politely on the cheek and gingerly walked in. It was a strange atmosphere. It was great to see my brother but there was no real explanation as to why he had distanced himself so much from us all. Looking back, he had been absent for most of the family gatherings (always an excuse not to come) and then suddenly he had turned up to this one. When Stacey invited him for the party it was more in hope than anything else. She didn't actually think he would turn up. Olive wasn't too impressed.

"How's your shit pads these days?"

"Mum!" said Belle disgusted in her mother's tone.

"It's okay, Belle. They're incontinence pads," explained Derrick seriously. "We deliver them. The business is doing well. Look outside the window. That's my Merc." Derrick looked pleased with himself.

"Whatever," said Johnny pouring scorn on his brother's attempt to show off.

"Derrick, have an éclair," said Stacey attempting to diffuse a situation. She then turned to Olive and attempted to inject some humour. "What are they mum?"

Olive was silent.

"They're half price," said Stacey in mocking tone.

"Of course," said Derrick ruefully. Derrick ate the éclair carefully so as not to get any cream on his smart suit.

"Are you sure you are not selling insurance?" said Johnny. It was clear that there was still no love lost between them.

"Pay no attention," said Stacey. "We're pleased to see you." And with that she started to set the table. It was Stacey's idea that we all bring along something to eat…something that we had made. Olive had come down with something and didn't really fancy going out. In no time the table was full of all sorts of goodies including Olive's favourite – chopped and fried fish which she had made herself. It was a recipe passed down from her mother, Annie. Olive didn't talk about Annie much and I only remember seeing her a couple of times. She suffered from early onset dementia and died when I was a boy. I know that she had a hard life. Raising seven children and being married to Ernie could not have been easy. By all accounts money was scarce and Ernie used to drink a lot which probably pushed her over the edge.

Olive often said that Annie was hard work. She was withdrawn and never communicated much with anyone but as Olive would proudly state, "She made a bloody marvellous chopped and fried fish." Olive's demeanour often perked up at the mention of this dish. I could imagine her there in the kitchen as a child helping Annie chop up the fish and grind in the matzo meal. She would be a model of concentration helping her mother delicately form small balls of goodness ready to toss in the frying pan.

Olive didn't have much of a legacy that was passed down from her parents but Annie's gefilte fish was a treasured part of her Jewish inheritance and ours. It was a family favourite and now everybody tucked in, relishing its distinct flavour. A few beers later and everybody was chilled. Apart from the odd glance through the window to check if his Merc was okay even Derrick relaxed. It wasn't back-smackingly warm hearted but we all got along fine. To a degree.

LOST AND FOUND

There is some lime green on my painting. I realise that it has come off my sleeve and smeared over part of the background. I tut and get the cloth to wipe it off and then I stop. It works. It needs to be modified but the colour works. It sets off a particular skin tone on the right hand side. I delight in my happy accident but you have to be open to these moments and take advantage.

After Olive's birthday I went back to Johnny's place. Whenever I am about to cross the threshold of his "love nest" as he calls it I have to take my shoes off. I don't think too much about the socks that I'm wearing, who would? On this occasion they were black, very cheap and slightly threadbare and that was fatal because apparently they left a few dark tiny threads on his pristine, immaculately hoovered white rug.

He went all irritated cursing and cussing as he spent five minutes picking up the remnants of my footsteps. He then marched into his bedroom and immediately marched back out clutching a pair of his best moccasin slippers. He then thrust them into my midriff. "Here! You gormless bastard!" I looked at the rug and couldn't see a thing.

"Don't you think you're being a bit anal," I said, "a bit domestic like."

He shrugged my comments off.

"You know you're the type of kid who'd be the first one to piss on a nice virginal patch of snow."

"Well you may be right but at least it wouldn't be random, I'd probably do a Jackson Pollock, maybe Autumn Rhythm. That'd be easy to do. Just wave the old pecker around a bit and it would be a damn sight better than your scrawny effort!"

"Arse'oles," said Johnny and we both laughed. And then he thought.

"Are you givin' me some verbals back?"

"It's teaching."

"What is?"

"I think it's made me a bit more bolshie. That and Olive."

"Olive!"

"Yes Olive. I think I'm becoming her in the classroom. There was this girl the other day – she can't stand me and as I lined up beside her in the dinner queue she turned to her friend and said she thought she could smell something…meaning me. I looked at her and said lookin' at that nose love I think it's too close to your arse."

"Jesus," said Johnny. "It's not like you. Did it get you into trouble?"

"Well it could have done but some of the other kids laughed. None of them liked the kid anyway and she just stormed off. But it wasn't just what I said. I had Olive's timing. I could feel it. There have been other times which I am not gonna bore you with but when I've said or done something it's her all over. It's like she's done some kind of astral projection and taken over my spirit."

We both looked at each other and screamed in mock horror "AAAGH." And then the doorbell rang.

"Jesus Christ, Terry. What are you doin' 'ere?"

"I've found him, I've found him!" Terry spluttered as Johnny opened the door to let him in. "You'll never believe it. He was on my bus. He's been on my bus for ages. Usually it's car keys or golf balls that you find when you've stopped looking but this time it's a person. All this time, I never knew. I never knew. You don't look closely at faces when you're drivin'. You go people blind, that's what happens when you're a bus driver – people blind."

"What are you on about?" I asked, mystified by his excited outburst but Terry kept rambling on.

"Maybe it's a subconscious thing. Maybe this time, that's why I looked up. I looked at his face. There was something vaguely familiar. I didn't realise. It was Frank! "

"Frank?" said a bemused Johnny.

"Frank Tapper," blurted Terry.

I was so shocked I couldn't utter a word. Terry was also quite breathless but a large intake of air allowed him to slow down a little. He then continued, "I looked closely at his bus pass and there it was. Frank, Frank Tapper. I very nearly choked on my mint imperial! Frank, it's me Terry. Terry from the youth club, I said. He just smiled and here's the thing – 'I wondered when you would recognise me,' he said'."

"Bloody hell. The little tinker," I laughed.

"I know" said Terry in full agreement. "He's been on my bus for the last few months and never said a bloody thing." Terry rarely swore unless he was very agitated or very excited. As he was both I was surprised he restricted himself to "bloody."

"We had a bit of a chat," added Terry, "but it was brief. He was getting off shortly but he was happy to give me his phone number. I said you wanted to talk to him and he was fine with that. He looked bloody good for a seventy five year old. Better than me."

"That's not difficult," Johnny said smiling at Terry.

There was a meek ironic smile back. "Very funny."

"Oh by the way. 'Ello Johnny. It's been a few years."

"'Ello Terry. Nice to see you. You ugly bastard."

"Thanks. Same to you."

It was a good friendly Mancunian exchange.

Meeting Frank

I was quite surprised when I heard Frank on the phone. His voice seemed assured. It didn't quite fit with my last recollection of him. There was something else. He had a slightly different accent, a mixture of Mancunian and something American. The conversation was short but I could sense that he was as intrigued as I was. We arranged to meet at his place the very next day.

I found the address that Frank had given me easily. It was a posh flat in Worsley. I rang the bell and almost immediately a voice from the intercom asked me to come up to the second floor and that the door was open. I cautiously stepped inside.

"Hellooo," a warm voice responded from behind the kitchen door. "Come in, come in. I'm just puttin' the kettle on. Fancy a cuppa?" Before I could answer, a small wiry figure smartly dressed in a cravat loosely dangled around his neck sprung out to greet me.

"How lovely to see you," he said warmly and with that he gave me a big hug and a small peck on the cheek. Frank's face was quite wrinkly but he still had all his hair. He had aged well but there was something quite different to how I remember him. He seemed lighter on his feet and perkier in his manner. He was very bright eyed, bushy tailed and surprisingly camp.

"Frank?" I said, not quite believing my eyes.

"Please my friends call me Frankie. I'm not what you were expecting am I?" he said grinning and then rather flamboyantly added, "Darling I am what I am!"

"Terry said that you were a little different from last time," I said laughing, "but I thought he was referring to you getting older."

"That I most certainly am," he declared, "but definitely none the wiser or at least I hope not."

I laughed some more and then we both sat down on the most stylish of chairs, sipped some Earl Grey and had what can only be described as a good old chat. It started with news about my father. Frankie was genuinely upset when I told him. "He was a dear friend, so loyal, your father. You must be very proud of him. He was a lovely man." It was strange to hear such genuine affection for my father. "He bailed me out a few times," added Frankie "Often when I was a little worse for wear." He saw the quizzical look on my face. "In the navy dear boy! He was a right scally then," he added. Frankie smiled to himself as recollections of a former life resurfaced. "And then of course we met again in your parents' house in Cheetham Hill." He sipped his tea again and then continued.

"I know that this is worlds away from Johnson Street." He looked around at the fine décor of his flat "But I absolutely loved my time there. Olive was fabulous." As he spoke I could see his face flush with excitement. "I loved her sassiness. She took no prisoners. She was bold." Frank sipped some more of his tea as he let his mind roam. "That time at the Beech Hill with Pat Gill," said Frankie wistfully "It was priceless." And then he looked directly at me and smiled. It was that same disarming smile he showed me when I first walked in "And what a handsome young man you have turned out to be. (Was Frankie flirting with me?)

"Not so young," I replied.

"Well, you are to me," he replied. "Anyway less of the small chat. I assume there's things you want to know." He took a breath and began.

"I don't want to be disrespectful to Ted and I am sure nothing would have ever happened but I think we did love each other. Your mother and me. Right now it's quite obvious darling why nothing would have ever happened...well not permanently, but back then I hid my sexuality well not just from your mother but from myself. Besides it was never anything you would be open about back then. I was far too responsible. The spirit of gay abandon had yet to descend on me." That last sentence was said with a touch of melodrama. There was a pause and then he got serious.

"But I didn't set out to do anything with Michael I..."

"He set you up," I interrupted. "My brother Johnny told me. Michael engineered it. You know that he faked an injury so that he could get you on your own? He told Johnny that he was gonna snog you."

Frank frowned a little. "Thank you for telling me that." He then paused briefly before continuing. "I did know that Michael had a crush on me and I must admit that I was flattered but before I knew it his arms were coiled round my neck and his tongue was buried down my throat." Frankie shook his head. "The little devil, eh?" I nodded and then he continued. "Just at the point where I was about to push him away Terry walked in. I know how it must have looked but..." he broke off for a second and then resumed "Terry does know that I didn't intend any of this?"

"Of course."

"Good. But here's the thing, when Michael kissed me I didn't break it off straight away. If I am honest a part of me liked it. It was sweet of him. I didn't really protest too much." Frankie's voice trailed off for a second. "Poor Terry," continued Frankie, "he was so shocked. I will never forget that look on his face. My instinct was to see him straight away, to tell him that it wasn't what it looked like but I wasn't able to get to him. And I am glad that I didn't."

"I am not sure I understand."

"I might have tried to explain it away. I would have said that it was all a silly joke by a young adolescent...a stupid mistake, which it was. And I may never have faced up to the simple truth, however repugnant it may have seemed, that I found men far more attractive than women. The shame of it all is that it took a young boy's kiss to do it but it was rather nice." A broad grin spread across his face.

I thought to myself that for all his mischief it was Michael who ignited the spark and set alight something that had lain dormant within Frankie but there was nothing sinister. Deep down I knew that. I just needed to hear it from the guy himself, although his account surprised me as did his evolution.

"In that instant," continued Frankie, "I knew I had to go. Leave. Not just the town but my job, the country, everything. I couldn't explain it to Olive because I couldn't explain it to myself." He laughed ironically.

"But you did leave her a gift?"

"Yes that's right. I said sorry in the note but I knew that she wouldn't understand." Frankie looked at me directly. "I'm afraid that I may have hurt your mother." There was real sadness his face. "I'm not sure that she will want to see me."

"I dunno," I said. "She can be quite hard. You left so suddenly but I did think she wanted me to find you. It's just that…"

"It's OK," said Frankie politely interrupting me, "you don't have to explain."

Despite my new friend's flamboyant exterior he had a real empathy and tenderness to him. He knew when to reign it in. I could see how people warmed to him.

"So what happened? Where did you go?" I asked, curious about his past.

"New York, dear boy, New York. Oh the adventures. I met Warhol you know!" And suddenly Frankie was off regaling me with tales of wild parties and young men. All of them very funny. It turned out that he fell in with an underground subversive activist gay rights group. He took great pride in telling me he was there at Stonewall. As I looked around his flat I could see pictures of him with a number of figures who looked famous. Pride of place was a picture of him with his arm round Alan Ginsberg!

"I was very fortunate," added Frankie, "that somehow I fell in with the wrong crowd. They were terribly debauched, lip smackingly sexy and courageously anarchic."

Frankie then asked me about the rest of the family. I gave him a potted history including the fact that I taught Ryan Giggs. Unfortunately he had no idea who that was. Towards the end of our conversation Frankie took another sip of his tea and then looked at me with a twinkle in his eye.

"And what about that young rascal Michael?" he said impishly.

It was a shock to the system. I didn't realise that Frankie didn't know. I should have guessed from the way he was talking about him.

"He died a long time ago."

"Really. How?" said Frankie clearly saddened by the news.

"I'm not sure. Some accident," I said. I was deliberately vague.

"That's a shame," said Frankie, "A real shame. He was a lovely boy."

"It was on the old railway track," I blurted out. I couldn't help it. Frankie deserved to know the truth. And for a moment there was a hint of regret etched across his ageing forehead for a life lost, that could have been so much fun.

"Yes a real shame," he added.

OLIVE'S VISIT

At first Olive didn't want to go. "What good would it do seeing Frank after all these years? Look at me now. I'm not exactly Rita Hayworth."

"It's alright. I've prepared him," I said. "I've told him you're an ugly cow now."

Olive responded with a smack across my shoulders.

"Look, it won't matter. He's not like that. He's not going to judge you."

Olive went quiet as she mulled over my comments and then she looked at me accusingly...

"You kept that bloody quiet didn't you? The visit and all?"

"Well, yes. What if he didn't want to see you?" Suddenly Olive looked concerned so I quickly reassured her. "Don't worry he's absolutely desperate to see you."

"Is that what he said?"

"Not in so many words but I know he does."

"Hmm," said Olive thoughtfully. "And you say he's battin' for the other side."

"Yes, but you're gonna get on like a house on fire. I know."

"OK. OK, I'll go."

Later on that evening I dropped Olive off at Frankie's. I decided to remain in the car as I didn't want to intrude on their first meeting. I parked across the road and watched closely as Olive walked towards Frankie's flat. I could see a little vulnerability in her manner as she glanced at me for assurance. She was just about to knock on the door when she checked herself. Her dress needed straightening so she straightened it.

She also flattened the creases out of her blouse and folded her lips together ensuring an even distribution of lipstick. She inspected herself in a small compact mirror, patted her hair and then turned to me. "Do I look OK?" she mouthed. I gave her the thumbs up. It was a side to my mother I'd not seen too often...a vulnerability. Suddenly I remembered.

"It's Frankie," I shouted, "Frankie."

"Arse'oles" yelled Olive defiantly. "It's Frank!"

She nervously pressed the bell and within a few seconds the door opened. Out popped Frankie's diminutive figure and he unashamedly gave Olive the most enormous hug. It lasted a long time. When they broke off Frankie glanced at me and smiled. I knew that Olive would be fine so I drove back to my place ready to pick her up in a few hours' time. I was expecting Olive to ring but it was Frankie's voice I heard on the phone later on that evening. A lot later than planned.

"You can pick Olive up now," said Frankie cheerily. "She's quite pissed but absolutely fine." I could hear Olive laughing raucously in the background but there were other voices too – all chirping away in lively fashion.

"It sounds like quite a party."

"Yes. Yes I suppose it is," said Frankie reflectively.

It turned out that his friends couldn't resist calling round. They'd heard so much about Olive. Frankie had talked about his Queen Boudicca with immense pride. She was quite legendary. I could see them all now gathered round – young and old, bright and bold sitting and kneeling at Olive's feet hanging on her every word. I know that once she got going she would have had them in the palm of her hand and when the drink flowed, I bet she was in her absolute element.

"Did you get a chance to talk?" I asked.

"Yes. Yes we did. My friends were very sweet and gave us some time together before they turned up but I didn't know it was going to be so lively," said Frankie laughing. "Have you ever thought of hiring your mum out at gay parties. She's an absolute hoot, a regular Diana Dors." We both laughed. "Don't worry she'll be ready in ten minutes," he added, still laughing. As I pulled up outside the flat, I could see several figures hugging Olive on the doorstep and wishing her bon voyage. They were excessive goodbyes that seemed to take forever but eventually Frankie prized Olive away and then escorted her to the car where we both managed to push her gently into the back seat.

Frankie then turned to me and thanked me. "We both needed that," he said quietly. "I've always felt guilty and she's always felt angry. Tonight's really helped." He then hesitated. "But I think there is something more. Maybe she'll tell you one day." Frankie didn't elaborate and before I could question him, he wished me good night and shook my hand warmly. I got in the car slightly baffled by his last remark.

Just as I was about to drive off, Olive wound the window down and thrust her arm out which held aloft a glass of Baileys that somehow she'd managed to sneak in. "A toast," she shouted. She then paused as a huge belch erupted from the back of her throat which caused her to falter. Undeterred, she raised her glass even higher "Cheers queers, you're me dears. I hope it slips in easy." And with that she knocked back the contents of the glass and promptly passed out on the back seat.

OLIVE/EVILO

The portrait might be complete. I stand back and contemplate the journey. I read somewhere that in a painting the beginning isn't always the start. The real beginning is when what is on canvas begins to reflect the truth. Similarly, this day I will count as the beginning. It is not the start but it is when the whole truth begins to emerge.

As I walked up to the hospital reception, I saw Nurse Clare and she recognised me immediately.

"Evilo will be pleased to see you," she said and laughed.

Clare loved that name and chuckled when she used it. Evilo – Olive spelt backwards, a fact that my mother loved. Of all the names she has been called or she herself had adopted, this was the one she secretly liked most of all. It certainly helped present an image of her that was quite scary. But in the short time that she was there, staff realised that there was more to her than simply a fearsome old git. Her stories were witty and entertaining. They were rich working-class anecdotes that revealed an insightful if sometimes cynical view on human nature.

A bladder infection and an appendicitis that had burst two days after seeing Frank had kept her in hospital for the past two weeks. At first we thought that it was a hangover as Olive was in bed for some time feeling awful. But when she took a turn for the worse, Belle decided enough was enough and an ambulance was called. I hadn't had a chance to talk to her about the evening at Frankie's. I was dying to know all the details. I was relieved that the secrets from the past had been unlocked but a feeling still persisted that something else was missing. I wasn't going to dwell on it. In fact I'd put it to bed as I approached my mum's ward.

"Hi mum," I said cheerily as I poked my head round the curtain.

"'Ello luv," she replied in her most generous Lancashire accent and gave me a hug and then winced.

"Oops. I shouldn't have done that," she said with a grimace and then clutched at her stiches. She looked around at the staff and, even in her pain, couldn't wait to get the next sentence out. "'E taught"…but then she strained to recall who it was that I did teach. In the end she couldn't remember so she asked, "'oo was it you taught again?"

"Ryan Giggs, mum," I said. I was slightly embarrassed as the staff had already heard it before.

"Art, 'e taught 'im art. Is it United 'e plays for?" But before I could reply, Olive answered her own question in a self-reassuring manner. "That's right. Manchester United." And then almost in the same breath she asked, "Are all the kids you teach still little bastards?" It never ceased to amaze me how in an instant she could turn a sweet conversation into a bomb blast. She used to love the ripples of shock that it caused. I tried to keep a straight face but she knew I found it funny. I could never quite hide my chuckles. The nurses too were used to it and secretly smiled whilst shaking their heads in mock disapproval. Just at that moment Johnny and Belle breezed in.

"Is she upsettin' you cos if she is I'll throw her out?" said Johnny.

The nurses laughed but Olive couldn't because of the stitches. I think my brother knew that. Belle smacked her brother on the arm. She also knew what he was up to.

"Don't be so cruel," she whispered to him. "You know that she can't laugh."

"Dragons don't laugh anyway," said Johnny disdainfully. Belle simply tutted and pulled out some grapes from her bag.

"Thanks luv," said Olive, grateful that her daughter was so thoughtful. She tossed a glance to Johnny who shrugged his shoulders. He hadn't brought anything and he wasn't particularly bothered. With most of the family there I decided to tell of some sad news that I had recently received.

"Oh, by the way. Bill Tanners died. Bill the policeman. You remember him?"

"Of course," said Olive but it was said in a perfunctory way. Not what I expected. Johnny was also strangely quiet. It was Belle who was the first to express any sadness.

"What a pity," she said but it felt as though she jumped in to fill a strange silence. I was puzzled.

"Blimey. I thought that there would be more of a reaction."

"Yeah, it's a shame," said Olive belatedly.

"Yeah," was all Johnny said.

"How did you find out?"

"Jenny, Bill's daughter…I met her a couple of times at art college, we kept in touch. She thought we'd like to know."

"Well, be sure to thank her for me." said Olive curtly.

I got the distinct impression that neither Olive nor Johnny wanted to dwell on Bill and so the conversation moved on. After that there was little danger of causing Olive pain through laughing but I wasn't going to let it rest.

JOHNNY'S PLACE

As soon as I stepped into Johnny's front room I came straight to the point. "What was all that about?" Johnny looked at me but didn't say anything. He evaded my question for a second whilst he passed me a bottle of beer.

"What do you remember about Bill?" he asked as he took a swig of Budweiser.

"I liked him. He was funny and he gave me a camera. Everybody liked Bill, didn't they?"

Johnny put his bottle down forcefully and looked me in the eye. "Did he do anything to you?"

"What do you mean? I'm not sure..."

"Of course he didn't," interrupted Johnny angrily, "Not to you anyway. No fuckin' way. You never got touched. Too fuckin' young even for Bill!" Suddenly I was the little boy again with an older brother venting his anger and frustration on me. And then as quickly as he got fired up he managed to calm himself down. He'd come to realise a long time ago that I was never the enemy.

"I'm sorry," said Johnny as though he were apologising, not just for his anger at me now, but for the anger of the past as well. He then gave a long sigh like a release of a pressure valve. "You were so oblivious. You had no idea and why should you? Bill fooled everyone. The good old family friend but you weren't just oblivious," said Johnny shaking his head, "You were..." as he searched for the phrase I knew instantly what it was.

"Bloody gormless?" I suggested.

"YES. You bloody well were," said Johnny shaking his head. "A bloody gormless bastard." He let a faint smile cross his lips as his brief anger at me dissipated and then continued, "I tried to be angry with you all those years ago but I never could."

"Don't worry. I still am bloody gormless," I said.

"No fuckin' kiddin'," replied Johnny sarcastically. "No. No, you're OK, our kid. It's not your fault." Johnny paused and then added, "That you're so fuckin' dozy!" I laughed sheepishly.

"Me and Derrick, possibly Stacey but definitely me and Derrick we were just his age. He was always fuckin' groping us, always." his voice trailed off for a second and then returned. "He was a fuckin' twat." The last part was spat out like some poisonous bile. Johnny didn't need to say any more. He just took another swig of his beer and shrugged his shoulders as if to say, "Well that was that...fuck it." But I still had questions.

"How could I have been so wrong about him? He seemed so..."

"Likeable?" said Johnny finishing my sentence and then added, "That's what these bastards do. They're wolves in sheep's clothin.' They're so fuckin' friendly and trustworthy, even I liked him." I saw Johnny wince at the admission and then he continued. "He was a policeman for Christ's sake. No one believed me. Stuff like that, no one ever believed you. The mere idea. With a copper, especially one as popular as Bill. No chance. And 'e fuckin' knew it."

"But didn't you tell mum or dad," I interrupted.

"Of course. I told Olive. That was stupid. She gave me a slap and told me not to be so disgusting. I knew that would be her reaction. You see I never really helped myself. I was always telling lies and getting into trouble. More mischievous than anything else but I never made things up and there's a difference," said Johnny adamantly. "I just hoped that she would believe me." Johnny thought for a second, "Maybe after Frank's

French fuckin' kiss with Michael she didn't want to believe any of it. In her words we were all being paranoid bastards."

"You said me and Derrick?"

"Well I know it happened to Derrick. Whenever Bill came round he went somewhere else pretty quickly and he had that look on his face. It was like looking at my reflection. I just knew. And what's more he knew I knew."

"Why didn't he say anything?"

"I don't know. You'll have to ask him. All I know is that when I told Olive he never said anything, in fact he said fuck all. He heard me and your mum arguing but chose to keep stum. I remember climbing up the stairs cryin' from Olive's slap. Derrick was at the top. He'd obviously been listening. I looked him straight in the eye and he said nothing. He just looked down. He should have been the one calling Bill out because he was older. He could have done something." Johnny shook his head and then his voice trailed off.

And then I got it. I realised that the strange dynamic that appeared between my two brothers had emanated from this one episode and it had festered away all these years eating away at them. Johnny blamed his older brother for everything. Derrick was a coward. In Johnny's mind he would have said or done something if he was in Derrick's shoes. He certainly would have stuck up for his brother. In fact he should have been the older brother.

And so from that time on, the younger brother usurped the traditional position in the family of the older one at every opportunity. Johnny used humour and his acerbic wit to ridicule the eldest, chipping away at his credibility consciously and subconsciously reminding Derrick of his failure to act all those years ago. Johnny was angry at what he saw as his brother's inertia. Derrick became the butt of Johnny's jokes and never gave too much back. He couldn't. In his own mind he deserved to be punished. And he was still being punished now, all these years later.

We laughed at the jokes and scorn that Johnny poured over Derrick but never realised the game that was being played out. After a while it just became the norm for Derrick to give in and smile meekly when his younger brother dished it out. We used to say that Derrick was a bit like Ted in that respect, he didn't like conflict either. Derrick never talked at Ted's funeral, Derrick never talked at many of our gatherings. He was rarely there. Johnny assumed the lead and his brother seemed happy for that to happen. That was the way it was and we never questioned it.

And I could see why my brother slowly distanced himself from the family who either didn't know or never understood. He made appearances from time to time but he had neither the wit nor the story telling ability to impress. Instead he used status and possessions to prove his worth. I used to think it was my older brother showing off, but now I see it as a compulsion with in him...a need to be seen as a success, a somebody with credibility who could somehow cover over the inadequacies of that thirteen-year-old bespectacled boy who "Let things happen." I wish I could have got hold of that callow youth and talked some sense into him. I would have embraced him and told him that he was loved but it was too late. I could see now how fear and inadequacy had gripped him and made him mute. I wish he had said something but he was too withdrawn and then it occurred to me.

"That's why I was his sporting bitch."

"What are you on about?" said Johnny.

"Derrick," I replied, "He used to take me out playing sports and stuff. I think it was to get us both away from Bill."

"Well I'm glad 'e did something fuckin' honourable," said Johnny sarcastically.

"You're being too hard on him. He was just a boy," I said, hoping that Johnny might soften.

"Am I?" said Johnny "Am I? The question was left hanging in the air. "We talk," he said icily. "What more do I want with him?" And it was in that moment that I saw Olive's grimace appear on my brother's face and I knew then that his mind was set. There was absolutely no way he and Derrick were going to talk about this shit – and would it have done any good? I remember thinking that some things need to remain buried in the past. They have each got on with their lives and it would not help or solve anything to talk. It would just rake up old wounds. They've never been close and they never will be.

"Does Olive realise? Surely she…"

"…will never admit she's wrong," said Johnny completing my sentence, "Not over this shit."

I reluctantly agreed. As Johnny took another swig of his beer. There was something that puzzled me.

"What about Ted?"

"Weak as fuckin' dishwater. He just sided with everything she said. Anything for a quiet life. You know dad. He was never strong enough to confront Bill even if he wanted to but Olive was."

It was strange how Johnny and Derrick seemed to attach far less blame to Ted because he was weak.

"All the while I thought it was something to do with Frank," I said.

Johnny laughed. "You thought he'd killed Michael. Remember?"

I nodded and smiled. I remembered my friend Nawab and his silly hypothesis that Michael could have been murdered by Frank and I believed him. I muttered the same thing that I said all those years ago.

"Fucking Nawab."

The lids of all my paint tubes lie scattered on the desktop. When I'm involved in a painting I can't take time out to put lids back on. Seeing them there…it would annoy Johnny for sure. If he was here now he'd have to go over and screw them back on. It's not just scattered lids. A paintbrush has gone hard. I forgot to leave it in soak. I'd been stupid.

It was never anything to do with Michael – it was just a coincidence that all the shit happened at around the time of his death. It made people feel shittier and fed my imagination.

Every family has got a pervert hidden away in their closet. I know that but Bill, he was good to me. Christ he helped me. That camera. I loved it. I didn't ask exactly what happened. I didn't want to know the details. I was still getting my head round the fact that Bill was…I couldn't even say it.

For a brief moment I was back there in Cheetham Hill seeing the past with fresh eyes. It gave me understanding but no resolution. There was a grim resignation that attitudes and lives were set. Johnny, Derrick and Olive…they were all civil to each other and that was that. I didn't really try to sort anything out, somehow it didn't seem my place. I don't think I could have helped anyway. I didn't have the skill set to unpick this one.

But Olive was happier. She had a spring in her step now that she had seen Frankie. But at the same time her good spirits were dampened by the fact that just recently he had become quite ill. "All that debauched living, my boy." Olive too was coming down with another infection probably caused by her operation earlier in the year. So between them they hadn't been able to get together despite their plans to meet up again.

I remember bringing Olive a book of old photographs of Manchester by Shirley Baker to cheer her up. I loved her work. She was the photographer I wished that I could have been. I had the idea that seeing those images of the areas that we grew up in would lift her spirits. Although it rekindled old memories, the urban decay that was so vividly depicted only served to remind her of her own mortality. Despite this, she still laughed at the faces of the "scallies" that played their childish games on the dirty grey streets of north Manchester.

I swear Johnny was there in one of the photographs – one of the scallies – a figure in the background running away as fast as he could. Knowing my brother he'd probably stolen a pair of knickers from the washing line that stretched over the ginnel. I pointed him out to Olive who smiled at the photograph. "It wouldn't surprise me," she said. There was a flicker of warmth in her response which faded quickly and then the shutters went up again. It was worth a try I muttered to myself as outside the rain began to pour. A minute or two earlier it was blue sky but now I could hear the rain drops splash annoyingly against the window. I didn't even need to look. It was almost as though the heavens had colluded with Olive to ensure that any bright spot was quickly extinguished.

That time was a low point for sure but there was still time for heroes and heroines to emerge. Sometimes, out of the blue, something can happen that can change the status quo, a drama, a crisis that can shift the balance and cause a crack to appear in the impasse. I wasn't aware such an event had actually happened but it had. At first it seemed insignificant on the grand scale of things. Of course it would have upset Derrick when he split up with his wife or to be more precise his wife left him but to the rest of his family it would not have registered. We never saw much of Janice anyway, and Derrick – he seemed a distant relative but that was about to change.

TOY SOLDIERS

Johnny was already quite pissed when he rang and asked me to come round for a few "Shiftas." That in itself was not too much of an oddity but when I heard Derrick's voice in the background sounding merry, I was already putting my coat on before the phone call ended. Johnny opened the door. I was barely inside when he laughed and shook his head.

"Wait till you see this," he said.

As I stepped inside the living room, several empty cans of beer lay scattered on the coffee table. Derrick sat looking at a computer. Johnny grabbed the screen and pulled it round so that I could clearly see the image. At the same time he shook his head and laughed.

"What the fuck is that?" he said looking at Derrick in utter disbelief.

"That's my profile," said Derrick in a strangely proud manner.

"Derrick, nobody's going to fuckin' date you looking like that."

As I sat there trying to take it in I had to agree with Johnny whilst trying desperately hard to contain my laughter. There was Derrick dressed in a German soldier's uniform smiling blankly at the camera, the reflection of his black rimmed glasses completely blocking out his eyes and slightly distorting his face.

"I thought women liked men in uniform," Derrick said with conviction and then added informatively, "I am a German foot soldier."

Johnny instantly replied, "Derrick you look more like a fuckin' toy soldier than a foot soldier you dopey bastard."

My brother's comment was said out of exasperation but it hit its mark. We couldn't contain ourselves and roared with laughter. Johnny shook his head. "You dopey fuckin' bastard," he repeated.

"It doesn't look that bad does it?" Derrick meekly protested. Johnny simply dragged the mouse and clicked a few times and pointed.

"Look. This is what you need."

It was Johnny's profile picture and it was classy. He was obviously on holiday, looking relaxed and leaning nonchalantly against an arch that was the front of some European piece of architecture. He was dressed in a light yellow sleeveless shirt and well-pressed trousers with an expensive pair of sunglasses held lightly by his side. He looked smooth and sharp without necessarily being a player which he most definitely was.

"Even I'd fancy you. You handsome bastard," I stated.

"Yeah, yeah. Ok. I see your point," Derrick said in humble fashion.

Johnny then took great joy in sorting out Derrick's wardrobe and his look. It was strange seeing them getting on. It took Derrick's marriage to fall apart for this to happen. Apparently it came out of the blue, his wife simply turned round to Derrick and said "I'm leaving you." There was nobody else involved. She'd just had enough. Derrick was distraught and for whatever reason turned to Johnny. Maybe he didn't want sympathy. He just wanted someone to tell him straight. Johnny was the right kind of person to do just that. He would have given him both barrels right between the eyes.

And he did. He really laid into Derrick and told him a few home truths about how cutting himself off and being this "Remote big I am fucker was a load of old shit." There was absolutely no chance that anyone was going to feel sorry for themselves. Johnny confessed that he got so angry he nearly smacked his brother. Derrick just took it.

Maybe that's what was needed. I guess it was like lancing a boil…the poison that had been stored up all those years came oozing out. There were no digs or sly jokes this time. Johnny launched a full-scale attack on Derrick – on his character, his attitude, everything. Derrick accepted the judgement and took his undeserved punishment. Hopefully for one last time.

Whatever was said worked as they were much happier with each other. The pain built up over a lifetime can never easily be taken away and in the continuing years it resurfaced from time to time but not with any great force. Johnny still took the piss out of Derrick but for the large part his jokes lacked the barb of earlier years. Bill Tanner was never talked about again until years later at Johnny's wedding where the whole picture was fully revealed.

After an hour or so kitting Derrick out in various outfits and personas, Johnny shouted from the top of the stairs, "What do you think, our kid?" Johnny was clearly proud of himself as his protégé glided down the stairs looking like a new man. The neatly groomed but ultimately dull figure of an aging man had been transformed. It didn't take much. The thick black-rimmed glasses were cast aside and bright but not outlandish clothes were added to bring out the best in Derrick's fair complexion. The slightly loose attire cleverly hid the paunch around his stomach. Johnny had also restyled his brother's hair combing it ever so slightly forward. The final touch was a pair of Ray-Ban sunglasses held loosely by his side.

"The tart with a heart," I said. We all laughed.

A photograph with the right posture and pose was duly taken and put on a dating website. It was no surprise that the hits came in immediately. To a seasoned pro like Johnny it was child's play. Derrick then enjoyed a bit of an Indian summer with the women with a little help from Viagra supplied of course by Johnny.

THE WEDDING

I think the portrait is complete. I see now what has been created or rather what has been revealed. Sometimes it is not until the end that I know what I have truly painted. It is the best part of her. She is full of joy, full of hope and for a moment she is free from the past. The eyes, the windows to the soul have life, but there is something else, a sadness that can only just be seen. Yes I say to myself. The picture tells the story but it's not quite the end.

It's a bright and breezy morning one sunny April in 2006 and I am back in Manchester. I am over for my brother's wedding. It is the first time I have been back since Olive's funeral two years before. Olive never recovered from a series of illnesses. Ever since the bladder infection and the operation for appendicitis there had been a slow decline in her health. It was a sad time for many of us. We all recognised what an impact she had on our lives.

It turned out that her visit to Frankie's was a last hurrah for both of them. Frankie was having treatment for some kind of bone cancer when we saw him. That week was a good week for him. He hid his illness well. But as both Olive's and Frank's health deteriorated they only saw each other once more. It was Frank who passed away first but shortly after Olive died too. At the end some of her fight had gone but even in death she managed to give us all a comedy treat.

Belle was with her in her last moments and apparently, just before she died, she awoke from a two-day coma, opened her eyes, sat bolt upright and demanded a shepherd's pie and a Bailey's Irish Cream. After an argument with the hospital staff, her wish was duly granted and a few days later she "Went." It was according to Belle, "Typical Olive."

It was a small gathering at the funeral. Olive would have been more than happy with that as she wasn't sentimental and would not have expected people to make too much of an effort to be there, particularly if the weather was rough. A small prayer would have been sufficient to commemorate a life no less ordinary. It was a bit more than that. There were a few blasts from the past that came to pay tribute and of course there were the stories. They were different to Ted's. His were full of pathos and comic tragedy whereas Olive's were full of belligerence and comic cynicism.

The best and the worst of it was that you couldn't keep her quiet. If she thought that there was ever the slightest injustice, as she perceived it, she would be there fighting not just for herself but for others, especially the poorest. And in that fight she was robust, opinionated and was not to be trifled with. I remember her haranguing "Powelly" the local vicar about my friend Ray's impoverished clothing. Just after a church service she marched up to him with Ray in tow and got straight to the point.

"What the pissin' 'ell's the bleedin' collection for?"

"I beg your pardon," said the vicar.

She grabbed Ray by the arm. "Look at 'im, 'es got no bleedin' shoes." And it was true the ones that Ray had on were virtually falling off, held together with a thick elastic band.

"I bet it's bloody loaded in that collection bag. Is it just for your own flock or is it to keep you in that big bloody 'ouse?"

"Mrs Sm..."

"Look at 'im (points to Ray) the church is supposed to 'elp children like 'im. You ought to be ashamed of yourself." Olive then gave Powelly the gorgon stare.

"And you lot," she turned to the well-dressed dearies stepping out of the church. "You lot are a load of old arse'oles. You call yourself Christians?"

Her accusation hung in the air like some poisonous squid ink blotting out a nice Sunday afternoon. I will never forget. The next day there were three parcels of smart jumble sale clothes and shoes delivered to our door with a note from Mrs Sattersthwaite. "We've arranged a collection. Hope you approve."

Even when her protests backfired or she was in the wrong Olive would be unapologetic.

"There is one thing worse than being talked about," she would say, "and that's not bein' talked about."

I once told her who said it.

"Oscar Wilde, mum."

"Who the bloody 'ell is he?"

"He was the one who said it."

"Well 'es nicked my material, the thievin' bastard."

"But he's dead, mum. He's been dead for a hundred years."

There was a slight pause and then a clear end to the conversation.

"Arse'oles!"

She could be incredibly funny but, like her father Ernie, a hard bastard. She loved people thinking of her in that way, a woman of very little sentimentality. My brothers certainly saw that side of her but they had a begrudging admiration for her resolve.

There should have been something more...a blast of horns a five-gun salute, something memorable but there wasn't. Still, I think even Olive would have been proud of Johnny...who got married for the first time at the age of fifty. The shame is that they never did resolve their differences. Olive could never bring herself to talk about "stuff" especially if she had to admit that she was wrong. She saw most things as a battle – it was a sign of weakness and it would be conceding defeat if she ever said sorry. She wouldn't confess that she may have been wrong to the person that battled her the most of all, her son Johnny. No, never.

If only Olive could have found a way to make things better like she did with Stacey that time when she went round to Mrs Haider's house. She found a way then without saying sorry but she could never do it with her sons. For Johnny's part he was angry with her a lot of the time. Who could blame him? It got in the way.

Derrick made some attempts to see his mother more often after his reconciliation with Johnny but it was hard going for both of them. Some progress was made but it was slow. A difficult bridge proved hard to cross. Putting all of this aside, my brother Johnny was about to get married!

We needed to get some last-minute bits and pieces for the "wedding do" so me and Johnny drove down to the new trading estate on Cheetham Hill Road. The site was unrecognisable from how it used to look. The old ginnels had gone, the Calypso Club was no more and the MacBride's prefabs had completely disappeared. Instead a new multiplex of small businesses had replaced what had largely been destroyed by the "great fire" some thirty five years ago. We stopped at one of them, a smart new digi-coloured shop and purchased a few party poppers and funny hats.

The new architecture was pretty uninspiring so we decided to have a drive around for old time's sake, re-visiting our old haunts and taking a trip down memory lane. As I looked out of the window of my brother's car, I could see Saint Luke's Church, now just a shell. In its day it housed a small congregation and was the base for Terry's youth club. Johnny was once apprehended there by the local vicar doing the dance of the seven J-cloths to an audience of young pubescent girls. It was a very suggestive dance which involved him being naked from the waist down apart from a tiny little J-cloth which he used to lift up suggestively eliciting riotous laughs from the young giggling females.

We drove past Smedley flats and the old Queens Road bus depot where Frankie worked for a time. Somewhere around this area used to be the old Finnegan's dance hall where we were introduced to ballroom dancing. I went once, never again. Derrick went for a couple of years. Johnny would have gone more but he got barred after a fight with the owner's son.

We took small detours through streets that had not changed much. Some of the old terraces still remained like fragments of a bygone age. At this moment I thought of Olive. I could understand how past events and experiences of north Manchester forged her personality. It provided her with a black humour and a darkly comic view of the world. It helped cultivate her ability to make anyone laugh at the bleakest of situations. In this gritty and uncompromising landscape full of life, Olive was that place and that place was Olive.

We drove along Cheetham Hill Road where we spotted some open ground where Olive's Offy used to be. Johnny stopped the car. We got out and walked across the croft, treading on turf where a thousand memories lay. We joked about the bags of rubbish we used to chuck out of the upstairs window when we were having a "sort out." We laughed as we could both picture our angry parents picking up the scattered debris of their belongings the next morning from the sodden grass. I looked over at my brother.

"I can still hear Olive cursing us under her breath and calling us 'a shower of shite,'" I said.

"Well, we were," said Johnny shaking his head and laughing.

"I bet if we digged this turf up we'd find half of our old stuff that we'd tipped out." My brother agreed and then added, "I once threw Olive's best scarf out of the window after an argument with her. She found it the next day round about here." Johnny stamped on the patch of grass to indicate the precise position.

"What did she do?" I asked.

"I said you'd done it," replied Johnny.

"She never said anything to me. I..."

"That's because you were the bloody favourite," he said laughing.

I laughed as well and begrudgingly admitted that there was some truth there.

"Fair enough." I said. And then added, "But you let me bloody know it!"

"That's true. That is true," he said, smiling to himself.

"You were like a bloody leech. The more I was pissy with you, the more you hung on. I couldn't fuckin' get rid of you. Fuckin' Bill didn't help," admitted Johnny.

And then I came out with it, "I think Olive knew about Bill. She must have."

"Why do you say that?" asked Johnny curiously. "She never fuckin' believed me."

"She cut him out of all the photos. At first I thought it was Frankie but it was Bill – definitely." I could feel Johnny listening intently as I elaborated on my statement. And then when I'd finished he asked me a strange question.

"What do you know about the accident with Bill?"

I struggled to remember anything. "Didn't he have some kind of fall?"

"Something like that," said Johnny quietly.

"I bet you were happy."

"Fuckin' ecstatic," replied Johnny, "Even better, after that I never saw him round at the shop again."

"I wonder why not?"

"Well, I have my own idea," said Johnny.

"Would you care to elaborate," I said intrigued by his announcement. Johnny raised an eyebrow.

"We're in Manchester now, not some bloody Sherlock Holmes mystery. Elaborate my arse."

Despite his annoyance with my vernacular Johnny happily continued.

"Basically it was Gary, our Belle's husband, a young policeman then, who came in the shop lookin' for Bill because he wasn't answering his radio. When he came into the back room he saw Bill collapsed on the floor and Olive sat on the chair beside him calmly smoking a cigarette.

"Hang on. How do you know all this?" I suddenly blurted out.

"Because I asked Gary about Bill's accident and he told me," said Johnny in a matter of fact fashion.

"When?"

"It doesn't matter," said Johnny, irritated that I was interrupting his story. He promptly ignored my question and quickly continued.

"Olive had already phoned for an ambulance and explained to Gary that Bill had slipped on some dog shit in the back yard. Gone arse over tit...,flat out. She said he must have hit his head on a paving stone, the silly bugger. But here's the best bit," said Johnny stroking his chin, "Gary asked Olive how Bill got in the back room if, as she put it, he was flat out in the yard. Apparently she said that when she went upstairs to phone for the ambulance, he must have crawled in."

"Really?" Johnny could see the frown on my face.

"Yeah. Really," said Johnny ironically. "Gary said that he was a bit suspicious at the time too. He said that he expected to see more dog shit on Bill's uniform. He noticed that there was only a tiny dollop on the sole of one of his shoes. He said he checked the yard after the ambulance crew had gone and it was full of dog crap. If he crawled or even if he fell, chances are it would be all over him. But," said Johnny raising a hand to suppress my questions, "if there was something that Olive had done, Bill never said a thing. When he was able to speak which was several weeks later he wasn't good and couldn't remember anything."

"Or chose not to say anything," I added. "Olive clocked him definitely without a doubt, right across the back of his head. Whack!" I was absolutely certain.

"I'm sayin' nothing," said Johnny, "Either way, he never came round to the shop after that!"

"That would be Olive's kind of justice. It would be just like her. No different to a slap to one of her kids who was bad mouthing her. She probably would have sat him down at the table, given him a nice cup of tea, smiled and then come up behind…wallop." And with that I slammed my fist into the palm of my hand. I thought for a second.

"Maybe a rollin' pin," I suggested.

"Maybe," said Johnny stroking his chin again.

"When do you think she realised about Bill?" I asked.

"Probably when Derrick told her and Ted."

I was shocked. "When was that? I thought he never said anything."

"Well he didn't, not immediately. It wasn't until much later on having felt so bloody guilty for not sticking up for me that he finally plucked up the courage to tell mum and dad. She never believed me but the fact that Derrick was saying something."

"When did he tell you that?" I asked impatiently.

"At the big bust up we had. You know just after his wife left him."

"But that means that Derrick…"

"Yes, yes," said Johnny waving away my exclamations.

"Shit! Does that mean you've forgiven him for…?"

"Christ our kid, you've been spending too much time with your mate Terry Evangelical Evans. Forgiveness? That's a bit much," he added sarcastically. "Let's just say we get on a lot better now."

"You know it could have been Ted that clocked him," I said. There was a pause as we both thought for a second and almost in unison we both said "Naaa." And with that we hopped in the car and drove off ready for Johnny's big day.

I step back. I'm not sure about the truth of the painting and then I remember a quote by Frida Kahlo: "I can only paint my reality."

As I helped Johnny with the last few arrangements for his wedding decorations, the conjecture surrounding Bill's "accident" started up again. In hushed tones we both offered theories into how it happened. But after a few drinks an element of farce descended on the scene as a Cluedo-esque game developed between the two of us.

"She did it. Lead piping in the kitchen."

"No, it was not a blow to the head, that came after an attempted suffocation by dog shit in the yard."

"No, no. It was her stiletto in the crotch and then Bill was force-fed Kimmy's special soup de shite."

"It was food poisoning caused by eating one of Kimmy's turds disguised as a chocolate." We both struggled to contain our giggles as Johnny suggested that it was one of Kimmy's walnut whip specials with brown sugar and hundreds and thousands sprinkled over the top.

"Bill probably keeled over in shock and horror once his teeth had broken the thin layer of crusted shit," pronounced Johnny.

And then it came to me. "What about one of Olive's rasping farts over the fire causing a noxious gas to erupt, knocking Bill out immediately." (more giggles)

"Not bad, our kid," said Johnny, "but I think she simply head butted him...the old Glaswegian kiss."

"I think you've nailed it there," I said and unable to contain ourselves any longer we burst out laughing. I broke first but Johnny nearly choked on his large glass of champagne.

I know that it was quite surreal to joke about such things but at the same time it seemed perfectly natural. It certainly was for Johnny. And whether he liked to admit it or not, it was a kind of humour passed from mother to son. Just then Derrick walked in dressed in a kilt.

"What the fuck. You're not coming to my wedding dressed like that!"

Derrick then pulled out a fake ginger beard and tartan cap.

"Oh, Christ," said Johnny. He then turned to me and asked me if I wanted to be his best man instead. "I'm not having this bad fuckin' comedian standing beside me," he added. "If it was something remotely fuckin' funny..." Johnny then turned to Derrick. "You don't need any of this ginger beard shit. Why don't you just come as yourself? Derrick the dick'ead. They'll be in stitches."

Derrick looked a little sheepish but when Johnny patted him on the shoulder they both laughed.

"OK. Just for Carol, your beautiful wife to be, I will dispense with the cap and beard," said Derrick begrudgingly.

Despite Derrick's attempts to hijack his brother's wedding (which was completely out of character) the ceremony itself went smoothly although Johnny was treading on thin ice when he cracked a few jokes at the blessing. Just as the registrar turned to them both and was about to say a few words Johnny interrupted him and said that he was only marrying Carol because he felt sorry for her. It was totally inappropriate but Johnny being Johnny he got away with it.

There were a few laughs but a quick dig in the ribs from Carol put paid to any more attempts by Johnny to impose his own unique brand of entertainment on proceedings. She would be more than happy to indulge him later on. She wouldn't want to stop him anyway. His anarchic humour and spontaneity were some of the reasons she fell in love with him.

Johnny and Carol had been together for several years. She had been married before and life had become incredibly dull during that time. Johnny represented some excitement. It started out as an affair which grew into something else. At first she wasn't sure what that was, particularly as it took her down some routes that were a little risqué. It was Johnny who introduced her to the swinging scene, a scene that she found quite thrilling at first. (Johnny told me all this) But over the last few years something deeper had taken root and they were more content with each other and saw less need for "outside interests."

After the ceremony had finished there were many hugs, kisses and handshakes followed by drinks that quickly flowed. And then came the speeches. Derrick's best man speech was strange but incredibly funny. It wasn't so much the attempted jokes…he did impressions of Johnny that were so awful they were good. But it was the surreal aspect of Derrick's story telling that revealed an anarchic side to him which belied his conservative image. My brother was a bit of a revelation. So much so that he upstaged Johnny who acknowledged this by raising a glass and toasting "the daft twat."

Later on I saw Johnny and Carol grab a moment. I watched as Carol looked at Johnny with soft brown eyes, her face flushed with excitement.

"You can stop that," said Johnny feigning dislike at his new bride's adoration of him.

"But Johnny, she is fucking loving you," said Jammi who'd sidled up next to my brother without him realising.

"Christ, Jammi. You're like creepin' fuckin' Jesus! Anyway, look at her – she's ugly," said Johnny smiling. Poor Jammi took it literally and his face dropped. Johnny knew that it would take too long to explain his kind of humour so he duly altered course. "Of course she's lovely." He turned round and grinned at Carol who acknowledged his compliment. Jammi looked satisfied that no harm was done and honour was intact. My brother then looked more closely at Jammi.

"Your front teeth. Christ, they're a bit manky. Is it the bastard sweets?"

Jammi nodded sheepishly "I am not looking forward to the bastard dentist. I am shitting myself to be going next month." Just then Terry Evans wandered in looking slightly lost.

"Oh, Christ," said Johnny as he spied his old youth club leader and family friend. "When are you getting changed Terry?" shouted Johnny.

"What do you mean?"

"Well 'aven't you 'eard, there's a wedding going on, not a bus driver's convention!"

I looked at Terry. His attire wasn't great but it wasn't terrible. Granted, his clothes were a bit crumpled, his brown pin stripe suit looked a bit dated and the charity shop overcoat that was a little big didn't help but Terry had made an effort. As others laughed, Terry then mumbled something about being "very funny." And then Johnny walked over and warmly shook his hand and told him that he was pleased that he could make it.

Suddenly Derrick leapt onto the dance floor and threw himself into what you could vaguely call a highland fling. It was, I suppose, a kind of "Scottish dance with a series of complex steps being performed solo." He was all alone on the dance floor, nobody wanted to get near him for fear of being injured through his flailing arms and kicking legs. I looked over at Stacey and, as

I caught her eye, she walked over to me. She looked a little concerned.

"I hope he'll be okay," she said.

"What do you mean?" I asked.

"I only gave him one pill," confessed Stacey. "He was a bit nervous of doing his best man speech and coming to the wedding in general."

"Christ, Stacey, he's drunk about two bottles of champagne as well. I thought your pill popping days had long since gone."

"They have. It's just that when he rang me the other day, he asked if..."

"Look at him," I said interrupting Stacey, "He's completely out of it. He's like Jimmy bleedin' Cranky on fuckin' acid!"

We both looked over to see that Derrick had now put on his false red beard and tartan cap. The arm of his glasses had partially broken leaving them just about hanging over his ears and nose. He was also jumping in the air to show off the most ridiculous Union Jack undies.

"Somebody rescue him for God's sake," I said, taking pity on my older brother.

But before either of us could do anything, the dance floor was invaded by nearly all the guests. Derrick's outrageous dancing had somehow ignited the celebrations. It was a sight to behold as hordes of fifty-somethings suddenly performed the Highland Fling to This Charming Man by The Smiths. Jammi looked on slightly bemused and pained. He saw this response to one of his beloved Manchester bands as a corruption of something he held sacred.

"Don't worry, Jammi," said Stacey sensing her husband's unease, "I'll get them to put Blue Monday on. They'll have a job doing that sort of thing to that track."

But it turned out to be a glorious night where all and sundry enjoyed themselves as only Mancunians can. We had a party!

Johnny was on his best form although for a time he was outdone by his older brother. It took so much out of Derrick that after his exertions he sat down at about 11 o'clock and went to sleep in the corner. We kept watch but he was fine.

It was late when we all sat around the table of scattered glasses and bottles. (Derrick was still out of it) The dancing had all but stopped apart from a few swaying around out of time with the music in a world of their own. Jammi and Stacey were two of those people. They were totally oblivious to everything but themselves. As some of the guests had started to leave, the music was turned down but Jammi and Stacey kept on dancing. Their beloved Smiths were still playing. "The rain falls hard on a humdrum town. This town will drag you down."

"It's tried to," said Belle.

"What?" said Johnny.

"Manchester. Cheetham Hill, Hulme, Moss Side. It's tried to drag us down. Do you not feel it sometimes?"

We all looked at Belle. It was a rare negative emotion from someone who was always so positive, but then it was understandable. Her life had not been easy for the last few years. She'd been diagnosed with cancer a few years back. The signs were there when Belle turned up to Olive's seventieth birthday party with a new hairdo. "The bird's nest" as Olive put it. It was an attempt to cover some hair loss. She hadn't been well for a few months and after a series of tests cancer was diagnosed. She never told Olive but the subsequent treatment left its mark. Amongst other things her face puffed out and her limbs became quite bloated, a fact that Olive was quick to point out as soon as she saw her.

"Christ all mighty, you've put on some weight."

"It's the chips mum," was all that Belle would say.

We all knew of course and, Johnny being Johnny, he called her the Michelin man. It worked as it caused Belle to laugh at herself. She would never wallow in self-pity anyway. As Olive's health deteriorated, Belle made sure that she visited Olive frequently despite her own illness much to the relief of my brothers. They didn't mind visiting once in a while but would dread the thought of spending more time with Olive than was necessary. The childhood scars left by skirmishes with the old battle-axe had left their mark.

Near the end, just before she went into hospital, it became clear that Olive was starting to suffer a little dementia. During that time I sometimes went with my sister to visit Olive. "Shall we do the rounds our kid?" Belle used to say to me in perky fashion. I knew what this meant. My sister had acquainted herself with Olive's favourite hiding places and knew that there would be stashes of five pound notes and other articles deposited there. She would give me the orders.

"You do the pillow case. I'll do the knickers draw." And sure enough wodges of £10 notes and remote TV controls were all found squirrelled away there. Olive always breathed a sigh of relief when we found her stash. She was happy in the knowledge that those "thieving bastards" (whoever they were) hadn't nicked anything. She would often be quite adamant that "they got to Joe next door. "He lost thousands, poor sod." Of course no such thing had occurred and there was no such person as Joe.

Belle always had a strong bond with her mother. For many years Olive was ever ready to throw a protective arm around her youngest. Belle didn't begrudge nursing her mother. She was simply returning what had been given to her.

Right now it was clear that there was something on Belle's mind. Her husband Gary, knew what it was.

"Why don't you tell them," he said gently. "You've held on to it for too long."

"What?" said Johnny.

"The past," said Belle, "The past."

Her words hung in the air and gently descended on all of us like a soft veil in the wind.

Can a portrait capture more than a moment in time? Can it embody something more than a fleeting impression? Can it ever truly capture the past?

BELLE'S STORY

The past. I can still hear those words of Belle's whispering softly in my ear. I realised then that it wasn't just about my past and making sense of it all. In all those years I'd not seen her. I mean properly seen her. If I'd just noticed a bit more. It was always Belle, it was her past that held the key.

"Evenin' Ol" came the cry and a familiar figure popped its head in. Whereas before, Ted found Bill's greeting friendly and affable it was now very irritating. At first he wasn't going to come down and see Bill but without realising it he got up and softly made his way down the stairs. When he arrived in the back room Bill was there slurping a cup of tea. Ted always used to laugh when Bill did that. It used to be endearing but now it was offensive. He was also making himself at home in his favourite chair.

"'Ello lad," said Bill warmly. Ted said nothing but smiled meekly. He was still thinking about what Derrick had told him last night about Bill. At first, like Olive, he thought it was ridiculous. He didn't want to believe it. Not Bill but then he saw how upset Derrick was and how hard it was for him to say anything. In his heart he knew. Johnny was easier to disbelieve. He said stuff about Bill in a scornful way to get at Olive. The two were always at each other. It was possible that Johnny could have made it up but not Derrick.

Ted admitted to himself that he was always in a world of his own. He knew how he could have missed it but Olive was always so cynical. Maybe (Ted paused) maybe she was having an affair with him.

"That's it," said Ted out loud.

"What's that," said Bill?"

Ted said nothing. It was as though Bill's voice came from a faraway place. And with that thought Ted got a little angrier. He didn't want his train of thought interrupted. When he looked back he could see there were times when Bill seemed a little false, but he'd dismissed it. Bill had been good to them, done them a favour or two…the car crash, turning a blind eye to a lack of documents, presents for the kids…but that was all a ruse to gain trust. Ted could see that now. That friendly charm was an act. Bill had taken him for a ride.

"Are you OK, Ted?" said Bill. Ted simply nodded and then picked up the rolling pin that had been left lying on the side.

"You're not going to hit me with that?" said Bill laughing.

Ted smiled meekly again and then walked round the back of Bill to where the chest of drawers was. He was never going to put it back, not really. Bill was still laughing when the rolling pin came crashing down on his head. It was a sickening blow that caused him to fall like a dead weight to the floor. To some extent all Ted wanted to do was to stop him from laughing. And he did just that. Olive came rushing through from the back yard toilet to find Ted in a trance staring over Bill's very still body. Ted still had part of the rolling pin in his hand slightly raised.

"Oh Christ!" said Olive as she walked in. It wasn't just the shock, it was a pained cry for her husband…a deep and heartfelt cry. Ever since Derrick had told them about Bill late last night, Ted had been quite numb and appeared unable to talk. He'd gone in on himself and Olive was genuinely concerned, worried that he might do something stupid. Ted was always so calm, so still, but she knew that under certain circumstances even he was capable of a "mad act." And now her fears had come true.

If only she'd heard Bill come in she could have got to him first. She would have done exactly the same thing as Ted. It needed to be her that did it. It was her guilt that needed to be assuaged. She'd refused to believe her son. She'd let her cynical guard drop and although she'd never had an affair with Bill she wanted to. Deep down there was always something but she'd dismissed it. How could she have been so stupid?

Olive lay awake that night unable to shake the rage and guilt that had engulfed her. She dreamt of various ways in which she'd do Bill in. It was no use going to the police. Whatever favours she did for them would count for nothing to cover up for one of their own. From her own experience, they were a load of lying bastards anyway. Olive could feel her anger rising again but quickly put a lid on it as she looked at the bewildered face of her husband.

She then calmly took the rolling pin out of Ted's hand and led him up the stairs to the living room. She kissed him tenderly on the forehead and said warmly, "Don't worry my dear. Sit down. I'll make you a nice cuppa." Ted nodded and smiled meekly but still looked blank. Olive stroked his cheek and stayed with him a little longer before moving slowly to the door keeping her eyes firmly fixed on Ted.

"Stay here," she said firmly.

Olive then went down stairs and checked Bill to see if he was still alive. He had a pulse! For a moment Olive wished he were dead as she looked at his ugly crumpled form. She bent over him and quietly whispered in his ear, "How did you ever think you could get away with it you fuckin' bastard?" That last venomous sentence seemed to release some of her rage and she felt better for it. Olive then stood up and pondered the situation. There was a good chance that Bill would not say anything for fear of what he had done being made public. There was also a good chance that he would not remember anything. Suddenly Olive had a sense of purpose as she raced back upstairs and phoned for an ambulance explaining that Bill had had a nasty fall and was unconscious.

"How did he fall?" came the voice from the phone.

"How did he fall?" said Olive repeating the question and then a word sprung out.

"Dog shit!" said Olive. "He slipped on some dog shit in the yard, went arse over tit and hit his head on the step. Poor bastard."

The woman on the phone seemed perplexed but accepted the explanation and said that help would be on its way in the next few minutes. Olive went quickly back down the stairs.

And then she thought…dog shit…I need to get some dog shit and put a dollop on Bill's shoes. Olive was quite attentive to detail. She made sure that shit of the right consistency was used and smeared a bit on the bottom of his shoes.

"How did he get in here?" Olive said out loud and then answered her own question. "Crawled in."

Olive surveyed the scene. It seemed OK. The rolling pin was upstairs out of sight. She lit a fag, took a long cool drag and sat down pleased with her work. Then Olive heard the rustle of the plastic curtain that guarded the entrance to the shop. She looked up to see a small figure standing there in the doorway all alone.

The little girl just stood there – not moving, just looking. Olive gasped in horror as she recognised the little girl's ashen face peeping out from the coloured ribbons of PVC.

Olive walked over to her little girl and instinctively gave her one great protective hug. She wasn't sure what the girl had seen. Now was not the time to interrogate her. Now was the time to be a good mother. Olive carried her daughter back up to her bedroom and poured her a large glass of Irn Bru. She gulped the orange brown fizzy liquid and then lay down as Olive tucked her in.

"Do not tell anybody what you have seen or heard. Promise me on your dad's and brother's and sister's lives. Promise me."

The little girl nodded.

"We'll talk again soon," said Olive gently. She then kissed her daughter's forehead and watched as her little girl closed her eyes ready to go back to sleep. Olive let out a big sigh as she braced herself for the next challenges. She had to keep an eye on Bill, be ready for the ambulance to arrive and she had to see to Ted, poor Ted.

Olive didn't expect Gary, Bill's young partner to knock on the door first. He'd tried to contact Bill earlier and had no luck so he called in on the off chance that Bill might be there. Needless to say he was shocked when he entered the back kitchen. Bill was still out cold with blood now oozing from the back of his head. Gary asked far too many questions. He wasn't convinced by Olive's explanations. He was still asking them when they loaded Bill into the ambulance. It took an eternity for everything to finish but, much to Olive's relief, eventually it did.

After they had gone Olive rushed up the stairs where she'd hidden Ted in the upstairs attic. She told Gary that Ted was out getting some bread from Warburton's bakery. There was no way that Ted could be risked. He was still in a state of shock and he could never be a convincing liar.

When she got there Ted was shivering. Olive brought him downstairs to the living room, sat him next to the gas fire and made him another cup of tea. She gently kissed his head again and clutched his hand. Olive was proud of him…of what her Ted had done for the family. That moment was the closest she'd been to Ted in a long time. Olive now knew that she would never leave Ted, however mundane life had become. She also knew deep down that this catastrophe would not change anything. In time he would go back into his own world and they would get on with their discordant lives. It would be as though nothing had ever happened.

THE GIRL IN THE DOORWAY

"I was the little girl in the door way," said Belle quietly. The one behind the curtain. And suddenly it was as though somebody had turned the TV down to listen to an important conversation, which it was. Everybody paid attention as Belle told her story.

As she went through events Belle didn't look directly at us but lowered her eyes to the floor. She managed to retain much of the detail...what Ted was wearing, what Olive said, the half a cup of Irn Bru that her mother had given her. She'd tried not to commit the event to memory but it wouldn't go away. In fact it clung on through the years and wouldn't fade. For a minute afterwards nobody said a thing.

"So let's get this straight," said Johnny after Belle had finished, "You're saying that Ted hit Bill over the head and Olive covered up for him."

"Yes, I suppose I am."

"Shit the bed!" said Johnny.

I was stunned.

"Why have you never told us?" my brother said slightly bemused.

"Because she promised Olive that she wouldn't," I said looking over at Belle who nodded meekly.

"Why now?" I asked.

"I'm not sure," said Belle, "Maybe it's to do with my own mortality. Look at me I'm not exactly healthy."

"You're fine," said Johnny. But it was said as much for his benefit as his sister's. Everybody could see that the cancer had taken its toll but nobody wanted to admit it. And Belle was quick to counter my brother's encouragement.

"No I'm not, not really." She paused and then stated earnestly. "But you all need to know about what happened." Belle paused again clearly finding it stressful to talk, and then she continued. "After mum died I was going to tell you but the time never seemed right. It never does but even though it's your wedding it seems right enough now."

"You're right," said Johnny reflectively.

"There's more," said Gary. "Bill might have died if it weren't for your sister." He paused slightly as he clasped Belle's hand. "After what happened, your mum and dad left Bill and went upstairs. Your sister who was all alone went up to Bill to see if he was alright. His face was bluish." He turned to Belle. "So you shook him?"

Belle took up the story and her nurse voice took over "It's a sign of an obstructed airway, probably his tongue. I think somehow what I did released the obstruction. He let out a gasp of air."

"Shit!"

"So if my sister hadn't have done what she had done, the old man could have been up for murder?"

"Probably," said Gary."

"Shit!"

Belle turned to face her husband. "You never quite believed Olive. You were always suspicious."

Gary nodded in agreement. "Olive's explanation didn't feel right," he said "But I was never going to voice my suspicions to Belle. How could I? I loved her and she was going to be my wife. I wasn't going to jeopardise that by saying that I suspect your mum of foul play." He then turned to Johnny. "It was only when you asked questions about Bill's accident that we talked or rather Belle did. It was after you'd gone...she opened up...told me everything…Oh my God it was such a relief for her to tell someone. Christ, I don't think you realise what a heck of a burden she's been carrying."

As Belle started to well up, Gary then put his arm round her and gave her an extra squeeze. Johnny moved close to his sister and clasped her hand.

"She's always wanted to tell you," Gary continued, "but never felt that she could. She loved Ted and wanted to protect him. She promised Olive. You know what Belle's like. She could not break a promise, but she knows it might have changed things. She's not blind. There's been such a lot of pain. All of this bottled up inside her for all these years."

We all looked at Belle who began to weep. This time Johnny didn't try to be funny. He never tried to deflect the pain with humour. Instead it was left to Jammi and Stacey. They had been merrily dancing away throughout Belle's revelations not having heard a word, oblivious to everything. Suddenly they grabbed our hands and attempted to pull us all up to the dance floor.

"C'mon you miserable bastards," said Stacey, "I don't know what you've been talking about but haven't you heard…it's a celebration. Someone's just got married!" Stacey and Jammi were drunkenly insistent and so reluctantly up we got. Within a minute there was a miraculous transformation in the mood as Belle threw off her wig, said "fuck it" and jigged around the dance floor bald and bold as brass.

Suddenly Derrick woke up and joined in. He was still pretty high and was still making us laugh. Johnny took the piss and before any of us realised, we were all there, brothers and sisters together…the Smiths dancing to The Smiths in complete and utter gay abandon. It was the best of times within the worst of times.

The aftermath

After the dust had settled a few things came to light. Bill suffered a fractured skull with some brain damage. His speech was slurred and there wasn't much feeling on his right side. There were other complications too, such as loss of bladder control. Although over time, Bill recovered some functions he was never the same man again. He had to come into the hospital regularly for treatment long after "the accident" had occurred…where Belle was his nurse. She confessed that she sometimes worked overtime with Bill no doubt trying to pay off a "family debt."

Belle once told me that one of the reasons she went into nursing was that a customer once collapsed in the shop when she was a little girl. No one was around and she desperately wanted to help but couldn't. She said that she didn't want to be in that position again…so she became a nurse. It was probably Bill she was talking about.

And then I realised the irony of it all. If it wasn't for Bill, the chief architect of all of our family's distress, I probably wouldn't have become an art teacher and my sister wouldn't have taken up nursing.

RAIN

From Northenden to Partington, it's rain
From Altrincham to Chadderton, it's rain
From Moss Side to Swinton, hardly Spain
It's a picture postcard of 'Wish they never came.
Beautiful South

"It always fuckin' rains in Manchester. If the Eskimos 'ave 'undreds of words for snow, we've got thousands for fuckin' rain," said Johnny. He gestured to the window which was continually being splattered, tat, tat, tat. "Listen!" he shouted. "It gets on my pissin' nerves."

"Why don't you move then?" I asked.

"Fuck knows," he said exasperated. "Maybe its cos I'm not you." Johnny then peered out of the window again. "We're not going to get a round in are we? I might as well put the golf clubs back in the bloody locker. And with that he trooped out of the door down to the locker room. A few minutes later Johnny trudged back up. "Fancy a pint?"

"Might as well," I said and as my brother went to the bar I found myself mulling over the stuff that was said at Johnny's wedding a few weeks ago.

"I can't quite get my head round how they carried on as if nothing had happened...Ted and Olive... because to all intents and purposes, that's what they did."

"I reckon that's why she never left him," I said as Johnny dished up two pints of frothy lager.

"What?" said Johnny quizzically.

251

"Olive. She probably saw what Ted did as something heroic like some lion protecting his pride. Because there's no other reason they stuck together for so long because I don't think it was love."

"I'm not sure," said Johnny. Olive found it difficult to show love but it doesn't mean to say that she didn't love. It was a rare concession to Olive from my brother. Perhaps he'd mellowed but then he got irritated. "She just couldn't admit that she'd fucked up. She could never admit that she was wrong and in the end it cost us and I find it hard to forgive her, even after all these years, I still find it hard." Johnny paused for a second. "Fuckin Ted. Who'd have guessed. And Belle, poor fuckin' Belle."

"I know," I said.

"What a fuckin' heroine."

"Yes, you're right."

And suddenly Johnny changed tack.

"What a daft fuckin' twat Derrick was though eh? But he was funny". And we both laughed. It would never do for Johnny to dwell too much on a depressing note and suddenly there were more funny stories about the family and one pint became three or four. Johnny didn't want to dissect events, neither of us did. It was just life. Shit happens. We just got on with having a drink and as Johnny returned from the bar and plonked the last pints on the table, he looked at me and sighed.

"What a bloody ridiculous family we are eh?"

"I am not so sure," I said thoughtfully. "I think we are perfectly normal what with people not talking to each other, arguments, resentments, dark secrets, hilarious episodes, funny funerals and a family friend who's a pervert."

My brother smiled faintly and reflected, "yeah you're right." There was a slight lull in conversation and then he turned to me. "What made you take up art anyway?"

"Is this a serious question or are you setting me up?" I replied with a hint of suspicion.

"No, no it's quite serious."

I looked into my brother's eyes. I believed him.

"I don't know. I think maybe I was trying to find things that are beautiful in a world full of ugliness."

"Christ, that's deep."

"Not really. Somebody else said it once. I think it was Bernard Sumner but it resonates with me."

"And did you?"

"Did I what?"

"Find anything beautiful."

I thought for a moment.

"Yes, yes I think I did."

A PORTRAIT

Over the next couple of years we were all pretty much a normal group of siblings just getting older. We didn't talk much about any of that stuff again. It wasn't that we swept it under the carpet nor did we avoid it. We just moved on. I had a few more questions but we were all in a decent place so I didn't ask. I kind of worked things out.

I think Derrick talked to Ted when he did because he feared that the same thing could happen to me. The camera, the gifts, the arm round my shoulder. He'd seen it all before with himself. And in their own way they'd always looked after me. Johnny used to tell me that Bill's police car was full of ghosts of dead murderers. It used to scare the shit out of me. "Whatever happens, if Bill asks you, never go in, these ghosts only show themselves to little boys and they stay with them for ever." Bill didn't ask me if I wanted to go in his car but I wouldn't have gone in. No chance. Not on my own.

And Derrick kept me away from Bill as much as possible. I can see that now but I often wonder why they didn't just tell me. But Bill probably told them that if they ever warned me then they would get into big trouble for planting such ridiculous stories into a young impressionable mind and maybe there was some veiled threat that something would happen to me if they breathed a word. Who knows? But they did protect me I am sure because I never got touched.

Despite living through slums, riots and bombings, I did find something beautiful in the ugliness but I still moved away from Manchester. Belle and The Smiths had it right…this hum drum town got me down. We all felt that way. Maybe it was a reflection of what we had all gone through but for whatever reason, I was the only one to leave. I left just as Manchester was getting interesting but I have no regrets. I paint the boats and the sea when the sun is setting but every so often I long to be back in the playground of my youth.

I think Belle might have moved too. A terrible burden had been lifted and she was looking to make a fresh start but unfortunately she never got the chance.

The doorbell rings. It is her sons. They have come to collect the portrait of her. I am not sure how they will react. They told me to do it in my style. I hope they like it. I take Craig and Simon upstairs to my studio where it is propped up on the easel. I have not looked at it for a few days and, as they open the door, I see it afresh with them.

I look at their reactions. Both jaws drop. I am not sure if it is horror or amazement.

I explain that it is at Johnny's wedding when she threw her wig off and danced the night away. I tell them that I took some photographs without anybody knowing. Both of them go closer and feel the texture of the paint and at the same time feel the face of their mother. They say nothing. I feel the need to explain further. There was a time at that wedding, I tell them, when Belle was free, defiant and heroic...not just full of goodness. Craig tells me to stop as a tear forms in his eyes. "It is her, it is all about her," he says "You do not need to say any more. The picture tells the story."

It is not all of the story but it is the best part. It is the part before she lost the fight. I remember her saying at Johnny's wedding "Look at me, look at how mortal I am." She knew she was dying. I can see that now. I look again at the ruddy cheeks, the uninhibited smile.

"The colours are fantastic," says Simon, "But I'm not sure that they will go with the wallpaper." He sniffs and sobs a little. I look at his face and his tears cause a lump in my throat.

"So change the wallpaper!" says Craig. They laugh and cry at the same time. Craig picks the painting up and inspects my signature. He turns the painting round and looks on the back. He sees some scribbled charcoal writing. "Is this the title?" he asks. He can't quite read it and looks to me.

I tell him that it's "The girl in the doorway."

"That's an odd title," says Craig.

"Johnny said that I should call it "Cancer Fuck off!"

We all smile.

"No, it's your painting," says Simon. "Your title. Girl in the doorway's fine. Just fine."

The end

Brian Smith

THE GIRL IN THE DOORWAY

Brian Smith

ABOUT THE AUTHOR

Brian was born and brought up in Cheetham Hill,
Manchester. Although he now lives in Dorset he still
considers himself a Mancunian. He has forged a career as
an art teacher and his greatest claim to fame is that he
taught art to Ryan Giggs. Brian has exhibited his own work
across the south west region. He is married to Deb and they
have two children. Brian didn't start writing seriously until
he was in his mid-fifties so there is hope for us all.

Printed in Great Britain
by Amazon